CONDEMNED

The Awakening of the Gift

A novel by Jessie Cabella

This is a work of fiction. Names, characters, businesses, places, events, locales, and incidents are either the products of the author's imagination or used in a fictitious manner. Any resemblance to actual persons, living or dead, or actual events is purely coincidental.

Copyright © 2020 Jessie Cabella

All rights reserved. No part of this work may be reproduced, scanned, photocopied, printed, or shared electronically without permission from the author.

Cover Design by OLIVIAPRODESIGN for the cover design.
https://www.fiverr.com/oliviaprodesign

ISBN: 978-1-7771937-0-6 (Paperback)
ISBN: 978-1-7771937-1-3 (eBook)

DEDICATION

This book is dedicated to my Grandma. Thank you for all of your support and for the endless hours you spent editing my manuscript. I cannot express how much it has meant to me to have you with me on this journey.

I love you.

CHAPTER

1

★

As I handed her the iced coffee, it happened... across the street a small boy blindly ran after the hacky sack he had accidentally kicked into the street. The taxicab that was screaming down the road didn't see him in time and....

The real world came crashing back into focus, and all I could think of was the boy and how I must get to him before it was too late.

"Hello?" The woman called out to me when I didn't answer her. "How much will that be?"

I dropped the drink and bolted out the door. I vaguely registered her shocked cries of protest as I sprinted past her and out the door. My brown apron flapped furiously in the breeze as I ran around moving cars towards where the child was playing, oblivious to what he was about to step into. I must get there in time. Please, let me get there in time! I ran straight up to the child and grabbed the hacky sack from him. No hacky sack, no accident, but we weren't in the clear yet.

He started crying immediately. I hesitated, fighting the urge to hold him close to keep him from moving any closer to the road. Two seconds later the cab flew by. I finally allowed myself to breathe a huge sigh of relief.

"Just what do you think you're doing?" I felt the mother's anger even before I heard her words.

Uh oh... I turned around to see his mother furiously stepping towards me.

She grabbed her son close to her and screamed at me to get away from her son. She sharply snatched the hacky sack from my grasp as she pulled him away and marched him down the street. I stuttered and stammered trying to think of how I could explain this logically... I came up blank.

"I um… I'm really sorry miss, I thought it was mine," I trailed off lamely, but she was long gone. I made my quick retreat towards the store, letting the murmurs and whispers fade as I closed the door to the café behind me.

The customer I had abandoned stormed past me with cold coffee splashed across her white blouse. I felt horrible. I never meant to stain her beautiful blouse. Any apology I offered wasn't going to undo what I had done, but I tried anyway. I even offered her a complimentary voucher for a future purchase on top of offering to make her another one free of charge. She wasn't having it.

"Your manager will be hearing from me. Absolutely disgusting behavior!" She shouted as she stormed out of the store.

I sighed and sank down into the nearest chair with my head in my hands. My boss, Jolene was pretty lenient when it came to my strange behavior. I had always wondered if she somehow knew why I did what I did (not that I'd ever ask), but I didn't know how long her kindness would last when I kept giving her so many reasons to fire me.

I started to clean up the spilled coffee and went about my closing routine. It was safe to say no one else would be coming into the café tonight. Way to go Quinn. I hated days like this. Why couldn't a single day go by without fate asking me to intervene? I just wanted the night to end so I could go home and close the door to the world—if only for a few hours. I looked at the clock, one hour before I could lock up…I stared at the clock, willing it to move faster. Too much down time meant too much time to think.

Tick… tock, tick… tock, every loud tick of the clock reminded how close the boy had come to being directly in the path of that cab. Two seconds. Two short seconds. What if I hadn't made it in time? I cringed remembering my vivid vision. But I saved him… this time.

What if one day my psychic flashes came too late? How would I live knowing I could've stopped it? It was too much stress. I was already starting to feel the intense emotional and physical exhaustion that came from the quick spike of adrenaline and overpowering fear that came with my premonitions. Oh, the joys of being a psychic teenager.

Worst. Gift. Ever. Forever trying to save people from themselves, but (as I quickly learned) not everyone wanted help or advice from a stranger. Since I always just "happened" to be around when disaster struck in this town, people avoided me as if my mere presence alone would cause immediate harm. How ironic.

People around here didn't like different. They liked predictable and mainstream. They'd probably have me locked up in a padded room for the rest of my life if they thought I believed I could see the future. Or worse, they'd never leave me alone and always be asking for insight into their lives as if I was some sort of novelty at their disposal... so I kept my abilities to myself.

Most of the time my gift—even though it was used to help people—made people steer clear of me. The people of Rosevale didn't see my actions as my means of intercepting fate, but the unpredictable and drastic acts of a rebellious, reckless, inconsiderate teen hooligan who was a bad luck magnet. Their words, not mine. Quite frankly I didn't think people still used the word hooligan but trust me —they did.

"There's Quinn, can you believe what she did yesterday? I heard she pushed a complete stranger to the ground for no reason. She's unhinged."

"Steer clear of Quinn, last week a man was standing near her and got his coffee knocked out of his hands."

"Quinn's in your class? I'd switch out, bad things happen when she's around."

I had gotten used to it for the most part though. It was better they hate me and avoid me than know about my ability. And it wasn't like I could just ignore what I saw. If I hadn't pushed that woman to the ground, she would have been hit by a load of lumber that was sticking out of the side of a passing truck and I saw that man having an anaphylactic reaction to the hazelnut in his coffee. It was either act on my psychic abilities and be ostracized, or not act on my abilities and stand by and watch as people got hurt. What choice did I have? I sighed again in frustration.

Glancing up at the clock I realized it was finally closing time. I slowly started cleaning, taking my time and making sure everything was spotless so there was one less thing for Jolene to be upset with me about. Once I was outside, I closed my eyes and let the cool breeze soothe my nerves. Focusing on slowing my breathing, I tried to let the cool night wash away the events of today.

The 20-minute walk home felt like an eternity. My body felt like it was getting heavier and heavier with each step I took as the mental and physical exhaustion started to hit me. As I walked up the stone path to my front door, I could see Gran in the kitchen and could smell her Sunday night black bean casserole wafting through the open window. I felt a small smile tug at my lips as I stepped into the front hallway. My house, my haven.

"Quinnie dear, is that you?" my Gran called from the kitchen.

"Yes Gran, who else would it be?" I kicked off my shoes and walked into the kitchen. I sunk down into my seat at the table with a small groan.

"Oh, well, you never know who's stopping by for a visit," she replied.

"And if it hadn't been me? What then?" I asked, slightly amused.

"Well then I guess I'd have to invite them in for dinner. Thankfully, I always make extras."

I looked at her incredulously wondering if she was serious, and knowing my Gran, she probably was. She turned and winked at me.

"That or hit them with this frying pan."

I laughed despite the residual tension left over from that night's encounter.

"How was work?" she asked. I just groaned again in response. "Uh oh, another night of saving lives and getting strife?" She came and poured us tea and sat down at the table with me.

That was why I loved my Gran, well, one of the many reasons. She was intuitive like me, but her talent was reading energies, not that it took a genius to see that I was upset tonight. She just… got me.

"They can't see I'm trying to save them… they just see me as someone who is bad luck or causing trouble. I wish they understood…"

"It's not easy being a modern-day superhero, sweetie. I wish I could say it gets easier, but until people become more accepting and realize that there is more to life that the black and white world they believe we live in, people like us, people with gifts will always live on the peripherals not quite able to blend in. We're hues of grey, Quinnie. We blur the lines they have gotten so comfortable living inside. It scares them. All you can do is hold in your heart the knowledge that you're making a difference and live your life the best way you know how." She stood up and gave me a kiss on the forehead before going back to check on our dinner.

"Would it be better if they just knew? Maybe then they'd see me as a help and not a hinderance."

Gran sighed. "We've talked about this, Quinn. The world would either use you for your gifts or use your gifts against you. You'll just have to make do with only me knowing your secret."

"I know you're right, it's just hard when people think of you as someone who is completely opposite of who you really are. And I don't like keeping secrets."

She gave my shoulder a sympathetic squeeze before serving our food. As we continued talking about our day my poor mood started to shift for the better. Or maybe she took my bad mood from me with her gifts, some days I was not quite sure.

By the time I finally curled up in bed I was feeling much lighter. I closed my eyes surrendering myself to the blissful slumber that would ward off the world off for a little while. I would need every minute of relief I could get because tomorrow… well, tomorrow I started my senior year of high school.

*　*　*

CHAPTER

2

★

My dreams, like most nights, were just swirling clouds of color with the occasional burst of a scene, never staying long enough for me to get a full grip on what was happening. In waking life this would normally be infuriating, except that these dreams were always accompanied by a complete sense of peace and an overwhelming feeling of safety. I couldn't explain it exactly.

Gran thought that these blurred snapshots were just my abilities seeping into my dreams, kind of like the leftovers of psychic activity. Regardless of what the dreams were or where they came from, I always woke up feeling calm, for which I was always grateful… though the peace was often short-lived.

Beep. Beep. Beep. My alarm went off again, starting to chip away at the remaining serenity and security I had felt upon first waking up. I rolled out of bed (almost literally) and into my favorite pair of hip-hugging jeans, paired with a white tank top and my favorite light blue cardigan. I threw my long, straight brown hair effortlessly into a high ponytail and made my way down to the kitchen.

Gran had an amazing breakfast laid out for the two of us: bacon, scrambled eggs, hash browns, freshly-squeezed orange juice and fruit salad.

Normally that would have been an incredible start to my day, but with school starting up again it felt more like a last supper than a scrumptious breakfast.

"How did you sleep?" Gran asked as I heaped piles of bacon onto my plate.

"Wonderful as always… then I woke up," I laughed. Gran smiled sympathetically at me. She was all too familiar with my anxiety about going back to school and back to the whispers and being avoided like the plague.

"Well at least you have Thomas and Elsbeth with you now that they're back from Florence," she said attempting to lift my mood. And it worked! My best friends were *finally* back from their family vacation.

Leave it to my only two friends in the world to ditch me for half of the summer. I rolled my eyes internally. I guess that's what happens when your best friends are also fraternal twins.

"Quinnie, you better hurry up." My Gran's voice broke me out of my thoughts. I had five minutes before I had to go meet Thomas and Elsbeth. I sprinted up the stairs, brushed my teeth, and hastily grabbed my bag before jetting back down the stairs.

"By Gran, love you!" I called out as I flew out the door. I heard her call back something in response, but her endearments were cut short.

I could see them waiting at the end of the street. As I rounded the bend I broke into a run.

"You're back!" I screamed as I threw myself onto the two of them. My attack was greeted with a loud "oomph" from both twins.

"Well hello to you too," Thomas replied, adjusting his glasses that I had knocked askew with my hug.

"Quinn, you will not believe how many cute guys there are in Italy. I've decided we need to move there. Like now," Elsbeth said with a huge grin.

The idea of never having to go back to Rosevale High does sound pretty enticing… I shook the thought from my head.

Elsbeth pulled her smartphone out of her backpack and started furiously scrolling through them as she told me about their adventures.

There were pictures of their family smiling at Piazza Della Signoria, pictures of the twins standing in awe outside the Cathedral of Santa Maria del Fiore, pictures of Ponte Vecchio, wineries, and so much more. They looked like they had so much fun! They had invited me to go along with them, and even offered to pay, but Jolene and Gran needed me back home. That and I wouldn't feel comfortable having them pay for me. The twins were blessed with parents who both had high-paying jobs. Don't get me wrong, Gran and I had always had a comfortable life, just not enough extra to take any vacations, especially if I wanted to head to university next year.

We kept walking with Thomas shouting the occasional warning about objects and curbs so Elsbeth and I could keep looking at photos while we walked.

Without even looking up I suddenly felt a palpable mood shift. A glance up from the phone confirmed what I already knew… we had reached the edge of school property. I quickly glanced back down at the phone, not wanting to meet anyone's eyes.

"It took a full ten seconds for anyone to notice we were here. They are off their game after summer break," Thomas pointed out.

"I hate that you've been ostracized too just for knowing me." I tried to keep my shoulders from caving inward. I didn't want to cower in front of my peers, but standing tall when you didn't feel accepted wasn't an easy task.

Elsbeth linked her arm through mine in a show of solidarity. "Who cares what these morons think? They say you're bad luck, but having you as my best friend makes me feel so lucky! One more year won't kill us," she said squeezing me closer. *And if it tried, I'd see it coming.* I added internally. To prove her point and show her solidarity, she yelled, "buzz off!" to the next person she caught staring at us. I laughed despite the guilt I felt.

"We're a team," Thomas added, coming to stand at my other side.

"Thanks guys." We walked in silence for a couple steps before I suddenly realized that we had been so caught up in talking about Florence we hadn't even compared our class timetables. We all unlinked arms as we all opened our bags trying to find our schedules for the first semester.

"I have Chemistry, Calculus, Biology and Geography," stated Thomas.

"Yuck." Elsbeth stuck out her tongue in distaste.

"While lame-mc-snorzeville is being bored to death, I'll be in English, Dance, Drama, and Visual Arts."

"This sucks!" I slumped my shoulders in defeat.

"Why? What's yours?" Thomas peered over my shoulder at my schedule.

"English, Chemistry, Biology, Writer's Craft." I grumbled, dreading facing the majority of each day without my two best friends.

"Well, you'll start your day with me," Elsbeth said cheerfully.

"And you have Bio with me after lunch," Thomas said, trying to match Elsbeth's enthusiasm.

"Yeah, but that means I'm without either of you for half a day in this hell-hole. Any chance you want to see if you can switch into my second period Chemistry class... best friend and lab partner ever?" I said tossing him my best puppy-dog eyes.

"No can-do Quinn, that's the only time that allows me to have calculus this semester and I need it as a prerequisite for next semester. Sorry kiddo. Can you switch?"

"No, same deal with me except with English. Ugh." We pushed through the front doors and headed upstairs to claim lockers next to each other.
Thomas turned to me as we walked up the stairs.

"It'll be okay, maybe you'll have assigned partners, so it won't be as awkward," he suggested. Thomas's comment was met by a swift swat from Elsbeth.

"Insensitive moron," she mumbled.

"What?" Thomas asked in confusion as he adjusted his glasses that had been knocked askew by his sister.

Realizing he had just implied no one would want to be my partner he quickly tried to backtrack his comment and became immediately flustered.

"What I meant was that it'll save you from having to, you know…"

"It's okay Thomas," I reassured him, "and hopefully you're right." I secured my lock on my locker and tugged at it twice to make sure it was closed.

The warning bell chimed in the hallway letting us know classes would begin in less than five minutes. Elsbeth and I said goodbye to Thomas and headed off to our first class. The English classrooms were on the fourth floor of the high school. It was not a big school, more tall than big.

At four stories tall it resembled a strange office building more than it did a typical high school. We chose seats by the windows at the back of the room where people were less likely to be involved in our business as I continued scrolling through Elsbeth's photographs. A few minutes later the class had filled up. Once the bell rang our teacher Mrs. Blanc, took attendance.

"Quinn Aurelia?" Mrs. Blanc called out.

"Present." Even though this was the first word I had spoken since coming to class, one single word—a word that I was *supposed* to say, no less—my voice was still greeted with whispers and harsh glances from many of my peers. Oh, the joys of being infamous.

Ugh. I groaned and buried my head in my hands.

"Ignore them Q, the ignoramuses know not what they do," Elsbeth said in her all-knowing teacher voice that made me smile every time she used it.

Her voice, along with the use of my nickname had me feeling a bit better, even if some of the students had yet to turn back around to face the front. Elsbeth had been calling me Q ever since we were in the third grade. She liked the way it sounded when she said, 'hey Q'. Like a mixture of 'hey you and thank you' and it just kind of stuck. Sometimes it still made her laugh when she said it.

"Elisabetta Mantello?" she called. I could feel Elsbeth's immediate annoyance at hearing her legal name.

"It's Elsbeth, Mrs. Blanc," she said through gritted teeth, "just like it has been for the past three years," she added under her breath.

Once Mrs. Blanc started her lesson, people finally turned around and stopped gawking at us. Last night at the café I just wanted time to speed up, but as I sat there beside Elsbeth who was doodling on her notebook, I found myself wishing time would slow down so that Chemistry wouldn't have to happen. But alas, time rolled on and before I knew it, the bell was ringing, and people were streaming out of the classroom.

"Well, I guess I'll see you at lunch... If I survive that is," I said to Elsbeth. She dramatically rolled her eyes and pushed me in the direction of the chemistry labs.

"You'll be fine. But, if you don't survive, I get your car!" she called as she danced her way to her next class.

Elsbeth had coveted my car ever since my Gran got it for me for Christmas. It was the one item I had that she didn't, but until she learned to drive, she didn't really have a use for one.

I hesitated outside the classroom door before going in, giving myself a pep talk, trying to convince myself to walk into the room. *It's one class, you can do it. Come on Quinn. You're used to this. Just ignore them the way you wish they'd ignore you.*

I took a deep breath and pushed open the door. The class was already pretty full when I walked in, with most people already paired up. I felt every set of eyes on me as I walked in. The emotions on people's faces varied from incredulous, to uneasy, to pitying, but not one smile. I chose the empty lab bench at the back corner of the room and plopped myself down in the seat, part of me wishing I had worn a giant sweater today so I could have hidden beneath the hood.

One of two things was bound to happen. Either the last person in the classroom was going to be stuck with me as a lab partner, or there would be an odd number and I'd be on my own. I was *really* hoping for the latter.

I was doodling on my notebook when a voice startled me. I looked up from my desk to see a boy standing directly in front of me with a kind smile on his face. I was so confused I didn't even register what he had said to me.

"Huh?" I asked, dumbfounded.

He laughed then said, "I asked if this seat was taken?" gesturing to the empty seat beside me. I looked around the room at the four or five other empty seats and looked back at him, too shocked for words.

"You mean here? Beside…me?" I asked, still really confused and not knowing what to make of this situation.

"Yes… me… sit… here?" he said drawing out his words slowly in a cave man voice with a smile still in his eyes. I knew everyone in the room was staring, but for once I didn't care. I was baffled by this turn of events and barely even noticed. *Why does he want to sit beside me when there are so many other seats? He must be new or something…*

"I probably wouldn't if I were you, but whatever." Trying to sound nonchalant, I flipped my hand absently in the direction of the seat, but I think I waved it too fast for the gesture to seem at all natural.

He sat down in the seat beside me, leaned back in his chair, looking completely at ease.

"This school's a lot different than my last one."

I nodded noncommittally trying to process what was happening.

"I'm Dominic and you are?" he asked.

Dumbfounded, I responded internally. Instead of answering his question, I took a deep breath and decided to spare his social status and tell him how the social hierarchy worked at Rosevale High.

"Um, I don't mean to sound rude at all, but you don't have to sit here and talk to me. I mean, I'm not exactly the most liked around here and since you're new to the school it's probably best to move now before it's too late."

He tilted his head quizzically as if pondering something for a brief moment before shrugging.

"I've never really cared what people thought. Let them think what they want, I don't scare easy," Dominic smiled with a wink.

"Your funeral," I said with a shrug. I could feel a slight smile tugging at the corners of my mouth.

He settled in and started setting his pencil case and notebook on the desk.

"By the way," he said after a moment, "you still haven't told me your name."

I told him my name was Quinn Aurelia and waited for him to cringe or flinch, but he didn't. Instead he told me his full name was Dominic Hunter.

"Two first names, huh? Cool," I said. He said neither name sounded very original and I joked that it was as if his names were just chosen at random out of a hat.

I surprised myself by letting out a small laugh.

"It's kind of true, but hopefully your parents put in more thought than that!"

"I somehow sense not," he said, breaking into another smile.

He launched into a story about his family moving here recently, but I found myself more focused on his features than his words. I couldn't help, but notice his shaggy jet-black hair, emerald green eyes (that put Elsbeth's to shame) and a pretty buff bod if my initial observations were correct… *not that I'm looking*.

His story was cut short when Mr. Linton came in to begin our class.

"Everyone please turn to the person next to you and introduce yourselves because you will be lab partners for the remainder of the semester. I hope you chose wisely!" Mr. Linton warned.

I shrugged at him and under my breath whispered, "I told you, you should have moved earlier."

He just chuckled and rolled his eyes.

Maybe this year won't be so bad after all…

"Sooooooooo," Elsbeth drawled as she put the back of her hand dramatically against her forehead, "was it as horrible as you imagined?" She pretended to faint against my locker.

"No, it was actually okay." I nudged Elsbeth out of the way so I could unlock my locker… except, it was already unlocked. *I could have sworn I locked this.* Peering inside everything seemed to be as I left it so maybe I just hadn't locked it properly after all.

"Elsbeth, did Quinn just say something about Rosevale High being actually okay?" Elsbeth mirrored his puzzled face when she replied, "Why yes, dear Thomas, I believe she did."

Elsbeth then turned to me, "who are you?" and without missing a beat Thomas continued, "and what have you done with our high-school-hating best friend?"

I just laughed, "high school isn't all that bad."

Elsbeth slammed my locker door shut.

"Spill," she demanded.

I relayed the entire story to them as we walked towards the cafeteria, explaining how Dominic seemed to voluntarily want to sit with me and didn't seem to care that my existence was not well received here.

"Whoa, either he is incredible, and you should totally date him, or he's certifiably insane… and you should totally date him," Elsbeth gushed after I finished my story.

"Date him? I just met him. Thomas, tell your sister she's crazy and that he wouldn't want to date me anyway."

But instead of agreeing with me I saw Thomas scrunch his nose in contemplation as we sat down at a table far away from the other students.

"Well… he did pick you out of a room of people and stuck around after he found out you're the high school's leper. I think he digs you," Thomas pointed out.

"*Digs me?* Seriously, Thomas. Who's to say I've even thought of him that way anyway? I know nothing about him. He's not even that good looking."

"Methinks the lady doth protest too much," Thomas said around a bite of his egg salad sandwich.

"Whatever. Drop it. Conversation over." I said trying to sound stern as I opened my container of leftover bean casserole.

"If you say so… he doesn't by chance have shaggy brown hair, does he?" Elsbeth asked.

"No, it's more of a charcoal than a brown, why?"

My spoonful of casserole paused by my mouth and I knew I had been caught. "I *knew* it!" Elsbeth squealed. "You totally checked him out. You *were* objectifying too much. And secondly, he's totally staring at you right now," Elsbeth said smugly.

"I think you meant *objecting* too much," Thomas corrected his sister. "Or then again, maybe not," he mused.

"What?" Elsbeth asked in confusion, completely oblivious. Thomas just shook his head. I looked over in the direction Elsbeth was looking and sure enough, there was Dominic eating with the popular crowd and staring directly at me. When I caught his eye, he smiled at me, before turning back to the group as someone tapped him on the shoulder.

I looked to see who has grabbed his attention and it was Mindy. *Great, of course it was Mindy.* In the saga that is my life, obviously, my arch nemesis would be the one vying for the attention of the only guy other than Thomas to acknowledge my existence. Melinda Thorne, the bane of my existence. Well, the bane of my high school existence anyway. Melinda Thorne, the thorn in my side ever since she arrived at Rosevale High last year. I had been trying to fit in my whole life; it took her all of five minutes to become the queen bee. She, more than anyone, seemed to get the most pleasure out of my being alienated by my peers and did everything in her power to make sure I stayed that way.

"I wouldn't worry about it too much," Thomas said, reading my expression. "He seems to be blatantly ignoring her." I looked back at the table. Mindy was giving him her classic 'smouldering eye' look that she gave any man with breath in his lungs. Then I looked over at Dominic, expecting to see the drooling look that most men give Mindy, but he wasn't even looking at her. He *was* ignoring her. *Ha!* I smiled to myself knowing she was working so hard with no results and that knowledge kept me smiling well through lunch.

The rest of the day passed by in a blur, with my mind drifting back often to Dominic. He seemed so confident and cool and collected and I found myself wanting to learn more about him. Even catching up with the twins after school was difficult to focus on. I was just so perplexed by this newest development. I found myself wondering if he'd be as happy to see me tomorrow as he was today or if Mindy and her minions had poisoned him against me. By the time I got home that night Gran was already asleep, but she had left a note on my pillow.

Hey Sweetie,
Hopefully your first day went well. If it did that's great!
If it didn't, there's always tomorrow.
I love you.
See you in the morning.
XO Gran

I put the note in the drawer of my bedside table directly beside the postcard I received from the twins two weeks ago from the leaning tower of Ponte Vecchio. I studied it for a moment cherishing the knowledge that at least three people in the world were looking out for me, even if the rest of the world could care less about my existence.

* * *

CHAPTER

3

✦

Two Weeks Earlier...

Cooper stomped down the hall of the Coordinator HeadQuarters towards the elevation pods, frustrated that the Magistrate had summoned him in the middle of an intense training session with his agility coach.

He stood waiting outside the pod launch, shifting his weight from one foot to another in irritation. He just wanted to get this meeting over with so he could get back in time for strength training and not waste his time with whatever lecture Nettie was bound to give him.

He stepped into the first available pod and gave the thought-command to be taken to the Magistrate's office on the 180th floor. The green laser scanning rings that were produced from a device at the top of the pod cascaded like falling halos over his entire body, confirming his identity.

Welcome Cooper, the words flashed upon the glass siding of the pod. *The Magistrate will see you now.* And with that, the pod shot up like a rocket taking him from the training facility on the 4th floor up to the second highest floor of the building in a matter of milliseconds. Normally, Coordinators just used thoughts to travel from place to place, but for security purposes, the only way to reach any floor of the Coordinator HeadQuarters was by elevation pods. Cooper hated the pods; it felt so unnatural to him to rely on something other than his own thoughts to get him to where he needed to be.

The golden wings tattooed on Cooper's back tingled as they always did when he was agitated; the magical ink embedded in his flesh reacted to his change in energy.

Cooper thought that finally becoming a Guardian and getting his wings would somehow change him—like maybe suddenly everything horrible that had ever happened to him would disappear, or at least feel more distant and less overwhelming, but that wasn't the case. If only these wings were made for flight... then maybe he could escape his past once and for all.

It wasn't that he wasn't thankful for the tattooed wings that covered the complete span of his back, because he was. The ink was composed of special compounds that enabled the wings to resonate at the exact frequency of the veil, allowing Guardians to pass through the veil unharmed.

Being given the gift of being able to safely cross the veil that separates his world from the human realm definitely had its perks; however, it didn't come with the complete freedom he longed for. Even though the honor of being a Guardian had given him a little more room to stretch his wings, he still felt like he was missing something; still waiting to find a meaning in what he did that was more than the obvious 'because it has to be done'.

Cooper stepped off the pod and quickly walked down the short hallway leading to the large oak double doors of The Magistrate's office.

"You rang?" Cooper drawled, as he sauntered into The Magistrate's office and plopped himself into one of the armchairs, knowing it would infuriate her.

"Cooper, really," Nettie said exasperatedly. "Could you please try to show a little more respect?"

"Sorry. You rang, *Magistrate*?" he drawled again, smirking a little.

Nettie just sighed to herself. She did note however, that Cooper sat up a little straighter.

"I have a new case for you."

Cooper leaned forward in his chair, resting his elbows on his knees, chin atop his clasped hands. Although his demeanor screamed nonchalance, Nettie noticed the fire in his eyes that always came to light when he was handed a new case that held the possibility of a new challenge.

"I'm listening," Cooper said, trying to hide the excitement in his voice.

In all of his nineteen years, Cooper had never been able to hide when he was truly interested in something. He had developed a poker-face for a lot of things, but not when it came to a prospective case.

Nettie paused for a moment. Careful to conceal any maternal feelings she had towards him. She couldn't help but notice how much he had changed since he was a boy… how much he had changed since… Pinching the bridge of her nose, she shook the thought from her head.

"I have a new case for you—"

"So, you said," Cooper interrupted.

"If you'd let me finish, I was going to say I have a new case for you that is different from any case I've handed you before, but if you're going to act like this, maybe I should give it to a more refined Guardian." She knew her comment would sting, but she needed his complete focus when it came to this case.

Cooper's jaw and fists clenched simultaneously. His tensed biceps were starting to stretch the cuff of his white V-neck T-shirt as he fought for control. Snapping at the Magistrate—even if she was a family friend—would not end well for him.

"I can handle it." Cooper clenched teeth.

"Good. Now this case is confidential, which means you cannot share any of the details with anyone."

"Covert Op. Gotcha," Cooper said, relaxing slightly now that Nettie seemed to be giving him the case.

"Be serious, Cooper. Not anyone. I mean it. Not your mom, not Cali, and definitely not Neil."

Cooper's best friend Neil was not as focused when it came to his job and the Magistrate could not afford anything to go wrong with this mission.

His voice softened. "I promise, Nettie. I won't tell anyone… not my mom, not my sister, and definitely not Neil," he said, serious for the first time.

"This case is a protection-based case. You will be with your Charge at all times ensuring her safety—no exceptions. Her survival and well-being are pivotal in the lives of many. There are those out there who seek to manipulate and destroy your Charge and you must insure that does not happen. She has a huge role to play in the grand scheme of things and her safety is of the utmost importance."

"Not a problem. Who's my Charge?" Cooper asked, envisioning a military operative, or a spy. Whoever it was, she must be important to warrant this much secrecy.

"Her name is Quinn. She is a seventeen-year-old about to enter her senior year of high school in a small town called Rosevale."

"Hold on just a minute!" Cooper said, jumping up from his chair, wings tingling in agitation. "You want me to *babysit?*"

"Her existence is pivotal in the lives…"

"…of many. Yeah, yeah, yeah. I heard you the first time. Why would I want to take on a case babysitting a teenage girl? If I wanted to do that I'd stay home with my sister, Cali." he fumed. Cooper's brows furrowed as he crossed his arms.

"It is not for us to ask why…" Nettie said, quoting the first line of the oath that all initiates must take upon being given their wings and accepting all the responsibilities that came with being a Guardian. The lilt in her voice and the pause told Cooper that she expected him to continue the oath.

"I am familiar with the oath, thank you very much," Cooper said, anger welling up inside of him.

Was he being punished? That was the only explanation he could think of as to why he was being stuck with a teenage female Charge. He knew his attitude was sometimes a problem, but he thought Nettie, of all people, would value his skills and be lenient with his behavior. He must've thought wrong.

"It is not for us to ask why…" Nettie repeated.

With that, Cooper huffed out a frustrated breath and recited the Guardian's Oath.

> *"It is not for us to question why.*
> *It is but our job to do or die.*
> *The Human race is in a fragile state.*
> *It's up to us to align their fate.*
> *Each human has a specific purpose in life.*
> *It's not our job to say what's wrong or right.*
> *And only if a life is prematurely in peril*
> *May we use our wings and step through the veil."*

"So, will you take the case or not?" Nettie asked, knowing full well he would do as he was told even if it was begrudgingly so.

"What could be so special about a seventeen-year-old that people would be out to harm her? And if you tell me *it's not for us to ask why* one more time, I swear I'm leaving." Cooper stared her dead in the eyes, daring her to deny his request for information.

"We are not sure why, but she can foresee events before they happen."

"Like the Virtualizing Animatron?" Cooper asked, referring to the high-tech computer system that HeadQuarters used to track and coordinate the millions of human destinies they were in charge of preserving.

"Yes, except without any technology."

Cooper started to pace the room before looking up and asking the Magistrate how that was even possible. She just shook her head and explained that she didn't know how the girl's visions were possible, but only that she could see death before it happened and must be protected against those who wish to harm or use her. After a moment of consideration, he stopped and faced the Magistrate. "Fine. When do I start?"

Nettie stood up and gestured for him to sit at her desk. He tried to suppress the shocked raise of his eyebrows before sitting down where she had just been. "Five minutes ago," she said succinctly. "You will find all the information you need in the file in my desk. I matched it to your brain frequency, so all you need to do is ask for the file and it will be uploaded into your long-term memory. Upon completion, the file in my desk will self-destruct. You know the deal Cooper—you cannot tell a soul."

"Understood, Magistrate." And with that, Nettie stepped out of her office to give Cooper time to upload his case file, as well as to give him ample time to brood over his latest assignment.

Cooper stormed home after leaving the office. The damn file had taken so long to upload to his long-term memory that he missed his last training session, which meant a lot of built-up adrenaline that had nowhere to go. He chose to walk home in hopes of burning off some energy. His mother and sister were in the living room when he slammed the front door behind him.

"Coop?" his mother called out, concern lacing her voice. "What's wrong honey?" she asked, rising from her seat and walking towards her son. Her question was met by a string of mumbled words that if she knew her son at all, were probably words better left unheard. Instead of pushing the matter further she gently steered him in the direction of the kitchen before pouring him a mug of tea.

Cooper flopped down at the table. The tea wasn't the only thing that was steaming at that moment.

"I heard he got called to The Magistrate's office," Cali said blinking up innocently at their mother.

"Shut it, Cali," Cooper growled.

Cali's face fell, making Cooper immediately regret directing his frustration unfairly at his sister, when she had nothing to do with the source of his anger. Cooper huffed out a big breath and ran his hands through his hair trying to ease some of the tension he was feeling.

"I'm sorry, Cali. I'm not upset with you. Just had a frustrating meeting with the Magistrate, that's all," Cooper said apologetically. Cali's face lifted slightly, still hurt, but also understanding. Her big brother wasn't someone who was easy to get to know, but she understood him better than most.

"What happened with Auntie Nettie?" his mother asked, leaning over the table slightly to add some honey to the tea, Cooper's favorite.

Cooper's mother, Candice, and Nettie had been best friends for as long as she could remember, and Nettie was very much like a second mother to Cooper. Candice knew it had been a difficult adjustment over the past three months for both her best friend and son, switching from the family feel they'd always had to the office dynamic where Nettie was the boss. It was hard for Candice, too, having her best friend as the Magistrate, presiding over every Coordinator in Crysthala, but they made it work.

"She called me away right in the middle of my agility training," Cooper stated. "She *knows* how much I hate it when she takes me away from training. Why couldn't she just wait another hour?" Cooper took the cup of tea in his hands to anchor himself to the spot so he wouldn't do something he'd regret. *Damn adrenaline, why won't it wear off?*

"Why didn't you just bi-locate so you could keep training while she talked to you?" Cali asked, confused.

"Don't they teach you anything in school? You can't bi-locate when you go to the Magistrate's office. She wants you to be 'all present' when you arrive, to insure you are fully focused on what she's saying—or in my case lecturing. The elevation pod won't move if it senses you're split," Cooper explained, using the slang term for bi-location.

"Believe me, I wanted to split." The double meaning was not lost on his family, causing all three of them to smile. All three of them broke out into smiles.

Although he couldn't split when he wanted to earlier, he was now using bi-location to be here with his family, as well as simultaneously watching Quinn, *who was presently walking to work reading a postcard she received today from Italy. How utterly fascinating*, Cooper thought to himself sarcastically, *such a great use of my time.*

His family couldn't know about this case though, so it looked like he'd be using his wings' capability to bi-locate until further notice. He had nothing to worry about because both versions of him when he was split, were breathing, thinking, feeling beings—like identical twin Coopers that were joined in the mind so no one would even realize it was happening. All he'd have to do was wish one or both of the Coopers somewhere and he'd arrive to that place instantaneously, his family being none the wiser.

"I'm sorry that she lectured you, Sweetie," Candice said and sensing that he had calmed down slightly asked him if he had done anything to warrant the lecture, knowing that he probably had done something to cause Nettie to intervene. She was a good leader and wouldn't be stern with Cooper if he didn't deserve it.

Cooper was about to argue and defend himself, but since he was lying anyway, he didn't see the point in risking getting his mother upset with Nettie. Instead, Cooper sighed.

"Yeah, probably. But it doesn't mean I like it."

He decided to attempt to shake off his frustration so he could enjoy an evening with his family. Well, his family and Quinn apparently. Tomorrow he'd go back to training—all while still watching her. Despite the fact that she wasn't a spy, he couldn't help but feel in slight awe of his teenage Charge.

Although she was just seventeen, she had done many incredibly brave things in her life, which was why it took the file so long to download. This caused him to miss his training session, sending him in to a tyrannical state that was now only slowly subsiding with his family's help.

He still didn't like this assignment, but he couldn't help but agree with Nettie that there was something extraordinary about this girl; not that he'd ever give her the satisfaction of knowing that she was right.

* * *

CHAPTER
4

Present day...

Day two in purgatory, I thought to myself as I went to meet the twins before school. Meeting Dominic had been a bright spot in my day yesterday, but who knew if he'd still be amicable towards me or whether Mindy and her minions had already poisoned him against me.

I had barely opened my mouth to say hello to the twins when Elsbeth launched into a million and one questions about Dominic, knowing full well that I hadn't seen him since I left her house last night.

"Do you think he'll ask you out? Where did he move here from? Do you think he has a brother you could introduce to me?" Elsbeth asked as we walked. Thomas was the one to roll his eyes this time. He was used to our incessant chatter, but that didn't mean he enjoyed it. I laughed at Elsbeth's intensity.

"Whoa, slow your roll. I've only talked to him for five minutes! He may not even want to get to know me, but I'll make sure to ask about a brother for you." I smiled at my friend. I wasn't about to tell her that I was wondering the same things myself this morning—minus the brother, that was all Elsbeth.

English went by in a blur with Elsbeth shifting in her seat the entire time. It seemed as though she was more excited than I was about my Chemistry class. When the bell rang at the end of class and Elsbeth jumped up and looked me up and down before starting to fix my hair.

"Stop it, *stop it*!" I hissed as I swatted her hand away. Her fussing was making me suddenly nervous.

"Don't worry your hair looks fine and your shirt is super cute. Go get 'em tiger!" Elsbeth encouraged me as we walked out of class.

"See you at luuunnnch," she sang with a wink as she sashayed down the hallway. I mumbled my goodbye and headed towards Chemistry. There was a knot in my stomach where there wasn't before, *thanks a lot Elsbeth.* I give myself a mini pep talk on the way to class and by the time I got to the classroom I was feeling a little more at ease.

Walking into the room I saw that Dominic had beaten me to class. I took a breath to steady myself, smiled, and walked to my desk.

"How was your first day at R.H.S.?" I asked him as I took my books out of my bag.

"Well the people I ate lunch with bored me, most of them too vain for my taste; too self-absorbed," he stated with distaste, "but there was a girl I met in one of my classes who seemed much more down to Earth, so there's that," he said smiling at me. I felt a slight blush creeping across my cheeks.

"Yeah, Mindy, Krista and the other socialites aren't exactly known for their humility, but stick with me and not only will I show you humility, but humiliation as well." I responded before internally kicking myself for sounding so idiotic. "My humiliation, I mean, not yours," I corrected. "I will be the one being humiliated. I didn't mean to make it sound like I was going to humiliate you…" I stopped talking abruptly, cringing inwardly.

He just smiled kindly at me, laughter in his eyes.

"You, Quinn, are one interesting character, and I like it. I'm glad I'm going to be your lab partner. I hope you're a hard worker though, I'm not about to get poor grades because of some rambling fool," he said lightheartedly.

"Top of my class, in grades anyway. I promise," I assured him, making the motion of crossing my heart.

"Then I think we'll get along just fine."

The heat in my cheeks increased at his words.

"People really dislike you though. Why is that?" he asked leaning towards me slightly.

"Let's just say I'm a bad luck magnet so people keep their distance," I replied candidly. Any follow-up questions he may have had got cut off by the sound of Mr. Linton's voice as he began his lesson on oxidation. I was relieved to see that he hadn't been scared off, *at least not yet.*

As we all filed out of the room after class, Krista—Mindy's second in command—made her way over to Dominic, calling out to him and asking if he'd be joining them again for lunch today.

"Save me, please," Dominic pleaded to me under his breath just as Krista reached us. She linked her arm flirtatiously through his as she waited for his response.

"What?" I asked him with a confused look on my face. Dominic just shook his head and turned his attention to Krista, removing her arm from his as he turned.

"Sorry Krista, I can't today. I'm having lunch with Quinn," Dominic replied.

His response literally had anyone who heard it stopping in their tracks, myself included.

Krista looked between me and Dominic with a look —that could only be described as horrified contempt—then said to Dominic with a cackle, "You'll be back eating with us by tomorrow. No one voluntarily eats with *that,*" she said, clearly meaning me.

She flipped her hair over her shoulder and walked out of the room. I was used to those kinds of remarks from her and for the past year, Mindy as well. I barely felt the sting anymore. However, I found I was slightly embarrassed that Dominic had heard the comment. It took me a second to work up the courage to look over at Dominic, afraid he had changed his mind. However, when I looked over, he didn't look disgusted or embarrassed he looked...bashful?

"I hope you don't mind," Dominic said looking at his feet. "I just couldn't stand the idea of having to sit through one more lunch with them so I thought I could sit with you and your friends? If you don't mind that is," Dominic asked raising his eyes to meet mine.

"If you want to voluntarily alienate yourself, suit yourself," I said to him, my stomach doing a little flip. I half expected Dominic to turn and bolt once we cleared the doorway, but instead he walked with me to my locker.

Elsbeth's eyes almost popped out of her head when she saw us together. I looked at her over Dominic's shoulder and gave her the 'be cool' look. Elsbeth composed herself and started getting her lunch out of her locker, one eye still on me and Dominic. Thomas walked up behind Elsbeth and was visibly startled to see someone leaning against his locker. I turned to them and said I invited Dominic to eat with us and asked them if that would be okay. Dominic corrected me by explaining that he forced his way in and didn't really leave me with a choice in the matter.

"But if you feel like I'm intruding though I don't mind eating somewhere else," he added.

"We'll have none of that rubbish," Elsbeth said.

"Of course, you can eat with us! We'd be delighted to have you join us, wouldn't we Thomas?"

Thomas was still a little bewildered and shook his head to clear it.

"Uh, sure. No problem bro," and putting his fist out awkwardly. Dominic smiled and gave props to Thomas.

Elsbeth and I met eyes and tried to stifle a laugh at the fact that Thomas just tried to be cool. Definitely did not suit him. The four of us headed down to the cafeteria. *The four of us—wow that sounded so strange.* It had only been the three of us for as long as I could remember…We sat down at our normal table, more eyes on us than usual. I could feel Mindy glaring at me, but I ignored it and sat beside Dominic.

Without a moment's hesitation Elsbeth launched into her personal inquisition of Dominic: where was he from, what brought him to Rosedale, did his girlfriend miss him now that he moved away, and how long was he staying. Elsbeth was a little breathless by the end of her list of questions. I kicked her shin under the table and glared at her for prying into his life when he had barely sat down.

"Ouch, what was that for?" Elsbeth asked rubbing her shin, confused as to why I was upset.

Instead of answering her I turned to Dominic and apologized, saying he didn't have to answer any of her questions if he didn't want to. Elsbeth looked at me open-mouthed, but after seeing the look on my face, she quickly snapped it shut and pouted realizing she had been overruled.

Dominic just laughed. "I don't mind really; I'm a military brat, so I'm used to much worse." He turned from me to Elsbeth.

"My family owns the vineyard on the outskirts of town. We used to move every few months, but I kind of just wanted to finish high school at one school and not five so we moved here. My dad's on leave right now and could be called back at a moment's notice. Hard, but that's life sometimes. No girlfriend," he added catching my eye, "but I'm hoping to stick around so maybe that will change?"

I could feel my cheeks burning under his gaze. Elsbeth squealed in delight at this new piece of information.

"The vineyard, eh? Does your family plan on making wine while they are here?" Thomas asked quizzically.

"My family and I want to try, but it's pretty new to us. I was working in the vineyard over the summer, that's why not many people knew me before yesterday. Grapes are high maintenance, so I didn't have much time to get out. Most of my time was spent tending to the leaves and monitoring the growth of the vines."

Thomas nodded in approval. The rest of lunch consisted of Thomas and Dominic talking about wineries and vineyards. Occasionally Elsbeth would join the conversation with a tidbit of information she remembered from their trip to Europe. I didn't mind so much that the boys did most of the talking.

It was nice seeing Thomas so animated, plus it allowed me to look at Dominic freely and have a side conversation with Elsbeth in the best way we knew how— through facial expressions and texting each other.

Dominic was able to keep up with the intellectual topics Thomas brought up and was surprisingly open when responding to Elsbeth's personal questions. Occasionally throughout lunch Dominic and I would lock eyes and I had to turn away for fear of blushing.

There was one moment when Thomas was ranting about the use of pesticides when Dominic's leg brushed up against mine. I was sure he'd pull away once the contact was made, but he left it there… and we stayed that way, knee-to-knee for the rest of lunch. By the end of lunch, I swear I could feel the heat from the contact burning a hole through my jeans.

At the end of lunch Dominic asked if he could eat with us again tomorrow, we all happily agreed.

✹

Cooper observed Quinn as she sat on her bed, staring blankly at her notebook. *What is she doing?* Cooper thought to himself, not quite able to figure out why she hadn't moved an inch in almost an hour. He was half inclined to step through the veil just to check if she was still breathing, but he wasn't allowed to cross to the human realm unless her life was in obvious peril.

Quinn jumped out of bed so fast, it startled Cooper, which was a very difficult thing to do. She then proceeded to pace her room muttering to herself, "words, words, words." This continued for the next five minutes. Then she stopped abruptly in the middle of the room, facing where Cooper was standing, staring intensely in his direction. Although he knew she could not see him, it still managed to unnerve him enough for him to take a precautionary step away from the veil.

It took Cooper a minute to realize she was probably working on her homework for Writer's Craft. She had to write a poem and read it in front of the class tomorrow and she was panicked. Her file told him she had stage fright, so even though she loved writing, her anxiety was through the roof… and apparently giving her writer's block.

With an exasperated sigh, Quinn flung herself onto her bed.

"I can't do it. It's impossible!" she said to the ceiling. "Stupid words. Who needs them anyway?" She frowned to herself. She went silent again, a scowl still on her face. Over the next few minutes he watched as her face softened and the tension in her face was replaced with the slightest smile.

During the past few weeks Cooper had grown very accustomed to that face of hers and had seen it often enough to recognize that she was finally done overthinking and worrying and had begun to find a solution to whatever problem she was figuring out. Then, without warning, Quinn shouted in delight before diving off the bed to grab her notebook and pen and began writing furiously. Cooper just shook his head. *Sometimes I just don't understand women…*

He relaxed a bit as he watched her write, noting that her scowl has been replaced by a soft glow. She wrote continuously for the next thirty minutes, pausing only briefly to pensively chew on her pen cap before writing again. She eventually put her notebook back in her bag and went over to her closet.

Cooper knew her routine enough to know that it was time for him to turn his back and allow her to get dressed in private. While his back was turned, he focused on opening his ears to their surroundings for any sign of trouble.

The first thing he heard was the hum of the game show rerun Gran had on the television downstairs. That accompanied with the rhythmic snoring told Cooper she had fallen asleep in her recliner. Extending his hearing further, he heard cars in the distance and something shuffling outside on Quinn's property. He paused to see if he could identify what it was, but unless Quinn went outside, he couldn't risk having her out of his sight while he investigated. Shortly after the sound stopped. *Probably just a raccoon.*

He waited until he heard Quinn climbing under the covers before turning back around to face her. Within minutes she was fast asleep.

Since Coordinators didn't need sleep, Cooper would stand guard the entire night. *Thank goodness for bi-location or I'd go out of my mind,* he thought to himself. He liked that he could be in his back property guarding Quinn, while simultaneously beating Neil at an intense game of pick-up basketball across town. *I wonder what Neil would say if he knew I was only half present and still whooping his butt!*

* * *

CHAPTER

5

My dreams were more vivid than normal. At first there was nothing but the usual swirl of color; until suddenly there was a flash and there clearly in my mind was this vicious snake, coiled and ready to strike with its eyes staring directly into mine. Then without warning the snake lashed out, fangs snapping at my skin, barely missing me.

Fear sent shockwaves through my entire body. The snake lunged at me over and over, barely missing me. I kept trying to back up and dodge the snake, but it was as if I just couldn't predict where it was coming from. It wasn't acting as I expected it to. I couldn't predict its movements. My panic felt like it was going to swallow me whole.

As its fangs were just about to pierce the flesh near my heart the image was suddenly eclipsed with the warmest golden light I had ever seen. I couldn't remember ever dreaming of gold light, but I wasn't about to complain. Even though my dream had been anything, but serene, that golden glow had me waking up feeling very peaceful indeed.

However, it wasn't enough peace to calm my nerves about my upcoming presentation. *Or to spare me from getting large bags under my eyes.* I groaned as I evaluated the damage in the mirror. Normally I didn't bother wearing makeup, but if I was going to be thrown to the wolves today in Writer's Craft, I might as well spend my last day on Earth looking my best. I grabbed my concealer and applied a generous amount to my face, trying to hide the fact that I looked like I had been in a fistfight last night, and lost… miserably. I tossed my backpack over my shoulder and raced downstairs and grabbed the bagel Gran made me. I was about to head out the door when Gran called out, "Quinnie dear?" I paused in the doorway.

"Aren't you forgetting something?"

I quickly walked back inside and gave Gran a kiss on the forehead.

"You're right, I'm sorry. Thanks, for breakfast!"

"Oh, you're welcome dear, but that wasn't what I was talking about," she said pointing at my shirt. I looked down, horrified when I realized that I had forgotten to change out of my pajamas. *I can only imagine the looks on everyone's faces if I had shown up at school in the cartoon-covered pjs Gran made for me.*

★

I was only half present in English class. My mind was on a million other things, but I was snapped back to reality by a not-so-gentle nudge from Elsbeth. *Ow,* I rubbed my arm where she had smacked it.

"Ms. Aurelia?" Mrs. Blanc called out. My head snapped up to look at my teacher.

"Yes Mrs. Blanc?" I asked, knowing my classmates' eyes were on me.

"What's the answer?" Mrs. Blanc asked, presumably for the second time. If only I had been paying attention to what she was saying. We were studying the works of Shakespeare so I answered with the first thing I could think of…

"Uh, to be or not to be?"

"Unfortunately, for you Quinn, that was not the question. Now if you would stop day-dreaming long enough maybe you would have known that we were talking about Romeo and Juliet, not Hamlet," she scolded.

"Sorry, Mrs. Blanc," I mumbled as I picked up my pen to start taking notes.

"Maybe you should just *not be* in our class," Mindy hissed from behind me. A few people chuckled.

"Maybe you should just *shut up?*" Elsbeth retorted, mimicking Mindy's snide tone.

"Good one Elsbeth, or should I say *Loser?*" Mindy asked, causing another round of giggles from our classmates.

"Ignore her," I whispered. "She's not worth it."

Elsbeth started scribbling notes with a little more vigor than before. I felt guilty that she was upset, as I normally did when someone I loved got dragged down just for knowing me. Eventually the class started focusing on the content again, but that didn't erase what had happened. When the bell rang, we headed out.

"I'm really sorry Elsbeth, Mindy is a total brat."

Elsbeth looked at me with a forced smile on her face. "Don't worry, little Miss Prissy doesn't bother me, I'll see you at lunch okay?"

I nodded and gave her a quick hug before heading to Chemistry. I beat Dominic to class and was thankful for the few seconds alone to allow me to push English class from my mind before I saw him. He sauntered into the room a few minutes before the bell, flashed me one of his stunning smiles and sat down beside me.

"Penny for your thoughts?" Dominic asked as he dumped a handful of loose coins onto the table for our lab assignment. I had been so concerned about my poem for Writer's Craft that I had completely forgot that I was supposed to bring pennies to class today for our experiment. I apologized profusely to Dominic, but he just laughed it off saying he brought more than we'd need so there was no need to worry. I still felt bad and mumbled another apology. He playfully told me to lighten up. My forgetfulness only soured my mood more and my mind was still on Elsbeth and wondering if she had been able to brush off our most recent Mindy encounter.

"You okay?" he asked. "You don't seem like yourself?"

And how would you know who I am? You just met me… I could feel myself wanting to push him away. It was too late to spare Elsbeth, Thomas, and Gran from being hurt by associating with me, but maybe I could still spare Dominic.

"I'm fine," I said dismissively as Mr. Linton began writing the experiment's procedure, and materials on the board. Before Dominic could say anything else, I got up to get our materials for the coin oxidization lab we were doing.

Mr. Linton came around occasionally to observe each group's progress. We worked in silence for most of the period to complete our assignment.

Dominic continued to attempt to engage me in conversation, but my responses were mostly monosyllabic.

He turned to face me completely. "Seriously Quinn, what's up? Did I do something to make you mad?"

I sighed, feeling apologetic. "No, it's not you at all. You've been nothing, but kind and I guess I just don't feel I've done anything to deserve it."

"You give me a reason to not sit with gossipy girls at lunch who were throwing themselves at me. That's reason enough to be kind to you," he said with a chuckle.

I felt a smile tugging at the corners of my lips. It was hard to resist his charismatic charm.

"Wow, somebody sure thinks highly of himself," I joked as we started to pack up. I could already feel some of my playful banter returning thanks to this charming boy and his smile.

✦✦

Cooper watched them laugh as they walked towards Quinn's locker. Thomas saw them and nudged his sister conspiratorially. Quinn was still out of earshot, but Cooper's heightened hearing allowed him to tune into the twin's conversation.

"Oh yay!" Elsbeth clapped her hands excitedly, "aren't they the cutest?"

Thomas agreed that objectively speaking, they were both very attractive people. Quinn's long straight dark brown hair was offset by the shaggy aspect of Dominic's black head of hair. His emerald green eyes a nice balance to her deep blue ones. He was taller than her and broad shouldered. The twins smiled happily at their friend. Cooper, however, couldn't seem to muster the same joy in seeing Quinn with Dominic.

Elsbeth seemed to be in better spirits when we all met up for lunch. We decided to give Dominic the inside information about each teacher and what he could expect from them. I was about to launch into the story about what someone found once in Mr. Linton's desk drawer when Elsbeth interrupted.

"Do you know what I think?"

No one bothered responding knowing that she wasn't really looking for our response.

"I think you two should exchange numbers so that no one forgets what they need to do for future experiments."

I have Elsbeth a *'what-exactly-do-you-think-you're-doing'* look, which was met by her innocent *'I'm-helping-you-I-swear'* look.

"I think that's a great idea," Dominic said reaching into his pocket. "What's your number Quinn? I'll put it in my phone."

I began to tell him he didn't need to add me into his phone if he didn't want to, but my words were drowned out by Elsbeth reciting my phone number for Dominic.

"I'll text you, so you have my number too," Dominic said, firing off a quick text to me. I felt my phone vibrate in my backpack and turned to go open my bag. He put his hand over mine to stop me.

"It's okay, don't worry about it now, you can always check it later."

The warmth from his hand lingered even after he pulled it away. Elsbeth beamed at me, proud of her masterful idea.

By the time Thomas and I were in biology, I could barely focus; my nerves were starting to become unbearable as next period approached.

Thomas looked over at me and whispered, "it'll be okay, just breathe. I'll take notes. You just focus on not passing out." He smiled at me and playfully bumped his shoulder against mine. I tried to smile back, but my attempt was feeble at best.

"Break a leg, Kiddo!" Thomas said as he patted my shoulder. I tried to smile, but it quickly faltered. I started heading towards Writer's Craft, but halfway there I turned and bolted into the bathroom.

I stood in the bathroom looking in the mirror. I tried to say my poem out loud to myself, but nothing came out except for a pitiful squeak. Leaving the bathroom, I walked to class, my feet moving of their own accord. I didn't know what fainting felt like, but I was thinking I might be about to find out. I got to class and sat in my seat staring straight ahead just willing Mr. Dufranco to be absent so we wouldn't have to present today.

Quinn looks like she is going to throw up, Cooper thought, eyebrows drawn together with concern. His concern was slightly for Quinn, but mostly for himself. He didn't handle people vomiting near him and was really hoping she wasn't going to spill her guts. Nowhere in the extensive history on Quinn that had been uploaded into his brain did it mention her being prone to nervous nausea. He really hoped she wasn't about to break her lifelong streak now. Although he'd only been Quinn's Guardian for a couple weeks, he had already learned a great deal about her that no file could ever capture.

From what he had seen Quinn was smart, funny, kind to her friends… and talked to herself when she thought no one was around. *That was the kind of stuff they needed to put in her file.* Cooper smiled to himself in amusement. *Some sort of warning would've been nice.*

Cooper continued to smile as he remembered how crazed she had looked pacing her room last night, searching her room as if her inspiration was literally hiding from her.

A little bit of Quinn's color had returned by the time Mr. Dufranco entered the classroom, only to drain again completely when she saw him.

"Okay class," Mr. Dufranco began. "Who'd like to go first?"

No one volunteered, so Mr. Dufranco called on the boy in the back row who looked like he was about to fall asleep.

"Go ahead," Mr. Dufranco said to him, gesturing for him to go to the front of the room.

The boy stood at the front of the room and dramatically cleared his throat and the class chuckled. *Well everyone except Quinn… she was just sitting like a Zombie.*

"Eh-hem," the boy started.

> "The sun is hot like lava,
> The moon is cold like ice.
> I ran out of time this morning,
> So hopefully this poem sounds nice."

The class burst out into giggles. Mr. Dufranco just frowned and scribbled something on his mark sheet. A few more people read their simile poems, all which were better than the first boy, but nothing exceptional as far as Cooper could tell.

"Quinn, you're up next," Mr. Dufranco said. Quinn visibly swallowed and slowly rose from her seat. All eyes followed Quinn as she walked to the front of the class. *She looks so nervous.* He found himself wishing that he could do something to help her feel calm.

★

I can do this, I can do this, I thought to myself as I walked up to the front of the room. I stood at the front of the class, looking at my peers and suddenly all I wanted to do was faint for real… anything to get me out of this situation. I stood there for a second with my eyes closed trying to center myself.

Suddenly behind my eyelids I saw the same flash of gold that I had seen in my dreams last night. I let the golden light envelope me, calming me. I looked up at my classmates and began to speak…

"Your words are like honey,
They stick in my mind.
Your words are like poetry,
Soft and refined.
Your words are like a four-leaf clover,
Lucky and rare.
Your words are like toolbox,
They build and repair.
You let me taste the honey.
You share with me your rhymes.
You show your leaves completely.
You repair me just in time.
Although some words sting,
And words can bite,
You remind me of what
The good words feel like."

I took a deep breath. Everyone was silent. I waited for the snide comments, but none came.

I paused a moment more unsure what to do. Mr. Dufranco started clapping.

"Exceptional job, Ms. Aurelia, quite exceptional indeed!" He beamed at me.

Slowly the class started clapping, not a lot and not for long, but enough for me to let out the breath I didn't realize I had been holding. I smiled and returned to my seat. *I survived! And they didn't seem to completely hate it.* I let myself feel proud for a moment before talking myself back down to reality. *This doesn't change anything Quinn, they still dislike you,* I thought to myself, not quite fully able to smother my smile.

It wasn't until I got home that I remembered Dominic had texted me. I quickly unlocked my phone.

Hey its Dominic, text me
back when u get this

That's it? I could've sworn it was going to be something more than that seeing as he stopped me from reading it earlier. *Just when I think I'm starting to understand this boy.*

After responding, I put my phone down on the counter and started heating up the leftovers Gran left for me. Wednesday night was her BINGO night. I heard my phone chime.

My heart stopped. I kept rereading the text until I was sure I wasn't dreaming.

I waited all of 10 seconds before responding.

I didn't bother responding because quite frankly I was still in shock. I called Elsbeth and Thomas immediately, knowing if I waited until tomorrow to share the news, they would both disown me.

After almost two hours on the phone I hung up. I tried to do homework, but I was too giddy to get any work done.

"I have a date; I have a date. I have a date!" I said in a singsong voice, as I danced around my room. I squealed and jumped face first onto my bed, kicking my feet in excitement while I screamed into my pillow. I didn't think I'd ever sleep again; I was too wound up!

★✦

Cooper couldn't help but laugh as Quinn danced around her room. She looked so happy, so carefree… *That and her dance moves were just horrible, but somehow it kind of worked for her.* It was amazing what people did when they thought they were alone. Quinn cranked her music, grabbed her hairbrush and started singing along to an artist that he did not recognize. Her ponytail was bobbing back and forth as she jumped around.

Cooper smiled to himself, *she looks so…* Cooper stopped himself short. *She is your Charge, Cooper.*

"Something, something, blah, blah, love me, love me!" Quinn sang as she spun around the room.
His smile faltered. He couldn't figure out why the idea of Quinn seeing Dominic seemed to bug him so much. *Since when do I care what Quinn does with her life?*

* * *

CHAPTER

6

I woke up feeling incredible! Not only were there no snakes in my dreams, but there was also this added feeling that I was not used to feeling. I felt… excited to go to school. *Whoa, I must still be dreaming, there is no way I am actually excited to go to Rosevale High.* Yet, there it was, that feeling; a tingling in my stomach. I got out of bed and headed downstairs trying to shake the feeling. Breakfast was already ready by the time I meandered downstairs. Gran's homemade apple cinnamon oatmeal was sitting waiting for me.

"Hmm…" Gran said in her all-knowing way. "Your energy is different this morning."

"In m-wat way?" I asked as I took a huge bite of toast, hoping Gran would drop it because I didn't really want to talk about it yet.

"Your energy is…lighter," Gran said with a curious look on her face.

"Streaks of copper flecked with a pinkish hue." She stood staring at me for a moment. Instead of looking happy about this discovery, she looked almost concerned about it.

She quickly covered her concern with a smile and said, "That's great sweetie!" She didn't ask follow-up questions and just went back to her cooking. Her reaction to my good mood confused me. *What could she have seen in my energy that made her look so worried?* I tried to convince myself that if it was anything serious, she would tell me.

Walking to school was a giggle-fest to say the least. Elsbeth was spinning all the different scenarios that could happen this Saturday and was already starting to mentally go through my wardrobe to figure out what she thought I should wear. Thomas was oddly quiet as we walked. I moved so I was walking in between him and Elsbeth and I asked him, "What's up?"

"Don't get me wrong, I'm happy that you're going on a date, Quinn, but you know I've always thought of you as my unofficial sister, right?" Thomas adjusted his glasses as he often did when uncomfortable or nervous.

"I know Thomas, you're like a brother to me too, and your opinion is important to me. Is it Dominic you're not happy about or the fact that I'm dating in general?" I asked, trying to get a feel for why he wasn't completely on board.

"I honestly don't know Dominic well enough to say whether I like the guy. He *seems* nice enough, but I'm just protective and just don't want you to get hurt. People at school haven't always been the greatest to you and I guess I just haven't met someone who is worthy of you."

I pulled Thomas into a hug. "Don't worry, Thomas. I'll be careful."

He chuckled, "You better, because there's no way I could take him in a fight. Well, no way I'd win anyway," Thomas said flexing his non-existent biceps causing us all to laugh.

"And hopefully you'll never have a reason to fight him," I said to him.

I was glad that he was looking out for me. Hopefully over time Thomas would warm up to the idea of Dominic and me. If there even was going to be a 'Dominic and me'. I guess I shouldn't get ahead of myself.

After English I headed to Chemistry, feeling a little nervous to see Dominic now that we had a date set up. We got to the door at the same time.

"After you m'Lady," Dominic said with a slight bowing gesture.

"Why thank you m'Lord." I curtsied awkwardly in response then walked through the door. Once we had settled, I asked him what the plan for Saturday was going to be.

"That is for me to know and you to find out," he said mysteriously, winking at me. I scowled at him.

Sometimes I found myself wishing my psychic abilities could be used to see my future. We didn't get much more time to talk in class because Mr. Linton was speaking really quickly today, so we all had to write faster to follow what was going on.

Dominic couldn't stay for lunch, he didn't say why, but it allowed us to talk about him without worrying that he would overhear our conversation.

"He sure is handsome," Elsbeth said.

"Yeah he resembles a fullback football player, strong, but more fit looking than a linebacker." We both stop and look at Thomas.

"Thomas… did you just make a sports reference?" I asked in disbelief.

"I think so?" I chuckled when I saw the startled look on Thomas's face.

"His bod certainly is delectable. His shaggy jet-black hair and his green eyes help with the whole 'high-class, bad-boy' vibe he's got going on," Elsbeth added.

"High-class, bad-boy?" I grinned. "I mean, I guess that's an accurate description?"

He did have a certain rugged charm. He was someone people probably would consider quite good looking, but not the body type of someone you'd want to run into in a dark alley.

The hairs on the back of my neck stood up. At first, I thought it was because I was picturing how scary Dominic would look in the right light, but when I looked up, I realized it was because Melinda Thorne was staring at me. *No, not staring*, I thought to myself, *glaring.* She got up and stormed out of the cafeteria.

"What crawled up her butt?" Elsbeth asked following my gaze. Thomas turned to look at what the fuss was about.

"Who knows, who cares," I responded, shrugging. "Maybe she is jealous that Dominic doesn't seem to be paying any attention to her, which is fine by me. It's about time she got a taste of what it's like to not be the center of the universe for once."

Even if that wasn't the reason for Mindy's hostility, it amused the three of us to no end to imagine that was the case. We finished lunch, threw out our garbage and put away our trays before heading to class.

My lock was unlocked again when we went to get our books.

"Did either of you go into my locker?" I asked the twins. They both shook their heads.

"Perhaps your lock is defective. Maybe you should invest in a new one," Thomas suggested. I just grunted in response and texted Gran asking her to pick me up a new combination lock for me. After re-locking my faulty lock and giving it three tugs to check it was locked, I followed Thomas to biology.

I loved having a class with Thomas. Not only did he take impeccable notes if I ever needed a sick day—which so far, I've never needed, but he was also quiet and didn't pry into my life during class *or ever really for that matter*. It was peaceful and comfortable with Thomas, which was a nice contrast to the energy-filled mornings I had with Elsbeth in English.

In Writer's Craft my classmates were back to ignoring me when I walked in, but I was sure if I messed up in some way the attention would snap back to me in a heartbeat. Any acceptance I had yesterday after reading my poem was long gone, but then again did I really expect that to last? I had hoped that maybe it would, but deep inside I knew that fantasy was no more than my wishful thinking. I went to my seat and took out my notebook. The more I thought about it the more I realized that I was okay with being invisible, I guess. I'd much rather be ignored than be constantly berated by my peers. I sighed and settled into my seat, hoping that Mr. Dufranco wasn't planning on assigning any more 'show and tell' type assignments.

That night I made dinner for Gran for a change. I started pan-frying some chicken breasts and chopped the vegetables I was going to sauté; green pepper, carrots, broccoli, cauliflower and onions with a splash of teriyaki sauce for taste. Gran came home from the Women's Shelter that she worked at during the day and smiled at me with such gratitude when she saw I was making us dinner.
As I cooked, she talked. Today at the Shelter, she worked with a woman who had just gotten out of a bad marriage and took her young son with her when she left.

Some days the stories Gran told were moving, but sometimes hearing stories about husbands and wives and fathers and mothers stung a bit because I had never met either of mine.

"Gran…" I began, but I trailed off because I never knew exactly how to bring up my parents.

"Tell me again about my mom and dad?" I asked, a bit timidly. I knew how hard it was for her to remember the daughter she lost. Gran smiled at me, a smile filled with sadness and love.

"Your mother was an amazing woman," Gran explained. "You got your creativity from her, that's for sure. She was dedicated to making the best life for you she could, but unfortunately her time with us was done and she was needed somewhere else. I don't know why things turned out the way they did, but I need to believe in my heart that fate had a reason. She loved you so much, Quinnie and would have done anything for you. I know that wherever she is, she is proud of you and watching over you. I like to think that those we've loved and lost, never really leave us."

She paused for a moment before continuing, presumably lost in thoughts about Grandpa Henry.

"Your Grandfather passed away when your mother was little and the only thing that got your mother and I through his death was the idea that he would always be with us, even if it couldn't be in the physical form."

"And my dad?" I already knew what her response would be because it was the same every time I asked.

Gran pursed her lips. "Your father, although a good man, lacked a sense of familial duty. He chose work over his family when you were very young, broke your mother's heart. I've never forgiven him for that."

"Have you ever thought to look for him? Maybe if I was to look into it, we could find out what happened to him and where he is now?" I asked.

"Sweetie," Gran said with sadness in her voice, "I've lived in this house for as long as I can remember, we haven't gone anywhere."

I could tell I wasn't going to get any new information from Gran tonight, so I dropped it and focused on finishing our dinner. Gran headed to bed early that night, probably because of the emotions I stirred up from my questions about my parents. I meandered to her office and turned on the computer wanting to check my work schedule before bed. *Assuming Jolene hasn't taken me off the schedule entirely after the incident earlier this week.*

As I waited for the ancient desktop computer to warm up, I looked out the window. It was dark out and the streetlights were just turning on, casting shadows over the pavement. The large tree right outside the window eclipsed most of our view of the street. I wasn't sure what kind of tree it was, an oak maybe? Well whatever it was, it was very large with lush green leaves that were slowly fading with autumn's approach. I turned back to the computer and logged onto my work email. My work schedule was there, Friday night, Saturday morning and Sunday night. Perfect! I wouldn't have to switch shifts for my date. I'd hate to ask Jolene for a favor after the debacle at the café last Sunday.

I was shutting down the computer when I heard the snap of a twig outside and turned towards the window to see what caused the sound. It was probably just an animal scavenging for food, but I scanned the yard anyway. It was hard to tell with the shadows, but for a second I thought I saw an outline of a figure standing just behind the tree. My heart started to beat faster and I suddenly felt the urge to run for cover. I took a deep breath.

I blinked and rubbed my eyes wondering if it was just the light playing tricks on me. By the time I looked back out the window I saw nothing. *Maybe it was just my imagination.* I shook my head trying to clear it. *Way to get worked up over nothing, what are you going to do next? Duck for cover when bugs fly by?* I felt foolish for thinking that someone was outside my house. However, even though there didn't seem to be anything outside, I found myself checking the locks twice and shutting the blinds just in case, before I made my way upstairs to sleep.

Slade cursed as he pulled Viper behind the oak tree, barely finding cover before Quinn looked out the window.

"Watch where you are standing, she will be sure to see us if you are not careful, you insolent fool!" He pinned Viper against the tree, staring angrily at his partner, shoving Viper's shoulder into a branch in the process.

"I do not understand why we are still standing here!" Viper complained, pushing Slade with a force that almost knocked Slade backwards a step.

"She is right in there, all alone. Let us get rid of her and be done with this. Why are we waiting when she is within our grasp?" Viper hissed in the darkness.

They had searched the globe for her and had started to doubt if they would ever find her. All they knew was what the prophecy told them: there was a girl who if allowed to reach her nineteenth birthday, would end the race of the Reapers as they knew it. So, they endlessly wandered the Earth for any signs of a girl capable of bringing the end to an entire race of people. It wasn't until recently that they finally heard whisperings of a strange small-town girl who seems to be causing trouble. They knew they had to investigate further. Sure enough, upon casing Rosevale, they discovered a girl whose hospital records indicated that her birthday coincided exactly with what the prophecy foretold. It was amazing how easily it was to threaten hospital personnel to do what you wish—that was, with enough force.

Finally, she was within their grasp. Viper was getting sick of all this waiting in the shadows and would much rather strike out at the creature threatening the Reaper's very existence instead of standing idly by watching as the girl got closer to her nineteenth birthday.

Slade understood Viper's frustration, but also knew if they acted impulsively it could mean disaster for the Reapers… or worse, punishment from the Temptress. Slade sighed and slightly loosened his grip on Viper before speaking.

"We have waited seventeen years, what are another few weeks? I, for one, want to know what it is about this human girl that could possibly threaten us." After all the strife this child has caused us, do you not want to make her feel fear? Make her feel pain? I want this to be slow; payback for the years of my life she has taken from me," Slade smiled menacingly. Viper frowned at first and then slowly smiled a smile matching Slade's volatile intensity.

"Fine," Viper finally conceded, "but not too long, I cannot restrain myself forever."

"It will not be long now, Viper. Trust me. The Temptress will tell us how to proceed soon."

They waited until all the lights inside the house were off before fleeing down the street and out of sight.

* * *

After school on Friday, I went home and got ready for work. I was a little nervous about having to face Jolene after Sunday's debacle. How would I explain last weekend's events in a way that wouldn't make me sound mentally deranged? *Maybe I thought I saw a long-lost cousin across the street?* No, that wouldn't work. Jolene knew that I didn't know my extended family. *Maybe I forgot to turn off the stove at home, making me spill the customer's drink on my way out the door… because my oven is obviously that important?* Shoot, that wouldn't work either. I worked my bottom lip as I tried to think of some plausible way to explain my behavior other than, 'hey sorry about Sunday. I had a psychic flash that I felt compelled to act on.' Ugh, why was it that the truth sounded even lamer than my sudden—yet completely fictitious—stove dilemma?

I took a breath before pushing open the door of Cup O' Joe's. Jolene was behind the counter. She turned to face me, but before she could even open her mouth to speak, I started talking.

"Jolene, about Sunday… I'm really sorry! I can explain. You see, my cousin's stove was… I mean not my cousin, I don't know if I even have cousins, but there was a problem with my…" I said, my words tumbling over each other. Jolene just put her hand up to stop me. I quickly shut my mouth and braced for what she would say.

"Quinn, stop. Please," she said firmly. "I received a phone call on Monday from a disgruntled customer saying you threw a drink on her before running out of the store."

She paused before continuing. "She was very insistent that I fire you on the spot."

I bowed my head and started to untie my apron to turn it in when she said, "but one disgruntled customer isn't enough to have me firing my favorite employee."

I looked up at her in surprise. "Wait, I'm *not* fired?" I asked, not quite believing my ears.

"No, you're not fired, but you will be if you don't get your butt behind this counter and help me with this muffin batter," she said with a smile.

I rushed behind the counter to give her a hand. Once I was elbow deep in batter, she turned to me and said with a laugh, "Your cousin's stove? Really? Come on Quinn, you can do better than that." My face was warm with embarrassment,

"Yeah," I said agreeing with Jolene. "Definitely wasn't my best excuse ever." As we worked on the batter, I studied Jolene from my peripheral vision. She seemed eerily unfazed that I ran out of her store, leaving it unattended and making a customer upset. It was moments like that where I wondered if she had somehow clued into the real reason behind my behavior. But there was no way I could verify this without potentially spilling my secret, so I again found myself condemned to silence.

A few minutes later Jolene went to clock out. She was almost out the door when she reached into her pocket and called out to me.

"Oh, and before I forget, here," she said, tossing something at me. I caught it swiftly and opened my hands to see what it was. It was a hacky sack. My jaw dropped.

"Funny, I didn't even know you played." She winked at me before walking out of the store.

"I thought it was mine," I mumbled pathetically as she stepped through the doorway, laughing.

I was just walking into my house after work when my phone chimed. It was a text from Dominic asking if we were still on for our date tomorrow.

What's tomorrow?

I was in a good mood and feeling especially sassy and perhaps a little coy as well. My phone chimed indicating he had responded.

I texted him my address and was about to put my phone away, when I realized I didn't know when to be ready.

I did a little pirouette before calling Elsbeth. She answered on the first ring. "Elsbeth, I need your help. I don't know what to wear on my date tomorrow."

Her response was not any English word or sound I was familiar with and I only heard the click of her phone as she hung up. *I assume that means she's on her way over?*

She barged through my front door moments later and thundered up the stairs.

"Okay, time for me to work my magic!" She tore through my closet hemming and hawing to herself before spinning around to face me. She blew a loose strand of her long curly locks out of her face and put her hands on her hips before announcing, "It's official. Your closet is not date ready. We're going shopping tomorrow!" I groaned slightly, but knew she was right.

The next morning on the way to the mall, Elsbeth let me in on a little secret of her own. Apparently, I wasn't the only one with a boy in my life. She had met a boy. She didn't know his name yet though, because they had met on an online artist's forum for people who were passionate about the art of painting.

"His username is ShowMeTheMonet," she beamed. "Isn't that clever?"

I smiled to myself, knowing that my response wasn't needed in order her for to continue

"He's studying classical art. How cool is that? An older guy," she said on a sigh.

Elsbeth had a pattern of becoming enamoured with a guy, only to lose interest a few days later. It'd be interesting to see how long this present infatuation lasts. She told me not to tell Thomas, and I didn't want to rain on her parade about this new boy, so I chose to steer her into the first dress shop I saw.

We started leafing through the clothes racks immediately. I wasn't seeing anything that remotely screamed, *Quinn.*

"What about this?" Elsbeth suggested holding up a little black number, barely age appropriate, let alone weather appropriate.

"Uh… no," I told her, putting it back on the rack.

"Are you kidding?" Elsbeth said with a touch of anger in her voice. I was a little startled at her tone. "It's not that I don't like it, I just don't think it is first date material."

"No, no-no, not that." She waved her hand dismissively, *"that,"* she said pointing across the store.

My eyes followed her hand as she gestured across the room—Mindy and her other worker bees, Krista and another girl who's name I didn't remember were in the store too. Thankfully they hadn't noticed us yet.

"Do you want to leave?" Elsbeth asked me, wanting to avoid a potential unpleasant interaction with Mindy.

"No," I said, surprising both of us, "let's stay. We have just as much right to be here as they do." Elsbeth stared at me for a moment with a questioning look on her face.

"Alright, if you're sure…"

"I'm sure," I responded, hoping I sounded more certain than I felt. I kept looking at the clothes when I saw it, the perfect dress: an emerald green short sleeve dress, very flowy, yet casual enough for a date. It would also look great with my black cardigan if I got too cold. I held it up to show Elsbeth when I heard Mindy's voice from behind me.

"Well, what do we have here?" Mindy said with a sneer as she and her two minions approached the clothing carousel.

"Go away Mindy," Elsbeth said, more irritated than angry. Mindy ignored Elsbeth and looked at the dress in my hands.

"Buying a dress are we, Quinn?" Mindy smirked. "How cute." Krista and the girl with the forgettable name laughed at Mindy's comment. Elsbeth just rolled her eyes.

"It just seems silly for you to spend money on a dress when everyone knows it'd be impossible for you to look good." The three of them snickered again on cue.

Elsbeth went to speak, but I got there first.

"That's funny," I said, looking at Elsbeth before turning back to Mindy, "I was just about to say the same thing about you. And you might want to get that checked out," I said pointing at a non-existent blemish on her face.

"It looks infected," I added with mock concern. Mindy self-consciously touched her face before looking at Krista, who shook her head to reassure her leader that her face was still flawless. She let her hand drop to her side and glared at me.

"You better watch yourself, Quinn. You have no idea what I'm capable of," Mindy threatened before turning on her heels and strutting out of the store with her two lemmings in tow. Elsbeth just looked at me with a dumbfounded expression on her face.

"Where the heck did that come from?" she asked.

"I have no idea," I admitted, still a little shell-shocked. "But if that was her reaction to this dress, then it's definitely the one I should wear."

★_★

Cooper watched as Mindy approached Quinn. Melinda Thorne was one of the key players outlined in Quinn's file. She had apparently been making Quinn's life hell for the past year, and on many occasions went out of her way specifically to cause trouble for Quinn.

He had seen many 'Mindys' in his day. All of the Coordinators who were bullies like Mindy on his side of the veil, ended up sorting files or inputting data in an office, never anywhere where they would be in charge of someone's physical well-being—for obvious reasons.

People like Mindy found pleasure in making someone else's life harder, the exact opposite of what Guardians stood for. Cooper knew all too well how vicious girls could be. Heck, he'd even dated a few Mindy-types in his time, not that those 'relationships' lasted for very long.

But never in his experiences—on either plane—had he encountered someone quite like Quinn. Even with the added information her file provided, Cooper still couldn't figure her out. When he saw Mindy approach, he was *sure* that Quinn and her friend would just leave the store, but she surprised him.

Quinn was constantly surprising him. Just when he thought he understood her, she'd show another facet of herself that just added to the confusing depths. And this was no exception. Nowhere in her file or in the two weeks Cooper had been with her, had she ever shown any signs of self-preservation or ever standing up to Mindy or those like her. *Just another piece to the puzzle that is Quinn,* Cooper thought to himself.

No wonder she needed a Guardian. She had no regard for her own safety, but today she showed that somewhere deep inside of her was a fighter. *Now if only she realized how capable she actually was, then maybe she wouldn't need me to watch over her and I could get back to focusing on my training instead of trying to figure this girl out…*

He wanted to be irritated, but his complaining was starting to lack the edge it first had when he was assigned to her case; curiosity starting to override his previously harbored contempt. Then he remembered Quinn had her date later and suddenly he was brooding all over again.

I heard a car pull up at exactly 5pm. *That must be Dominic!* I walked down the stairs and grabbed my black cardigan. Dominic honked his horn once. *Oh my goodness, this is actually happening.* I took one last look in the mirror before going outside to meet him. Dominic was waiting in his car when I walked outside.

"Nice ride," I said to Dominic as I lowered myself into his car. It was very low to the ground, but had lots of legroom, which made up for the fact that I felt like I was basically sitting on the road. *Thankfully this dress is a little on the long side.* I pulled the dress even farther over my knees.

"Thanks, I love her. She's awesome."

"Did you just refer to your car as a female?"

"Indeed, I did. Feeling jealous, Quinn?" He smirked.

I looked at him evenly. "No, but if you'd rather have a date with your car… I can just get back out," I said with a shrug reaching for the handle and pushing the door open. *Who is this confident girl, and where did she come from?* I thought to myself. Normally I was not this bold. What was *up* with me today?

He leaned over and grabbed my hand to stop me from leaving. "I'm sure you are a much better conversationalist than she is."

Instead of responding, I just closed the door, leaned back against the leather seat, and buckled my in.

He revved the engine of his black Italian car—whose make and model I had already forgotten—and sped down the road.

I gripped the door handle as he sped down the street, slightly unnerved by his speed, but wanting to appear cool.

"So, where are we going?" I asked in a tone that I hoped sounded calm. Instead of answering, he just grinned charmingly at me and put his finger to his lips indicating it was a secret.

Part of me wondered if I should have insisted that I knew where we were going before I got into his car, but I had my friend tracking app on and I knew Elsbeth would be watching it like a hawk awaiting my return home. A few minutes later we pulled up to what I assumed was his family's vineyard.

"Wow…" I breathed as I took in the gorgeous surroundings. A few of the trees had already started to fade from green to the many shades of fall.

"My thoughts exactly," Dominic said looking right at me. I felt the heat of my blush stain my cheeks. I was still not used to this kind of attention. Dominic was the first boy other than Thomas who had ever complimented me. With Thomas it didn't feel the same as when Dominic said complementary things… I was never nervous with Thomas, but I was always a bundle of nerves when I was with Dominic, even if I did a passable job at hiding it.

He hopped out of the car and went to the trunk to grab the blanket and basket before calling out to me, "Well, are you coming or not?"

I know I've never been on a date before, but isn't he supposed to open the door or something? I thought to myself before stepping out of the car. *Well, he may not be the perfect gentleman, but he did make a picnic, that has to count for something!*

We walked through the rows of grapes with Dominic pointing things out along the way as we headed to the hill at the far side of his property. I mostly just nodded as he talked, too busy taking in all the beauty to really care how to check a leaf for signs of disease.

It took us maybe ten minutes to walk the span of the fields. The weather was just warm enough that being outside was pleasant without being too warm or too cold. Dominic laid the blanket down near the top of the hill so we could look out over his entire property.

Dominic opened the basket and pulled out some sandwiches, crackers and cheese, some fruit and some packets of gummies.

"I didn't know what you wanted so I kind of grabbed everything from my cupboard."

"It all looks good, thank you," I said, picking up a sandwich and taking a bite. We ate in silence for a few minutes. Eventually, the silence starting inching towards uncomfortable. Dominic finally spoke, ending the quiet. "I'm glad you said yes. I wasn't sure you'd go out with me," Dominic confessed with his eyes downcast. I almost choked on the bite of food in my mouth.

"Are you serious? If either of us should be surprised, it should be me, not you."

Dominic lifted his eyes to meet mine. "I could tell right when I saw you that there was something different about you. It's like you were exactly who I'd been looking for…" He lifted his eyes to meet mine. "I'm sorry," he added when he saw my surprised expression. "Was that too cheesy? Too early?"

"Well maybe a bit of both, but I don't mind." I could feel my heart beating against my rib cage as a smile spread across my face.

✦✦

A picnic, scenery, cheesy words… man, was this guy schmaltzy. Cooper rolled his eyes. *What's he going to do next, wait for the sun to go down and slow dance with her under the moonlight to a song only they can hear?*

Cooper didn't trust this Dominic guy. He seemed to be trying too hard. Cooper couldn't place the feeling inside of him. It was almost as if he was… no, it wasn't possible. Cooper didn't get jealous. Cooper never let himself close enough to anyone to feel anything more than physical attraction, but he still couldn't shake this feeling; half of him wanted to punch Dominic in the face and the other half wanted to say, 'screw my obligations' and walk away from Quinn and this whole mission… anything other than having to watch Mr. Cheese spread it on thickly with Quinn eating up every bit of it.

They sat on the hill talking and laughing even as the sun started to set. The warm splashes of color danced their way across the sky; rich purples, reds and oranges made for a perfect backdrop for a perfect date. Suddenly Quinn's eyebrows drew together, and her hand came to rest on her forehead. *Uh oh…* Cooper thought to himself, his senses suddenly becoming alert. *Here we go again.*

★

"Are you alright?" Dominic asked me.

"Just a headache, nothing to worry about." *No, no, no… this can't be happening. Not now.*

Dominic's house was just off the main street in town, but it would take at least five minutes to get back across the field if I ran fast, but I didn't even know where I had to go yet.

"Can I get you anything?"

The buzzing started before I could answer him. The vision started slowly at first, still picture after still picture, like an animated flip-book. Then the pictures all moved faster. At first, I didn't recognize what I was seeing, but then I knew exactly where I was needed.

"I'm sorry. I have to go," I said hurriedly to Dominic as I scrambled to my feet and kicked my sandals off, knowing I'd run faster without them.

"Here, I'll clean up and I'll drive you home," Dominic offered.

"No, it's okay. I have…I have…I have to go!"

I took off down the hill and through the rows of grapes. I could hear Dominic yelling after me in confusion, but I knew this couldn't wait.

In my vision it was dark, so I knew I still had a few minutes before tragedy struck. I pushed myself harder, the sandy earth making it difficult to get a good grip. I replayed the scene in my head as I ran.

The stoplight at the corner of town was broken. The bus driver was texting and didn't notice the light change; neither did the transport truck traveling perpendicular to the bus, both heading towards the exact same intersection, neither slowing down.

The sun was hanging low in the sky by the time I reached the road, almost completely out of breath. A cab was approaching so I stepped into the road, not daring to risk the cab passing me by.

Cooper stepped towards the veil ready to push Quinn out of the way of the cab. He was about to jump through the veil when the car came screeching to a halt.

"Damn it, Quinn," Cooper cursed out loud, running his fingers anxiously through his hair. The adrenaline pumping through his veins had the golden ink of his winged tattoo vibrating in response to his anxiety and frustration.

"Rosevale Library," I huffed to the cab driver as I jumped in the passenger seat. "And HURRY!"

He peeled away, pushing his foot to the floor to get me to the library as fast as he could—that or he just wanted me out of his cab, but quite frankly at that moment I didn't care which it was as long as he got me there in time.

The sun has just dipped below the horizon. I threw a twenty at the cab driver telling him to keep the change as I flew out of the car. *How am I going to stop the bus?* I panicked as I stood on the corner where I knew the collision was about to take place. I turned my head and saw the transport coming down the road in the distance to my right, which meant the bus was going to be coming straight down the road in my direction. Sure enough, as soon as the thought crossed my mind I saw the bus barreling down the road.

Think Quinn! You don't have time to call the cops or fix the light… Think! I started waving my hands frantically up and down trying to get the attention of the bus driver, but nothing happened. The transport truck was getting close to the intersection and the bus still wasn't slowing down. It was fast approaching so I did the only thing I thought might work. I ran into the middle of the road, flailing my arms and screaming at the top of my lungs for either vehicle to stop.

★★

Cooper jumped through the veil arms stretched ready to push Quinn out of harm's way. The bus screeched to a halt and Cooper quickly retreated through the veil so she wouldn't see him.

"Damn it, Quinn!" He yelled again, pacing furiously behind the veil. He had half a mind to just walk right back through the veil and shake her until she understood just how stupid and reckless she was being with her life. Didn't she realize how valuable she was? How… irreplaceable she was?

★

It took all my energy not just to collapse to the ground and cry, tears of fear or joy at this point I didn't know. I really didn't think that bus was going to stop. I heard the transport truck speed down the road behind me and breathed out a sigh of relief. I bent over with my hands on my knees and my head down trying to catch my breath.

"What the hell lady?" the bus driver screamed as he stood beside the bus. "What were you thinking jumping in front of a bus like that?"

"You weren't slowing down and the light is broken," I huffed, head still feeling a little too dizzy to stand up just yet.

"Oh jeez," the bus driver said looking past me to the intersection. "Thanks, but you and that boy should really be more careful," he said looking down the street to my left.

"What boy?" I asked, looking down the street, then back at the bus driver. He might have thought I was crazy for jumping in front of a moving vehicle, but at least I wasn't seeing people who weren't there.

Instead of answering my question the bus driver just asked if I was getting on the bus or not since he was already stopped. I shook my head in response.

"Suit yourself," he said as he climbed back on the bus. I heard him on his radio informing other buses of the broken stoplight. I quickly moved to the sidewalk and let the bus pass now that the coast was clear. I picked up my phone and called the police station and told them about the burnt-out light as well. I didn't know how many times I could step into traffic tonight and still survive.

Next, I called Gran to come pick me up before going to sit on a bench to wait for her. Gran didn't even ask me what had happened when she saw me. My energy must have told her I wasn't in the mood to talk to anyone. I felt my phone vibrating: missed calls from both Elsbeth and Dominic. I couldn't face either of them at that moment, so I just turned my phone off. I'd deal with them tomorrow.

* * *

CHAPTER

8

★

On Monday morning, Cooper walked along the cobblestone path from his neighborhood to the Coordinator's HeadQuarters. Just as humans had government buildings and office buildings, Coordinators had HeadQuarters. All Coordinators went there everyday for school or their daily jobs; one general hub for all of the Coordinators. Cooper could have easily teleported to HQ, but he knew he needed the walk to shake off the sour mood that had been lingering since Saturday.

Cooper looked up at the 181-story, seamless glass building and couldn't help but be in slight awe of its vast beauty. No building like this existed on the human plane.

Both sides of the veil were carbon copies of each other topographically—the world that the Coordinators lived in had the exact geographical landscape as that of the human world, except the Coordinators had chosen different landmarks, houses and buildings. The grand HeadQuarters building was so tall its highest floor literally was in the clouds. It was a powerful sight to behold, *which is the exact opposite of how I'm feeling,* Cooper thought as he pulled his fingers through his short, sand-coloured hair.

HQ was buzzing with activity when Cooper walked in. Although Coordinators didn't need sleep to survive, they tended to keep a similar workday schedule to that of the human realm they protected. HeadQuarters was where all Coordinators spent their days. Those under the age of fifteen, like Cooper's sister Cali, were in school all day on the first two floors of the building. The fourth floor was the training center for all the current and prospective Guardians to perfect their skills—that was where Cooper and his best friend Neil spent most of their time. Not only was it a place to train, but also a place where Cooper could take his mind off things. While his other self was watching Quinn, he was going to do everything in his power so that *this* Cooper didn't have to think about her.

Neil was already warming up when Cooper entered the simulation training room on the fourth floor. Each week the simulation room was programmed to project a different scenario Guardians might encounter on the Earthly plane. These high-tech simulations included computer-generated objects and obstacles that were tangible so the Guardians could interact with them in an authentic way. The variety of obstacles were intended to test their mental and physical acuity as well as give them a taste of a real emergency situation involving their Charge.

Cooper saw that this week's simulation was programmed as a busy city center with traffic buzzing around. There were computer-generated people as well—all holograms—but not in the traditional sense of the word.

Like traditional holograms these images were made from a light source, which was projected into the training arena; however, they were solid to the touch, which enabled the Guardians to interact with them in a life-like fashion, but also allowed the technological team to shut down the simulation if something were to go awry.

"Look what the cat dragged in!" Neil called out to Cooper, punching him in the shoulder. "We have a doozy of a course ahead of us this week," he said, looking out at the illuminated course in front of them.

"Hopefully this week they won't have to shut down the whole course because of you. That stunt you pulled last week in the faux Appalachian Mountains caused a giant avalanche. They had to start digging you out because it was taking too long to shut down the entire simulation," Cooper reminded him.

"An avalanche because of *moi?*" Neil's face was a statue of mock surprise.

"That is *impossible!*" he said in a poor French accent.

"Who else would have been dumb enough to yell, 'yahoo!' at the top of their lungs while racing to intercept their Charge on a snow-capped cliff?" Cooper said accusingly, but with humor in his voice.

"I was excited," Neil said with a shrug. "I couldn't help myself."

Cooper just laughed. According to the display on the wall, Neil was scheduled to tackle the course first. The course scenario changed slightly for each Guardian's turn, so those waiting on the sidelines wouldn't get as many advantages.

"Don't mess up this time," Cooper warned. "I want a shot at it today. I don't want to wait around because you decide to make this simulation your playground."

"Don't worry man, I got this," Neil said, with a big goofy grin on his face. Neil took his place on the painted line just outside the simulation zone. This outer wall of transparent, shimmering light simulated the veil. The Guardians were to use their knowledge of protocol as well as their learned skills to decide when to intercept and walk through the veil and when to hang back. The tasks started off easy with each day's simulation becoming increasingly more difficult as the week went on.

Neil stood with his nose almost pressed right up against the shimmering simulated veil; eyes squinted with intense focus, scanning the area for his Charge. His Charge was a male in his mid-forties, wearing a bright green business suit, while all other pedestrians were dressed in black. Cooper laughed to himself. *If he can't keep track of his Charge in this situation there is no hope for him!*

Neil's Charge was walking down the street about to step into the road but neglected to look both ways. Neil grinned and with a loud "aha!" reached through the veil and flicked the lock on the man's briefcase, causing all the files to spill out onto the cement. The man paused to collect his belongings as the van flew by, missing Neil's Charge. The spectating Guardians all chuckled and gave a round of applause. Neil turned and took a dramatic bow. "Thank you, thank you."

Cooper was up next. It took about a minute for the technicians to reprogram the scene for him. He stood rigid and alert just outside the veil, immediately spotting his Charge... a twenty-something girl wearing a bright pink dress, amongst a sea of grey-clad pedestrians. The girl was wearing headphones and bobbing along to her music, dancing her way down the sidewalk. She didn't realize the light had changed and started to walk across a busy intersection. A motorcyclist was speeding down the road, weaving in and out of traffic. He started honking his horn when he saw she was about to step in front of his bike, but she couldn't hear the horn over her headphones.

Cooper's mind flashed back to Saturday night and without thinking he jumped through the veil and pushed his Charge out of the way. The simulated girl looked up from the street in surprise before fading away.

Cooper was breathing heavily, adrenaline surging through his body. It wasn't until the entire scene faded, leaving him looking at the wooden floor of the gym, that he was brought back to the present. He looked up at his classmates, all of whom wore matching expressions of shock on their faces. Cooper had always been the head of his class, always followed protocol, yet here he was causing a simulation to be halted when he unnecessarily pushed his Charge. Cooper got up off the ground and walked back to where Neil was standing, flabbergasted.

"Dude, I know you're intense and all, but next time don't you think it'd be easier to just knock the earphones from her ears, so she hears the horn? I know you haven't been with a girl in a while, but no need to go all grizzly on the poor hologram and pin her to the ground. You gotta relax man," Neil said, putting his arm around his friend in a show of comradery. Cooper said nothing in response and just stared blankly ahead for the remainder of class.

After training, Cooper went directly to the little basketball court in his family's backyard and spent his evening there. Starting at one end of the court and running his way to the other, Cooper dribbled the ball towards the basket, jumped up and in one fell swoop dunked it into the net. He dangled off the rim for a moment. The muscles tensed in his back to keep him hanging there; his body covered in a thin sheen of sweat. The luminous ink of his tattooed golden wings was glowing brightly against the dark backdrop of the evening sky, a complete contrast to Cooper's dark mood.

Cali looked out the window at her brother. He had been shooting baskets in their backyard since before the sun went down, and it was now almost 9 p.m. *I haven't seen Cooper this worked up in a long time,* Cali thought. She walked outside and sat on the grass at the edge of their basketball court.

"Hey Coop, you've been out here a while. Is everything alright?"

Cooper heard his sister talking to him, but didn't acknowledge her, at least not yet. He was still too worked up to say anything, plus how could he explain it to her?

Hey, Cali, actually everything isn't fine. I can't seem to stop thinking about this girl. I think about her so much, even holograms of girls remind me of her. I know the protocol and she shouldn't even be an issue because she doesn't even know I exist. You see, I'm her Guardian, she's my Charge, completely off limits. She can't see me. She'll never know me and yet, I still can't seem to shake her from my mind. Oh, and the mission is top secret and I can't tell anyone about her. But other than that, I'm great!

His hair was starting to stick to his forehead since he had worked up a sweat being outside for so long. He blew his golden-brown hair out of his eyes before turning to his sister.

"Just a rough day in simulation training, that's all."

Cali looked at her brother. It was clear that class was not all that was bugging him. She might only be fourteen-years-old, but that was fourteen years of knowing her big brother and being able to tell when he was holding something back.

"Coop, seriously. I'm worried about you. I haven't seen you this way since…" she gulped, not being able to say the words—the wounds still seeming too fresh for both of them.

"Well…in a while," she finished.

He looked at his sister standing there, so small in comparison to himself, her sadness plainly showing on her face. He tossed the ball onto the grass and went over and sat beside her. Her eyes were still downcast, replaying the painful memory. He put a finger under her chin and raised her face until he could see her eyes.

"I'm really okay, Cali. I know it doesn't seem like it. I've just been a little … off, for the past two days and today's training didn't help. I made a stupid mistake. That, and Neil's been on my case about how I'm not seeing anyone and it's just grating on my nerves... that's all," he said. Her face perked up at the mention of potential girl problems because that at least was a topic she could help him with.

"Ugh, not you too," Cooper said playfully bopping his sister on the head, wishing there was something she *could* help him with. She scowled and tried to duck, but she didn't quite make it before Cooper ruffled her hair. She stuck her tongue out at him then broke into a smile. Cooper grinned back.

"Seriously, Coop, I know you've never had trouble finding a girl to date, but you haven't been with anyone in a while. Isn't there anyone you might interested in?" Cali asked with her eyebrows raised.

Cooper's mind flashed to Quinn dancing in her room and then to Quinn standing nervously in front of her classmates. He paused before responding.

"There isn't a single Coordinator that's caught my attention, Cali. Sorry to burst your bubble," Cooper answered honestly. "What about you? Any boys I should be threatening to beat up?" Cooper asked jokingly, but to his surprise his sister blushed.

"Well, there is this one boy in my class, but I don't think he knows I exist," Cali said dejectedly. "And even if he did," she added hastily before her brother could interject, "I wouldn't tell you yet because I know you can't help but act on your big brother instincts sometimes."

He thought about pushing the matter more but realized that maybe it was best that he didn't know— one less thing to think about. That, and technically Cali didn't owe him any honesty seeing that he was keeping his business and personal life private from her too.

They sat in silence for a while watching as the stars came out of hiding and scattered themselves across the wide expanse of sky.

Cali looked up at the millions of stars, comforted by their presence. "They say the stars are clearer here than they are in the human realm. I wonder if it's true?" Cali mused.

"It's true. I've seen it. Even the starriest skies on the human plane pale in comparison to the number of stars we can see here. It's because of all the light pollution over there."

"I can't imagine not being able to see the stars. Tell me more about the humans," Cali pleaded.

"Well, they can't travel by thought like we do. They travel by a kind of pod with wheels, called a vehicle. It takes them several minutes to get from one place to another."

"That sounds horrible." Cali wrinkled her nose. "What about bi-location? Can they be in two places at once like the Guardians here can?"

"Seriously, Cali, don't you pay attention at all in Human Anthropology? They should be telling you all about the humans in that class." Cali just blushed.

"Ah, I see. The boy is a bit distracting. Well, to answer your question, no, they cannot bi-locate. They can only ever be one place at once. The closest humans have ever gotten to bi-location is cloning, but that takes a long time and never seems to turn out exactly like the original."

"I can't wait to become a Guardian!" Cali beamed with excitement.

"You still have four years to go, Cali. You just turned fourteen last month. Plus, if you don't start paying attention in your classes, you'll never pass your final exam," Cooper chided. Cali bowed her head in shame, knowing she should really start focusing in class if she ever wanted to become a Guardian like her older brother.

He bumped her playfully on the shoulder telling her she was going to do great as long as she focused.

Cooper wanted to lighten the mood, so he grabbed a handful of grass before walking over to the edge of his property that boarded the veil before throwing the grass at it. The grass exploded and fizzled into a bright flash of light as it burnt up before turning to dust and falling to the ground. Cali laughed in delight at the mini light display, grabbed a handful and tossed it at the veil.

This thin wall of vibrating energy was the only thing that separated the two worlds. To the Coordinators of Crysthala, this veil appeared transparent, except for tiny vibrations that gave the veil the appearance of heat rising off asphalt. To humans however, the veil was invisible. It existed at a frequency too high for the human eye to perceive. When something came in contact with the veil that did not match its frequency, it burned up instantly just like the grass had.

Coordinators like Cali and Cooper had been raised knowing about the existence of humans and the veil, as well as the dangers of touching the veil. Because the veil resonated at a different frequency than the rest of the matter on both planes, anything that touched it would break apart, molecules splitting left and right until nothing was left except the low hum of the veil and the sparkling light show it produced. The only reason Cooper could safely pass through the veil was because of the special properties in the ink of his Guardian's wings. The Doyens had used their alchemist knowledge to create a compound that allowed the special ink to change Cooper's frequency to safely travel through the wall of energy unharmed.

Many toys and insects have been lost to the veil from the human side. The only thing that seemed to keep humans from coming in contact with the veil was a sixth-sense they all seemed to have, suddenly forgetting something or turning around without any conscious knowledge as to why.

Cali looked over at her brother's wings, the gold ink shimmering like moonlight. *These wings are incredible,* Cali thought, completely in awe of their immense power. *They are so detailed... they look like they could be real.* The tattoo covered the entirety of Cooper's back. Cali touched the top of the right wing and felt the inked feathers move beneath her fingertips.

"Cooper! Get your sister away from the veil, right now!" their mother, Candice, screamed from the front door.

"Party's over," Cooper said. He picked Cali up and threw her over his shoulder, carrying her back towards the house as she kicked and laughed. They were both still laughing when they walked into the house. Candice had both hands on her hips and was angrily glaring at her two children.

"You'll both give me a heart attack one of these days, I swear it. Cali, you know how dangerous the veil is for a non-Guardian. I'm disappointed in you."

Cali looked down and pushed a piece of grass from her shoe around on the floor.

"And Cooper," Candice added, "you are older and know that Cali doesn't have her wings yet. You mustn't be so reckless!"

"Sorry mom," they both said in unison. Cali reached up to kiss her mom on the check, while Cooper leaned down and planted a peck on her other cheek.

"Now get out of my sight the both of you," she said, her voice softening as she waved them away with her dish towel.

Cali ran out of the room before her mom could change her mind about punishing them. Cooper went back outside and flopped down on the grass. He put his arms behind his head and looked up at the stars, hoping that maybe if he lay there long enough the Earth would help him feel grounded again and maybe the stars would give him the clarity he was looking for. Cooper had many people in his life that loved him and cared about him and would help him in a heartbeat, but he was sworn to silence. Never in Cooper's life had he felt so lost, alone and so completely out of control. Both sides of his split selves sighed in unison: *What am I supposed to do now?*

*   *   *

CHAPTER

9

★

I woke up way before my alarm and was seriously contemplating contracting an array of fake illnesses—anything to keep me from having to face Dominic. He texted me on Saturday after I ran off, and again on Sunday. I just told him I was really sorry, and I'd explain on Monday. The thing was, it was Monday and I still had no idea what to tell him. I came downstairs for breakfast and was surprised to see Elsbeth and Thomas sitting at the breakfast table. Thomas looked exhausted, and Elsbeth looked pissed.

"Hey guys, what are you doing here?" I asked as I sat down. Gran was at the counter putting on more pancakes for our guests. Gran always had more than enough food to go around, so I knew their presence wasn't a burden to her, even if it was a surprise to me.

"Well, since you ignored my phone calls all weekend, I had to come over and make sure you weren't dead!" Elsbeth said. "But obviously you're alive. What's the deal, Quinn? What happened on your date and why won't you tell me?"

"I didn't tell you about it because I'm trying to forget it," I admitted, putting my head in my hands.

"What happened?" Thomas asked with concern in his voice.

I retold the first part of the date in detail, right up until my vision. "Then suddenly I got super-panicked about the whole thing and just kind of… got up and left," I continued, shamefaced.

"You just left? In the middle of the picnic?" Elsbeth asked incredulously; not understanding what would possess me to leave in the middle of a date with the school's most eligible bachelor. Gran however looked over at me with deep understanding and sympathy.

"I regret it now obviously," I said. Gran gave my shoulder a supportive squeeze before putting the pancakes on our plates. "I guess I just freaked out. I've never dated anyone. I guess part of me isn't used to kindness from people other than you three. It was overwhelming and perhaps just seemed a little too good to be true," I told them. It wasn't a complete lie, I *was*, but that wouldn't cause me to leave in the middle of a date.

"You can't help feeling scared. Have you talked to him since?" Thomas asked. I explained that I told him I'd tell him today, but I also confessed that I didn't exactly know what to tell him.

"Just be honest," Elsbeth suggested.

"Even if he doesn't fully understand why you left, he'll probably appreciate the truth." *The truth*, I thought to myself bitterly. *Sorry I bolted Dominic, but I had to go run in front of a bus. Care to go out again?* No, that wouldn't work. So, it looked like a slight variation of the truth would have to do. Technically I was scared. Technically, I did run because I was afraid, but not because of the date or because of Dominic. I ran because I had to do everything in my power to stop that accident. My stomach was in knots knowing that my actions on Saturday might have just ruined my only chance at having a boyfriend in a town full of people who disliked me.

"Hey…" Dominic said tentatively as he sat down in Chemistry. He spoke in the same tone of voice one might use when trying to coax a baby animal closer without scaring it off.

"Are you okay? You left pretty quickly on Saturday."

'Pretty quickly' being the understatement of the century. I can't remember a time when I've run that fast.

"About that…" I started, not exactly sure the exact words I wanted to say, even after spending all of English class going over and over them in my head.

"You probably think I'm crazy, running off like that without any explanation. It's just that..." *Ugh, this is so embarrassing.* "That was kind of my first date ever. I got overwhelmed and I just kind of...bolted. I regret it now though, because before my irrational fears took over, I really was having a good time."

I paused before looking at him, giving him time to digest all the bull crap I just fed him. When I looked up, his face was scrunched in confusion... or skepticism, I couldn't tell. After what seemed like the longest five seconds known to mankind, he finally turned to look at me. His brow was furrowed as he began to speak.

"I completely understand you feeling unsure and uncomfortable. But next time, can you let me drive you home instead of sprinting off into the night?" Dominic asked, with a smile that didn't quite reach his eyes. I told him I would do my best.

"Any chance you're free for dinner tomorrow?" he asked me. I immediately agreed that dinner sounded perfect. I just hoped that everyone else in Rosevale could fend for themselves for one night, while I tried to have a life of my own for once.

★

As we were sitting down for lunch Thomas looked from me to Dominic, his eyes silently asking me how our conversation went. I just nodded and smiled. Unlike his twin sister, that small interaction would be enough to hold him over until I could explain the full story to him later.

"Hey Elsbeth," I said, leaning over the table conspiratorially. "Look who's wearing a new dress today?"

We both looked over to where Mindy was sitting. She was wearing a dress, which almost matched the exact silhouette of the one I bought for my first date with Dominic. We both laughed, not that Mindy would ever understand the irony of that moment. At our laughter Mindy turned to us and glared at me. *I will never understand why that girl hates me so much. I've done nothing to her—well, with the exception of catching Dominic's attention.* I must admit it felt good to have something she coveted.

★

Mindy's choice of outfit also amused Cooper. He smiled right along with Elsbeth and Quinn at the realization that Mindy was wearing almost the same dress that Quinn was supposedly buying to look prettier. *Not that Quinn needed fancy clothes to be beautiful,* Cooper thought, then immediately kicked himself for letting his professional demeanor falter *again.* He could not afford to make any mistakes, not when it could cost him his job… not when it could cost Quinn's safety.

★

Elsbeth came over after school to help me decide on an outfit. We invited Thomas to join us, but he respectfully declined being subjected to the inner workings of our female minds and closets.

"Do you know where he's taking you tomorrow?" Elsbeth wondered. I just looked at her. "Oh, right, it's Dominic, so he's probably keeping it a secret. How romantic!" she mused.

"Or annoying," I mumbled as I searched through my closet. I didn't know how fancy or casual I should dress. Dominic's family seemed pretty well off, but I didn't want to assume something fancy. Without knowing where we were going, it was impossible to even start to narrow things down —so I texted Dominic asking whether we were going somewhere jeans casual or ball-gown formal.

Haha although im sure u'd look amazing in that, something like last time is fine.

★

I heard Dominic's sports car drive up at precisely 5p.m. and I hurried out the door to meet him. If I made him wait, he'd just honk the horn again.

"I hope you like Italian food," he said as I lowered myself into the car. He backed out of the driveway, placing his arm behind my headrest as he reversed. I felt the touch of his hand on my neck.

"I love Italian food." Other than Gran's cooking, it was my absolute favorite thing to eat—probably because my two best friends were Italian.

The drive there was mostly filled with small talk and observations about our surroundings as we wound our way through the town. I noticed that Dominic had a tendency to take his corners more sharply than necessary—a little reckless—but he always seemed to be in control, so I didn't worry too much.

We pulled up outside a beautiful Italian restaurant, right along the river that ran through town. Dominic turned hard to the left and slid into a spot close to the entrance.

We got out of the car and as we walked towards the door, I looked up at the sign. The restaurant was called *La Farfalla*.

"La Farfalla, that means butterfly, I think?" I said to Dominic, trying to remember all the bits of Italian I had learned from the twins over the years.

"Very good," Dominic replied with a smile. The sign above the restaurant was a gorgeous golden-colored butterfly, with the name scrawled beautifully through the center. I paused for a moment and found myself entranced by the butterfly's mesmerizing golden wings.

"You okay?" Dominic asked, placing his hand on my lower back and gently guiding me forward.

"I was just admiring the craftsmanship of the sign, that's all," I said, letting Dominic lead me through the doorway. I felt compelled to look back at the sign, I but resisted and continued into the restaurant.

He walked up to the maître d' and gave his name. We sat down and I gazed out the window at the river, watching as the sunlight danced across its surface. I sighed in contentment.

"Is something wrong?" Dominic asked, misreading my sighing. I quickly explained that it was a pleasant sigh, not an unhappy one. He seemed to relax a bit. He looked over at me with a slight glint in his eye.

"You seem pretty smart. Pop quiz. How do you say butterfly in French?" he challenged.

"La Papillion," I answered back confidently.

"And in Spanish?" he challenged again, a devilish grin on his face, thinking that he had stumped me.

"La mariposa," I responded without missing a beat. Dominic looked surprised.

"What can I say, Gran loves watching Spanish soaps." I shrugged with a huge grin on my face.

"Well played, Quinn. Well played. What about in Romanian?" he asked with a self-assured smile.

"Uh… how in the world would I know that?" I said with a laugh.

"De fluture," Dominic said swiftly.

I just looked at him with my mouth agape.

Dominic just lifted one shoulder in response. "I've basically lived everywhere. You pick up a lot of things when you travel as much as I have."

"That is crazy! I can't imagine living a life without having roots. I can't say I love Rosevale, but it has been my home for as long as I can remember. Where has your favorite place been so far?" I asked, curious about all the places he had been, *and how many girls he had probably met and been with…* The thought had me feeling very insignificant and incredibly inexperienced.

"It's this tiny little town. You've probably heard of it. I didn't think I was going to like it at all, but then I found this girl, who made all my travelling worth it," he said, taking my hand in his.

"Handsome *and* charming," I said to him. "What ever will we do with you?" I smiled at him and tried to hide my blush.

Chatting with him felt easy. He was very interested in getting to know me, which was something I wasn't used to. I had to stop him occasionally just so I could ask him something! It was a pleasant change and slightly uncomfortable at the same time because it was unfamiliar territory for me. When the waiter arrived to take our dessert order, I was so full I was afraid I wouldn't be able to stand up when it came time to go.

Dominic ordered for himself in flawless Italian, "Un torta della nonna, per favor."

"E per la bella ragazza?" the server asked, with a smile so charming it almost rivaled Dominic's. I blushed as I always seemed to do when I got complimented.

"Niente," I said in my horrible Italian accent.

"Un tiramisù per la bella ragazza," Dominic interjected curtly. The waiter nodded and left our table.

"If you don't want to eat it, you can take it home. No one should pass up dessert." His voice carried a little bit of an edge that I wasn't used to hearing from him. 'Plus, their dessert here is delicious," he continued, "I want you to get the whole experience." Dominic smiled at me. All signs of his previous irritation seeming to spontaneously evaporate. I smiled tentatively.

I only got through a quarter of my tiramisù before pushing the plate away.

"I can't do it…too full." I slouched back in the chair.

I waited while Dominic finished his dessert. That was when the headache hit. *Please not again,* I pleaded internally, just wanting to get through one full meal with Dominic without having to leave. Images of *La Farfalla* flashed through my head, except it wasn't from my current vantage point. I saw in my mind a table across the room where a woman took a bite of her pasta, not knowing that they made a mistake and put shrimp in it instead of chicken. I saw her throat closing as she collapsed onto the ground…

She is deathly allergic to seafood!

And with a flash, the image disappeared. I quickly scanned the restaurant trying to find the woman from my vision. She was sitting across from a sign for *Il Bagno*. She didn't have her meal yet, but I could see the server approaching. I turned to Dominic and hastily excused myself, saying I had to go to the bathroom.

The waiter was just putting the plate in front of the woman, which was sure to mean *morte* if I didn't stop her. I quickened my pace and just as I was passing her table I fake tripped, which turned into me really tripping and tumbling into her table. I crashed into her table; cutlery and glasses went flying and thankfully so did her plate.

"I'm so sorry!" I said to the shocked woman. "I wasn't watching where I was going. I've ruined your meal."

I looked at her pasta, which was now scattered across the floor, completely ruined. She looked like she was going to start yelling at me.

"I'll buy you another shrimp penne," I quickly promised as I stood up and started brushing myself off. The woman looked from me to the pasta then turned to the waiter.

"*Shrimp* penne?" the woman shrieked. "I told you I am allergic to shrimp! I ordered the *chicken* penne," the woman screeched.

The waiter apologized profusely and hurried back to the kitchen, returning moments later with a broom.

Dominic rushed over and helped me up. "Are you okay?" he asked, pulling me to my feet. I brushed the leafy salad greens off my dress.

"I'm so embarrassed! I ruined her meal." I didn't have to fake embarrassment because I genuinely was horrified that Dominic witnessed that.

"Lucky you did. Looks like you spared her from getting sick," Dominic said, with a strange look on his face.

"I guess me being clumsy isn't such a bad thing after all." I laughed, trying to lighten the mood before excusing myself to go to the bathroom to clean up.

When I got back to the table, Dominic was taking a one-hundred-dollar bill from his wallet. He said something in Italian as he handed the money to the server. He thanked Dominic and tucked the bill away before leaving to go to another table.

My eyes widened when I realized that Dominic must have just told our waiter to keep the change. *I didn't realize he was rich enough to throw $100 bills around like it was nothing.*

When we got to my house, Dominic put the car in park and looked at me. I suddenly felt nervous. I had no idea what the expected goodbye was… *Should we hug? Shake hands? What if he goes to kiss me and we bump heads?*

"I had a really great time," I told him nervously, knotting my fingers in my lap.

The tension was building in the car. Dominic leaned towards me and I held my breath. I closed my eyes and felt his lips brush mine. Our lips had just touched when I felt the car lurch forwards. Dominic and I snapped apart.

"What the hell was that?" he wondered aloud.

We both looked around for what could have caused the sudden jarring of the car, but there was nothing around.

"I have no idea, but maybe it's a sign that I should be going." I reached for the door handle and turned back around and gave Dominic a quick peck on the cheek before climbing out of the car. I thanked him again for a wonderful night.

I walked into my house and closed the door before letting out an excited squeal.

"He kissed me, he kissed me," I sang to myself as I danced around the front foyer.

"Who kissed you, dear?" I turned around to see Gran standing in the hallway, a bemused look on her face.

"Uh…Dominic," I mumbled, blushing. No point in lying to my Gran, especially since it was probably written all over my energy field anyway.

"Hmm. Well if this Dominic character is going around kissing my granddaughter, I think I should meet this boy," Gran said.

She tried to make her concern sound playful, but I could see that she was serious.

"You'll meet him eventually, Gran. Promise!" I ran past her and up the stairs, closed my bedroom door and threw myself on my bed as a fit of giggles overtook me. *I can't believe I just got my first ever kiss!* I brought my hand to my lips remembering the pressure of his mouth against mine. With how isolated and limited my social life had been my whole life, I had never really let myself imagine what it would be like to go on a date with an attractive guy—or any guy for that matter. I figured I'd have to wait until college or university before I knew what a date was like. I kept replaying the night over and over again.

With a huge grin still plastered on my face, I reached over into my purse and unlocked my phone. I knew that if I didn't text Elsbeth letting her know how it went I would never hear the end of it. I texted her quickly letting her know I was home and that it was awesome, promising to tell her and Thomas all the details tomorrow on the way to school. *Now that was an amazing second first date!*

* * *

CHAPTER
10
★

I pushed myself harder than I ever had, knowing I had to get away. I fumbled my way through the darkness, running blindly. All I could hear was the sound of my own erratic breathing and the crunch of my feet against the dirt and rubble. The hairs on the back of my neck were standing so tall it was like they, too, were trying to escape. It couldn't be far behind... Whoever or whatever 'it' was. Or was there more than one?

I didn't have time to think about what was behind me. I stumbled over something on the ground. I quickly righted myself and continued to move my feet faster, faster. I saw the outline of a man standing in a pool of light up ahead. He was screaming at me to hurry.

"Run, please!" The voice was panicked. I ran faster, knowing that I must get to him, knowing that the only way I'd be safe was if I could get to him before they got to me.

Dominic, I heard myself think—his name had me running faster. The light around the figure was so bright I couldn't make out his face when I finally made it to him. I only felt his strong body as he wrapped me in a tight protective and loving embrace. A feeling of complete contentment filled me. The fear left my body, being replaced by an emotion I had never felt before.

It was like butterflies in my stomach, but ten thousand times stronger. The feeling made me so happy I wanted to weep. I felt whole, I felt invincible. Never had it felt so right to be cocooned in someone's arms. I was safe in his arms... I was safe with him.

I woke up in a haze, confused and exhausted. I looked over at the clock. 3 a.m. *What was that?* Never in my entire life had I had a dream like that. That dream was more vivid than ever before. Normally my dreams were colors or pictures, but tonight... tonight they were a full-fledged horror film. It felt real—the fear, the panic, my muscles protesting as I pushed them harder. My body ached as if I had truly been running for my life. And those arms... That feeling... My heart warmed at the memory. *What could it all mean? Who was I running from?* I stared at the ceiling, still wrapped in the warm tingly sensation. But even with the warm fuzzies, I was also feeling a little uneasy for some reason...

My instincts were suddenly urging me to stay quiet. Without opening my eyes, I slowed my breathing down so I could hear my surroundings better. I could hear the clock down the hall slowly ticking, and a car in the distance. *But what was that?* I listened harder trying to hear the sound that was coming from my front yard. I heard a twig snap and the distinct sounds of a whispered conversation.

I froze, not knowing what to do. Maybe it was the fact that I had a scary dream, but whatever it was outside had me pinned to my bed afraid to move. I listened harder, trying to hear what was going on outside, but I couldn't hear anything. I kicked myself mentally and told myself to get a grip. It was probably a neighbor's television or something equally as harmless. I rolled over so I was facing the window and closed my eyes again, willing myself to fall back asleep so I could feel those strong arms once more.

☠

Slade and Viper stood at the end of Quinn's driveway. All the doors and windows were locked, with no way in unless they wanted to make a scene.

"Let us go in and grab the girl," Viper suggested for the umpteenth time.

"Be quiet," Slade growled in irritation.

"Why? She cannot see or hear us with our jackets on. The Temptress had the thread for the embroidery charmed specifically to cloak us from humans, you know that," Viper pointed out in confusion.

"I am not concerned that she will hear us," Slade huffed in exasperation. "I am concerned about what I will do if I have to keep hearing you whine about harming the girl when the order has not yet been given."

"But we would be in and out before her precious grandmother had a chance to call for help," Viper insisted.

"The Temptress told us to wait. She wants more information, as do I. We need to know what we are dealing with before we can plan our attack. Any other mission and you *know* I would be smashing through her glass window and ending this, but this is too important, Viper. Seventeen years we have been trying to locate this one girl. If we rush this, it could mean the end of all of us. You have heard the prophecy. We cannot afford to act rashly," Slade chastised.

"Has the Temptress acquired any new information yet? We have been watching her for a while, Slade. She seems harmless if you ask me; there is nothing special about her whatsoever so let us just get this over with so we can go home," Viper offered. "I am tired of this."

Slade's phone vibrated as he pulled it out of his pocket. It was the Temptress.

"Yes, Mistress?" Slade said into the phone. Viper leaned in closer so that they could both listen to the call.

"We have some new information. Keep your phone on you at all times. Keep your heads low and stay out of sight. Do *not* bring unneeded attention to yourselves. I will call you once I know more." Viper threw a small branch in frustration and it snapped against the pavement from the force of the impact.

"We should leave. I cannot stay here for much longer without doing something I will be punished for later," Viper hissed as they disappeared into the shadows.

★

I was not even at the corner of our street the next morning when Elsbeth started hounding me from a distance.

"Tell me *everything!*" she shouted, as she rushed over to me. "And don't leave a-ny-thing out!"

I spent the entire walk to school reliving the entire evening. I didn't tell them about the unexplainable car bumping thing, but I did tell them about the kiss.

"Oh my God, your first kiss!" Elsbeth squealed, spinning me around.

"But definitely not my last," I winked at her, causing her to squeal once again.

"So, you like this guy, huh?" Thomas asked with a smile on his face.

"I mean, what's not to like?" I shrugged. "He compliments me, he likes me, he's super handsome, and smart too."

I could see that Thomas was genuinely happy for me, but he also expressed some concern and wanted to make sure I wasn't rushing into something I wasn't ready for. I gave Thomas a sideways-hug as we walked and assured him there was no need to be protective or to worry. I could handle myself.

"I know you can," he said. "I just don't want to ever see you get hurt," he said sincerely.

"Pssh, stop being a mopey, buzz-kill," Elsbeth said to her brother before turning back to me. "You have a *boyfriend*," she squeaked delightedly.

"Well, I don't know if I'd say thaaat," I protested. I wasn't exactly sure what Dominic and I were.

"Oh, you totally are together," Elsbeth said confidently. I just smiled in response. She continued to gush on my behalf all the way through English. We got scolded a few times by Mrs. Blanc for distracting others with our whispers, but that didn't seem to deter Elsbeth in the slightest.

I walked to Chemistry, with a spring in my step that wasn't normally there.

"Well, hey there," Dominic said with a grin. He bumped his shoulder playful against mine as I sat down beside him.

"Well, hey yourself," I smiled back.

"What are you doing after school? I was thinking we could do something," he said. I explained that most nights I went over to the twins and that he was welcome to join us.

"Oh, sure, that sounds great. I'll just drive to your place after school and we can go over together?"

"Sounds like a plan." I couldn't stop the grin from spreading across my face. Elsbeth was going to freak out.

On the way to our lockers, Dominic took my hand in his and I had to stifle a giggle. It felt good to have his hand in mine. I asked the twins and Dominic to wait as I replaced my old lock with my new combination lock.

"Why does it need replacing?" Dominic asked me.

"I think my old lock was faulty and wasn't locking properly," I said. *Or someone had been breaking into it.* I pushed the thought away as quickly as it had arrived.

As we exited the staircase closest to the cafeteria, I spotted Mindy walking towards us. Her eyes homed in on our entwined hands and her eyes narrowed in displeasure. She smiled seductively at Dominic before purposefully slamming her shoulder into mine as she strutted by.

"Ignore her," Dominic said, casting an angry look over his shoulder at Mindy. I took my hand from Dominic's and rubbed my shoulder.

"That's going to leave a mark," I mumbled to myself. There was a sudden crash from behind me. We all turned around and saw Mindy sprawled on the ground. She shrieked in anger as she stood up, ready to punish whoever tripped her, except she was there was no one around.

"She must've tripped over her ego," Thomas said with a smirk.

"Serves her right for bumping into you like that. She must *really* hate the fact that you're with Dominic and she's not," Elsbeth surmised. "She's just used to getting everything she wants, whenever she wants it."

"People like her act from their basic emotions instead of considering the people around them. I'm with Quinn now, so I guess she's just going to have to get used to it," Dominic said, bringing my hand to his lips. I beamed at Elsbeth when we locked eyes. She wiggled her eyebrows as if to say 'I told you so' before composing herself.

I leaned into Dominic, trying to recreate the feelings I had in my dream. It felt nice to be beside him, but I couldn't capture the intensity I felt in my dream. *Oh, well, I guess it will take some time,* I thought as I snuggled closer to him. *Practice does make perfect, after all!*

★⋆

Cooper saw Mindy bash into Quinn and couldn't resist sticking his foot through the veil at the precise moment she walked by. When she stood up a tiny welt had started to form on her knee where it made contact with the floor. He felt guilty. Not about tripping her—she was asking for it. He felt guilty because that was not what his wings were intended for. They were not given to him so he could trip an unsuspecting human... *even if that human was unnecessarily cruel.*

He wished there was more he could do to make Quinn's life easier, but there wasn't, and it was torture having to stand by feeling useless. He had been struggling with what to do and his rash actions just proved to him that he was no longer able to stay objective. He had been searching for an answer and now he knew exactly what he must do.

Cooper walked up to the reception desk on the first floor of HeadQuarters. There was a large mahogany desk directly in the center of the room and behind it sat the building's receptionist who was also the Magistrate's personal secretary.

"I need to speak to the Magistrate," Cooper said to the woman behind the counter.

"And what shall I tell her is the purpose of this proposed meeting?" the secretary asked sweetly.

"Tell her Guardian Cooper says he needs to speak to her *now* and it cannot wait. She'll know what it's about."

"Yes, of course, Guardian Cooper." The secretary called up to the Magistrate, talking to her briefly before hanging up and addressing Cooper.

"The Magistrate will see you now. Please proceed to the middle elevation pod."

Cooper stormed over to the pod and waited for it to make its way down. The door opened and he stepped in and sent the thought-command for the pod to head to the 180th floor. The scanning rings were not their usual green color as they cascaded round him. Today the rings were rings of orange, as they always were when a Guardian was bi-locating upon entering the pod. He waited impatiently for the rings to turn green, indicating that he had been given special clearance.

Welcome Cooper. The Magistrate will see you now.

The text scrolled briefly across the pod before shooting upwards towards the Magistrate's office. For security purposes, Cooper normally wouldn't have been granted access to the Magistrate's office while bi-locating, but the pod had been reprogrammed to accommodate his arrival with the Magistrate's approval.

Cooper stepped off the elevation pod and walked directly into Nettie's office without knocking. The Magistrate was at the door as he entered.

"Cooper, what's wrong? Did something happen with Quinn?" Nettie asked with concern.

"She's fine," Cooper responded. *She's draped over Dominic with a big stupid grin on her face.*

The Magistrate relaxed visibly.

"Then what's the problem?" Nettie asked, not quite understanding what could've caused Cooper to come storming into her office in the middle of the day.

"You need to find someone else to take this case," Cooper said, shaking slightly. However, he wasn't shaking from anger. He was shaking because he was torn. He didn't want to leave Quinn's side, but he couldn't stand being close to her either. Being around her made him irrational and do things that he normally wouldn't do. He didn't like the way she made him feel and the way he acted because of those feelings.

Nettie paused to consider his request and turned away from him and walked towards her desk. She knew if he saw her face right now the confusion and shock she was feeling would be written clearly all over her face. Once composed she turned back towards him.

"You want off the case? Why?" Nettie questioned, sitting on the edge of her desk as she crossed her arms.

Because she drives me crazy. Because I'm on the verge of getting in too deep into a territory I've never been in and which there is no way out of. Because I can't stand *seeing her with Dominic.* But Cooper couldn't tell Nettie any of those things, not without the potential of serious consequences.

"Do I need a reason? I just don't want the case," Cooper said with exasperation, collapsing into the chair behind him.

Nettie studied him for a moment. *Why is Cooper so disgruntled? He has never gotten this way over a case. Sure, there have been many cases he hasn't liked, but he has always done what duty required him to do. What is so different about this case?* She studied the young man that she considered her nephew. He seemed confused and frustrated, as if he were fighting himself.

Then a reason started to form in her mind. *He's getting emotionally attached to his Charge,* but as the Magistrate, she couldn't voice her suspicions without having to write him up. *It's about time he started letting himself feel something again. Anything, even if it is for his Charge.*

She knew it was dangerous territory leaving him on the case if his feelings were developing, but as his pseudo-aunt she wanted him to feel again and knew his feelings would make him even more protective of his Charge.

However, she had to be careful not to push him too far or else he or Quinn could get seriously hurt. She went back and forth inside her mind weighing the pros and cons of keeping him on the case. She hoped it would help to open his heart and had to trust that his sense of duty was strong enough to keep him from making an irrevocable mistake. She quickly decided on a course of action.

"As you wish, Cooper. I'll assign another Guardian to this case." Nettie walked around her desk sat down, scrolling her fingers along the surface, bringing up a list of available Guardians. Instead of feeling relieved, Cooper suddenly felt sad. A part of him was really hoping Nettie would talk him into staying on the case.

"It looks like the only available agent is, Neil. I'll have my secretary bring him right up so we can fill him in on this case. He can take over immediately."

Cooper froze. *Neil would be in charge of Quinn's safety?* "Neil?" He said incredulously, standing up to face Nettie's desk. "Over my dead body!"

"Well it's either Neil takes over, or you stay on the case. There are no other options," the Magistrate said, as she folded her hands in her lap. "What will it be Cooper?"

Cooper's frustration was palpable. "Who was in charge of her safety before me? Can't they just return to this post?" He was desperately trying to find any solution that kept him away from the temptation and distraction she caused him.

Nettie visibly flinched at his question. Something about his words had upset her, but he was too worked up to care.

"It was Magistrate Raymond that watched her personally up until…" she said quietly trailing off.

Cooper stopped his pacing and stared at his aunt, flabbergasted. A Magistrate being split was unheard of except for in imminent emergencies.

"She is that important Cooper," answering the unspoken question written across his face.

The Magistrate could see his fists clenching and unclenching and his jaw working as he considered the choice before him.

"Fine. I'll stay on the damned case," he said, storming out of her office. He felt a little bit of relief spread over his body and a little bit of dread. What if he couldn't trust himself to stay impartial? How would it affect Quinn? How would it affect his job? There wasn't much he could do about it unless he wanted class-clown Neil to be Quinn's Guardian.

It looked as though Cooper was going to have to either face his feelings or push them down so deep that they would never be found again. He knew which option he should take; which option would be better for both of them, which option would hurt him less in the long run— but there was another part of him wasn't ready to let go.

He sighed in exasperation and pulled his fingers through his sand-colored locks. *This may be the hardest case I'll ever have. And not just because Quinn seems to value everyone's life except her own.* He stepped onto the pod, and went back down to rejoin his classmates, hoping that today's simulation training would go better than his last.

* * *

CHAPTER
11
★

Walking the hallways hand-in-hand with Dominic everyday was a great feeling. People still stared at me daily, but the difference was that I no longer cared. They could stare all they wanted; it wouldn't change a thing. I was dating the most attractive guy in my high school. And the cherry on top? He was also the only boy in our grade that had never made a play for Mindy, despite her best efforts. She glared at us constantly, but that only lightened my mood. Knowing I was with someone who wasn't interested in her just made my relationship with Dominic all the more satisfying.

The only unsatisfying thing about our relationship was how many times I got pulled away from him due to psychic flashes of someone needing my help. They were happening more and more frequently it seemed. So far it appeared I was able to convince him with my excuses. He didn't seem to suspect anything. He just thought I was clumsy and quirky, and occasionally flighty, which was fine by me. Even though those who cared about me seemed to accept me, I couldn't risk telling them the truth and having it end up being too much for them to handle. I couldn't bear it if I lost them. So, I just used my (mostly feeble) excuses and tried to move past each episode, so I could slip back into my routine and slip my hand back into Dominic's.

The next few weeks continued like this, Dominic and I walking to and from class together, fingers intertwined, him eating lunch with my friends and coming over every Wednesday and Sunday to do homework or just hang out. I was so happy. Time seemed to fly by as if I was walking on air and the world was stuck on fast-forward, not that I minded. Life before Dominic had just moved so slowly. Don't get me wrong—I was happy before him, but now everything was just a little brighter.

Cooper blanched as he normally did whenever Dominic's hand found Quinn's. *Gag me*. Cooper made an exaggerated vomiting gesture and rolled his eyes at the two of them, glad for once for the veil that separated them because it allowed him to respond in whatever way he deemed fit, even if it wasn't a way he'd ever respond if someone else was around. Dominic leaned down and kissed Quinn.

"Ugh," both Coopers grunted.

Cali heard her brother's sound of disgust from the other room.

"What?" Cali asked from the kitchen table. She was doing her homework while their mom was making dinner.

"Uh, nothing. Just thought of something gross I saw today," Cooper said, not able to explain to his sister that his other self was being forced to watch Quinn and Dominic kiss.

"Ew, then don't tell me. If *you* think it's gross then I'll probably puke," Cali said turning back to her homework.

"Believe me, this is gross, and I won't say a word," Cooper said as he mimed zipping his lips and throw away the key. Candice just smiled at her children as she continued cooking.

"Thank you," Cali replied, visibly relieved. "Hey, Coop?" Cali asked after a moment. Cooper lifted his head up off the couch in response. "Would you be able to help me with my essay for school?" she asked, her eyes pleading.

"Do I have to? I don't really want to do more schoolwork. I already had to do seventeen years of it," Cooper complained. Cali opened her big brown eyes and with a pout, unleashed the full effect of her puppy dog eyes.

"Oh fine!" Cooper grumbled as he rolled off the couch. "What's your essay on?" Cooper asked, giving in. He had never been able to resist his sister's adorable face when she begged like that. She was just too darned cute. Cali grinned triumphantly at her brother.

"It's on the veil. We're supposed to write about how it would look to a Guardian and explain where it's located and stuff, but I don't really understand how it works. Help?" Cali asked. Cooper mumbled something about just reading the darned textbook.

"Oh hush, Cooper. If she wants our help, then we'll give it. I can explain to you the basics of the veil, Sweetie," Candice said as she cooked. "But since I'm a Keeper and not a Guardian, I can help you understand how to monitor human lives and lifeforces, but your brother will have to help with the rest. Can you do that, Coop?" Cooper just grunted.

"That's my boy," she said, coming over to quickly kiss her son on the head. Cooper pulled away slightly, but not before allowing his mother to plant a loud smacking kiss on his mop of sandy brown hair.

Candice then turned towards Cali.

"As you know, the veil is a thin wall of energy that separates our world from the human realm. It vibrates at a level that humans can't see, but we can. However, even though our eyes are able to see the veil, it still resonates at a different frequency than us, which is why Coordinators who *aren't* Guardians, like you and I, need to stay away from the veil because anything that touches it that resonates at a different frequency will immediately start to burn and turn to dust."

Cali shuddered at her mother's words, remembering the grass she and Cooper had thrown at the veil and how it immediately exploded into a bright array of light and dust.

"But what exactly do you see when you look through it? I mean, I know I can kind of see the human world when I look through the veil, but what am I looking at?" Cali had never been allowed close enough to the veil— for obvious reasons—to be able to get a clear view of what the human realm was like. Even if Cali could get close enough, the human world only fully came into full focus when the Doyen's golden ink fused with its Guardian host.

Knowing this was a question better answered by Cooper, Candice looked at her son and signaled for him to continue.

"Well, uh, how do I explain this exactly?" He picked up a (mostly stale) doughnut off the counter then sat across from his sister.

"Take this doughnut for example. The inner circle is the veil," he said, tracing his finger around the circumference of the hole. "And the main doughnut part is our plane." He gently pinched the doughnut.

"Our house is built close to the veil," he said, pointing to a spot close to the veil, right along the inner edge of the pastry. "And HeadQuarters is here, farther back from the veil, for safety reasons." He pointed to a spot on the very outer edge of the doughnut—the farthest place from the veil before continuing.

"Only those with their Guardian tattoos are safe near the veil."

Cali took a moment to jot some notes down.

"Okay, but then how can you keep track of your Charge? What if from where you are you can't get to your Charge in time? What if on the Earth plane they live in the very center? How do you get to them then?" She questioned rapidly, putting her finger on the table directly in the middle of the doughnut hole.

Cooper chuckled. "Well, you see, once you are assigned a Charge, the veil becomes kind of like one of the fancy monitors at Mom's work, constantly showing their life in live time. Your Charge becomes the focal point and is brought in orientation closer to the veil. It's like an interactive screen where you can just step through the glass and into the scene. The world goes from spinning on its axis, to revolving around her," he said before quickly catching himself, "her… *whoever* you are looking after," he immediately corrected himself when he realized his slip up.

Oblivious to his Freudian slip, Cali asked, "but how does that work if there are multiple Guardians watching a whole bunch of different people?" Cali asked, brows pulled together trying to figure out how the veil worked.

"That's the magic of the veil and the magic of energy. What you think, controls what you see beyond the veil. You become attuned to their frequency, so you can home in on them alone, while someone else can just focus on whoever they are looking at. I don't know how to explain it, really; it's just how it works."

"Does it matter where you stand?" Cali asked.

"Not at all," Cooper responded. His other self was presently standing by a little clearing in the woods by his home that backs directly onto the veil, watching Quinn.

"Oh okay, I think I understand now," Cali grinned, picking up her pencil again.

"Good, but now you're on your own. There's no way I'm writing your essay," Cooper stated firmly.

"Pfft, thanks but no thanks. I've seen your writing," Cali said as she rolled her eyes.

Cooper grumbled in mock anger and started tousling his sister's hair, causing her to call out for their mom.

"Cooper, leave her alone," Candice scolded as she shook her wooden spoon at them. Cooper raised his hands in the air feigning surprise.

"I did nothing," he said. "I've been framed!"

His mother just laughed and went back to her cooking.

"What are you making, anyway?" Cooper asked.

"I'm trying out a new recipe for eggplant soup. I think it's going to turn out well." Cooper and Cali shared an uneasy look. Sometimes their mom's recipes were delicious and sometimes they were putrid. Hopefully this meal would prove to be better than it sounded.

"Mom, why do you insist on cooking? If we need energy, we can just sit in a field and use nature to replenish us. Why bother cooking at all?" Cali wondered aloud.

"Because it's delicious and it gives me a reason to make you two stay home longer at night. Plus, just because you don't *need* something doesn't mean you don't want it."

Ain't that the truth, Cooper thought to himself as looked at Quinn.

I smiled down from my bed at Dominic, who was sitting on the floor of my room. This was how we were every Sunday afternoon, the two of us cooped up in my room working on homework. I couldn't believe that it was almost Halloween that meant that Dominic and I had been together for almost two months.

I was still not used to having a boyfriend, and yes, that was what Dominic was, *my boyfriend.* When we weren't at my house, he would come with me to the twins'. He seemed to get along with Elsbeth and Thomas, for which I was thankful. I didn't know if I could stay with someone who didn't get along with the people who were most important to me, but so far that hadn't been an issue.

Dominic and I were in my room reading chapters from our textbook and taking notes—or at least he was taking notes. It was hard to concentrate when he was in the same room as me. He was a complete gentleman, though, which kind of drove me insane. He wasn't a big fan of public displays of affection, so in public the most we normally did was hold hands. I wish I could say that when we were alone, he tried to jump my bones, but no such luck. We would kiss, but never any crazy make-out sessions.

Some days I just wanted to shake him and say, *"snap out of it! I don't want you to be a gentleman, you idiot!"* I sighed impatiently. Looking across the room at him, I chewed the end of my pen cap as I traced the outline of his face with my eyes.

"I can feel you staring at me," Dominic said without looking up, a smile playing on his lips.

"Nuh-uh," I said, looking back at my book.

"Yeah-huh," Dominic replied.

I looked at him again, this time he looked up and met my eyes.

"See?"

"You caught me." I leaned down to steal a kiss. Dominic complied, but then pulled away.

"We really need to finish this chapter before I have to go home for dinner."

I pouted at him, my feelings more hurt by his withdrawal than I let on.

"Aw, don't give me that look. You know I'd love to kiss you all night, but we need to be responsible," he said, giving me another quick peck on the lips. After a brief moment, I nodded and looked away. I was not content with his response, but I knew there was no changing his mind.

"Quinn," he said pleadingly. I turned my gaze back to him. "Please don't be upset. It's not you. We just can't afford to get into the routine of slacking on our homework."

In my mind I started thinking about all the adventures he'd been on; all the people he'd met and wondering how far he had gone with them. I couldn't help but wonder if I somehow just didn't measure up to the other girls he'd liked around the world. I couldn't quite shake my fear that I wasn't the same caliber of girl he was used to dating.

He saw that his responses were doing little to ease my worries so he leaned up and gave me a longer kiss then said, "I want you; can't you see that?" I nodded again, not trusting myself to speak. "You are the only one I want, Quinn." He paused, searching my face for any sign that I believed him.

"Do you remember what I said to you in Italian at La Farfalla?"

I thought back to our date. I recalled that he had said something to me in Italian, but when I asked him what it meant, he hadn't explained. "No," I answered honestly. "I don't remember the exact words."

"I've been to many places in my life, but never have I met someone like you. At the restaurant I said to you 'L'ho trovato finalmente. Lei è il mio.' Do you know what that means?"

I shook my head, not even wanting to guess.

"It basically means that there is nowhere I want to be, but here with you. I said it so you know that when I'm with you I think of no one else." He rubbed his thumb across the back of my hand. I felt my heart melt a little and I instantly felt foolish for doubting him. He linked his hands with mine and said to me tenderly, "Il mio," before kissing me once again.

★

Gran got home just as Dominic was pulling out of the driveway.

"Was that Dominic?" Gran asked as she walked in the front door.

"Yeah, he had to go home for dinner," I explained.

"I still haven't formally met that boy. I think one of these Sundays he should stay here for dinner so we can have a proper sit-down and I can get to know him."

"I'll mention it to Dominic, Gran. His family seems pretty adamant about family dinners together, though, so he's normally not able to get away for meals." Even to my own ears my explanation sounded a bit like an excuse.

"Hmm…" Gran said to herself, as she started taking food out of the fridge for our dinner. Her tone made it seem like she, too, thought I was just making excuses for Dominic. Gran then switched topics, asking me about work and school and the twins—basically anything other than talking about my boyfriend. Gran needed to meet him soon or I feared her opinion of him would forever be tainted.

* * *

CHAPTER
12
★

As the twins and I meandered down the hallway to our lockers, we noticed that the walls were plastered with bright orange posters.

Rosevale High's Halloween Celebration This Friday at 7pm.
Come in Costume for a Hauntingly Good Time!

I rolled my eyes as Elsbeth squealed.

"Ooooooooh, can we go please, please, please! I've been working on a costume for months and really want to show it off," she begged. I knew that if Thomas and I didn't go, there was no way she'd go alone. Thomas and I both grunted, showing our complete dislike of this idea. Dominic got to my locker just in time to hear our protests.

"What's wrong?" He asked as he put his arm around me.

"Just the school's Halloween dance. Elsbeth wants us to go," I said rolling my eyes again.

"Does that mean you don't want to go? Because I was thinking it'd be fun for us to get all dressed up and check it out," Dominic said with a shrug, "but if you don't want to go... we don't have to."

I'd do almost anything if it meant getting to spend more time with him, which I suspected he knew. He was already smiling in victory before Elsbeth added the cherry on the cake.

"Plus, think of how jealous Mindy would be if she saw you and Dominic slow dancing."

Just imagining the look on Mindy's face when she saw Dominic and I was enough to sway me.

"Fine." I let out an exaggerated sigh. "We'll go."

"Oh yay!" Elsbeth said at the same time Thomas groaned, "aw man!"

Thomas knew that he could stay home if he wanted to, but also knew he'd regret missing a group excursion.

"But I don't even have a costume," Thomas complained.

"That's okay, neither do I. We can all go out after school and hit up the costume shop," I suggested, knowing that Elsbeth wouldn't let me get away with not taking her, so I might as well make an event out of it.

"Can you come with us after school today, Dom?" I asked him. He liked shopping just about as much as I did—which was basically as much as I'd like standing stark naked in the middle of a frozen lake in the dead of winter with all of my classmates skating around me. I shuddered at the mental image I had just created.

"Uh, yeah, I guess I could come with you. I do need a costume," Dominic agreed reluctantly.

Elsbeth cheered excitedly. She was the only one of us that was remotely thrilled about costume hunting. The rest of us were hoping the school day would drag on just a little bit longer to spare us from having to shop at all. Unfortunately, that didn't happen.

When we arrived, the costume shop was full of people: children, adults, teens, couples… every kind of person was milling about the store. Pieces of costumes were scattered on the floor, the shelves in complete disarray and some shoppers were even trying on costumes in the middle of the aisles because the line for the dressing rooms was too long. It was a complete zoo.

I guess that was our punishment for shopping the Monday before Halloween. There were so many costumes I didn't even know where to begin. Scary costumes, funny costumes, clever costumes, provocative costumes—they were all there.

"You and Dominic should totally wear a couple's costume, like Mr. and Mrs. Claus or Adam and Eve!" Elsbeth said, as she thumbed through the costumes.

"What about Clark Kent and Lois Lane?" Dominic suggested. "You'd look great in a skirt and I could deal with being a superhero."

"Dom, Clark Kent is an alias. He's really Superman. If you just go as Clark Kent people won't know who you are. You need to wear the proper outfit or people will just mistake you for someone else." I said, shaking my head at him. "But if you were to wear the leotard…" I trailed off, wiggling my eyebrows at him mischievously.

"Oh, no way, lady. You're not getting this guy into tights," Dominic said, pushing me away from him. Elsbeth vocalized her support of my costume idea.

"But what will I be?" Thomas interjected, looking lost and confused as he tried to sort out all the different costumes.

"I think this one would be perfect for you," Elsbeth said holding up a costume. We all laughed when we saw that she had chosen a Robin Hood outfit.

"If Dominic doesn't have to wear tights, then neither do I," Thomas stated matter-of-factly.

"Well then, what about this one?" I offered, holding up my costume pick for him.

He looked at the simple white and red striped shirt and the red toque and smiled. "Now, that's more like it."

After a bit more tweaking of Dominic's costume, we all went to the checkout to pay for our choices. I had to admit; once we had our costumes, I was actually looking forward to the dance a bit... but only a little bit.

★_★

Candice poured two cups of tea, one for herself and one for Nettie. It wasn't often that the Magistrate got time away, so when Nettie called and said she had Monday afternoon off, Candice jumped at the chance to spend some quality time with her best friend.

The two of them sat in Candice's living room, looking out the window watching Cooper and Cali as they practiced sparring together.

"Those kids work so hard," Nettie observed, as she sipped her tea. "Both so determined and dedicated to their craft. It's really refreshing to see."

"If only more were like that," Candice agreed, "but some of them are less like Cooper in the responsible aspect and more like..."

"...Neil," they both said in unison with a laugh.

"Don't get me wrong. Neil's a good kid," Nettie added. "He just lacks the focus and dedication to the job that Cooper has. He'll be a great Guardian too once he matures a little."

"Sometimes I wish Cooper was a little less serious, though," Candice said sadly. "He had to grow up so fast."

Nettie's face mirrored Candice's sadness. Both women temporarily lost in the memories of the heartache their families had experienced over the years.

Candice turned to her friend and cautiously asked... "Any word on Raymond?"

It was a very sensitive topic and she did not want to pry, but also knew that she was the only one Nettie had to talk to about her husband.

Nettie's face hardened at the question.

"He's still missing. It's been over six months, Candice. I've started to give up hope that he'll ever come home."

Knowing there were no words that would comfort her friend she let the conversation fall away.

"At least we still have them," Nettie said, smiling tenderly at the children she loved as if they were her own.

"They are the only things that keep me going. I love those two—they are my entire life," Candice said, her eyes misting.

"You've done an amazing job with them, Candy. I'm proud of those two."

They smiled and watched as the two siblings went through various training scenarios.

Outside, Cooper stood facing his sister, both of them a little out of breath from their sparring session. Cooper was helping Cali with her coordination, while also helping her study for the academic and theoretical portions of her Coordinator aptitude test that she would be taking within a year's time. This was the most important test a Coordinator would have in their lifetime. The results would indicate which career stream she would be advancing in: Keeper, Doyen, Healer, Clerk, or Guardian.

There was nothing Cali wanted more than to become a Guardian like her brother and Cooper would do everything in his power to help her get there.

"So, what do you do if your Charge is going to step in front of a moving vehicle?" Cooper asked, thinking back to his time with Quinn and the horrible experience with the simulation training.

Cali ducked as Cooper's fist swung towards her.

"Um... try to get either the driver or your Charge's attention in a non-violent manner. Like tipping their coffee cup so they have to pause or have their paper swept up in a gust of wind?" Cali suggested, looking to her brother to see if her answer was acceptable. Her slight pause earned her a swift kick to the knees and she almost lost her balance.

Once she recovered, Cooper tossed out another situation where a Charge was about to trip on a toy and fall down the stairs.

"Distract them or kick the toy out of the way. That was too easy. Give me another one." Cali lunged at her brother, but he easily side-stepped her attack and she landed with a thud on the grass beneath them. She jumped back to her feet and spun to face her brother, ready for his next attack. Cooper smiled at his sister.

"Okay smarty-pants. What about if your Charge is driving and they are about to swerve into traffic?"

"Um..." Cali scrunched her eyebrows in concentration, trying to picture the scenario in her mind.

She took a step back out of his immediate range while she thought. "Wait. Why are they about to swerve into oncoming traffic? Are they asleep? Or are they distracted?"

"Asleep," Cooper replied. He felt proud that she had caught the need for distinction as he closed the gap between them.

"Turn on the radio or honk the horn to wake them up," Cali said.

"And if they were distracted?" Cooper asked.

"Toss a rock at the window? Gently of course," she added with a smirk.

He continued firing off scenario after scenario, all of which Cali responded to perfectly and quickly. His theoretical situations started rolling out faster and faster as she tried to keep up with his scenarios while still dodging his blows.

Cooper lunged and tackled his sister to the ground. He paused and looked seriously at his sister.

"What if your Charge is held at gunpoint?" Cooper asked. Cali stilled beneath him and hurt immediately flooded her eyes. She pinched her mouth closed and shook her head, trying to wiggle away from him.

"I can't… please." Cali's voice began to shake.

Cooper's own heart was hurting as he looked at his sister, but he needed to hear her say it… needed her to promise.

"You can, Cali. I need to know you'll be okay. Please." His face mirrored the pain that she was feeling. She started to sob so Cooper let her up and pulled her into a sitting position before wiping away her tears.

"I can't lose you, too, Cali."

★⋆

It was two years ago, on a day just like today when it happened. The sun was shining; Cooper was seventeen and was at home sparring with Neil in the backyard when they got the news. Carlton, Cooper's father, had been assigned as a Guardian to a government official on the human plane. He had been on the case for over a year and had felt a kinship with his Charge.

When his Charge was held at gunpoint, Carlton didn't even think. As the man pulled the trigger, Carlton jumped in front of his Charge to block the bullet. His brave, yet foolish act had cost Carlton his life and caused Cali and Cooper to lose their father… all for a man who never even knew Carlton existed. The shining sun and chirping birds seemed so wrong after hearing of his father's passing. How could the sun still be shining with his father dead? How could the birds still sing, when such a brave and loving man was gone forever?

It was after that day that Cooper changed. He had to step up and become the man of his household and with it, took on all the responsibilities and stresses that he shouldn't have had to deal with so young. It made Cooper more guarded. He locked his emotions away tightly and vowed never again to show any weakness. His family needed him to be strong. His father would want him to be strong, so he toughened up and tried to move on with his life.

"Cali, please…" Cooper begged, gripping her shoulder tightly.

"I would cause a commotion behind the shooter, forcing him to turn away from my Charge and if I could, I would find a way to make the gunman drop the gun," Cali said, fierceness now clouding the pain in her eyes.

"And never, under any circumstances will you ever jump in front of them," Cooper said sternly.

"Never," Cali's voice echoed the promise.

He pulled his sister in close and held her as another wave of tears overtook her. He stared hard into the distance, willing his tears to stay away, but wasn't quite able to stop a single tear from escaping. He quickly brushed it away. Some days he hated his father for being so reckless, but today he just missed him and wished that he was there to tell him what to do or what to say.

There were so many things his father never got to teach him. All Cooper could do was focus on what his father had instilled in him. He must be strong; he must be brave. He must keep his family safe and make his father proud. Nothing else mattered. And in that moment, with all the loss he felt, the only thing that brought him a shred of happiness was the picture of Quinn's smiling face that danced in his mind.

* * *

CHAPTER
13
★

It was dusk and I was walking through a vast valley. All the flowers in the valley were wilting, all the colors dark and muted with decay. I ran my hand along the flowers, and they crumbled in my hands. The dirt of what once was beautiful, slipping through my fingers, covering the ground. I heard a rustling in the grass and turned around. I could not see anything with the approaching darkness, but I could hear something moving along the ground; a low sound like the scraping of sandpaper.

I backed away instinctively from the noise, unsettled because I could not see where it was coming from. That was when I saw two beady yellow eyes glowering in the night; two horizontal slits, staring directly at me. I didn't see much at first, only the eyes. Then I saw it more clearly: a green snake, poised, waiting to strike.

Before I could take another step back it lunged at me. I turned to run, but before I could get away, I felt its fangs sink deep into my flesh. I stumbled and fell, shocked and in pain. The snake was still biting hard just below my collarbone and right above my heart. I started to feel woozy and disoriented. I watched in horror as the snake's fangs walked their way up my chest towards my neck. Each fang pierced me one at a time as the snake moved closer and closer to my face.

I started to feel nauseous and felt my body start to weaken. Then in a flash of light the snake was ripped away from me and tossed into the night. The next thing I felt was his strong arms as they pulled me into an embrace. I lay there on his lap, terrified that I was going to die.

He took my hand in his and whispered my name over and over again, a soft plea for me to hold on, to stay with him. I felt his fingers lace through mine. My pulse beat faster and my hand started to tingle, whether from his touch or the venom, I wasn't sure. I turned his hand over and easily found the scar just below his left thumb. I traced my fingers over the familiar mark and felt the tiniest bit of relief knowing that if I died, he would be the last thing I ever saw; my love for him being the last thing I ever felt. The numbness soon took over my entire body and I felt him press his lips to my forehead tenderly, one last time. Then everything went dark...

I shot upright in bed gasping for air, my hands flying to my chest checking for any signs of pierced flesh along my collarbone. I sat back against the headboard of my bed and tried to catch my breath. I turned on my bedside lamp, not wanting to be in the darkness for a moment longer. As my breathing slowed, I looked around my room.

I'm fine. I'm alive. I'm safe. Nothing's wrong. I'm fine. I'm alive. I'm safe. Nothing's wrong. I repeated these words over and over again like a mantra until I calmed down. I rolled over and pulled the covers in tight to my chest. I closed my eyes and tried to remember the feeling of being safe in his arms —the feeling of knowing he would keep me safe.

I could almost feel the slight pressure of his lips on my forehead. I opened my eyes, for a second almost thinking I'd see Dominic there... but it was just me alone in my room. I left the light on for the rest of the night, afraid that the darkness would consume me if I let it. So, I left the light on to keep the darkness at bay.

Cooper saw Quinn tossing and turning before suddenly gasping and sitting straight up in her bed. Her hair was in disarray and her eyes were open wide with fright.

What did she dream about that made her so scared?

She looked like she was shaking as she pulled her covers up under her chin. She lay there with her eyes shut tightly. Cooper's heart clenched, hating that she was so afraid and so alone and wishing he could be there for her, to calm her down and let her know that he'd never let anything happen to her.

He leaned through the veil briefly and brushed a light kiss across her forehead, wishing he could hold her in his arms and reassure her that it was just a dream, but knowing there was no way she would ever even know he existed.

★

I heard Gran milling about the kitchen as I walked downstairs for breakfast. She had the television playing in the living room and the sounds of an old game show drifted through the kitchen. Gran loved watching old reruns. When I went to sit down there was a box on the table and the box was...moving?

"Uh, Gran?" I looked at the mysterious package skeptically. "Why is there a box on the table? And why is it moving?"

"Oh! Quinnie, dear. I didn't hear you come down. Don't be frightened, just open it," Gran said with a gleam in her eye.

Gently lifting the lid, I peered inside. I let out a very uncharacteristic squeal as I picked up the tiny ball of squirming fur. The kitten tilted its little head up to look at me and let out a soft 'mew' before giving my face a lick; its rough tongue tickling my chin. I giggled and snuggled my face into its soft fur.

Gran walked across the room and stood beside me.

"I wanted to get one for you in September after your difficult first week of school when the psychic episodes ruined your plans over and over again. But the breeder said her new litter wouldn't be ready to take home until late October. She called me last night to say I could pick up the little guy this morning." Gran was grinning from ear to ear.

"He's so cute and soft and fluffy," I cooed as I petted his fur. He was mostly white with a brown face, almost like he was wearing a mask, the hazel-brown of his eyes matching the flecks of hazel in his brown mask as well as the brown spot on his back.

"What are you going to name him?" Gran asked me, smiling as she watched me cuddle my new kitten.

"Theodore," I declared. The name just popped into my head. I didn't even have time to question it. "Theo for short." Theo nuzzled against me almost as if to show his appreciation for the name.

I looked up at the clock and sighed. Gran followed my gaze and spoke as if anticipating my next question.

"Not to worry, Quinnie dear. The shelter said I could keep him in my office while you're at school until we're comfortable leaving him at home."

I reluctantly passed Theo over to Gran. He settled against her chest almost instantly. I knew he'd be in good hands. Gran then told me I needed to stop by the pet store after school and pick up the rest of the supplies for him.

"I left some money for you on the table in the foyer. Now get," Gran chided as she playfully pushed me towards the stairs. I quickly took out my phone and snapped a picture of Theo to send to our best friends' group chat.

As expected, both Thomas and Elsbeth couldn't stop gushing over the newest edition to my family. Gran said she'd leave the Shelter early to drop Theo off at home for when I got there. Dominic was waiting for me as I got to school so I pounced at the chance to tell him about my little Theodore.

"Gran got me a kitten!" I said, grinning from ear to ear. I reached into my pocket to show him the picture on my phone.

"Oh, cool," Dominic responded absently, his tone not as excited as it should be if he actually thought it was 'cool'.

My face fell a bit. "Thanks for the enthusiasm…"

"Sorry, Quinn, I'm just not a huge fan of cats, dogs…or any other small cuddly animal for that matter," Dominic said shrugging, "but I'm glad you're so excited. That's good."

"Who doesn't like small cuddly animals?" I asked incredulously.

He shrugged half-heartedly. "I had a tarantula once, and a snake and a lizard, but never anything that you could really pet."

I could feel my excitement deflating at his lack of interest. Feeling there was nothing else I could say to propel this conversation forward, I just let Dominic link his fingers through mine as he steered me down the hallway.

★

I couldn't tell you what happened at school because all I could concentrate on was getting home to see Theo. Once I got home, I immediately rushed over to his crate and picked him up. I put his collar on him before snuggling him into my neck. He started purring like crazy. Theo tried to make his way around the room, stopping to bat at anything that moved, including his collar, which made him fall over every time he tried to attack it. He was still a little clumsy, so he fell a lot—so much for cats always landing on their feet. Maybe it only applied to full-grown cats? Or maybe Theo was already taking after me. Poor cat, I hope that wasn't the case.

"Hello?" I heard Dominic's voice call from downstairs.

"I'm up here!"

Theo was exploring my room and I didn't want to leave him alone in case he got lost, or stuck, or got his little paws on something he shouldn't—like my clothes.

"Shut the door, shut the door!" I said hurriedly, not wanting Theo to escape. Dominic rolled his eyes and shut the door behind him.

Theo turned to Dominic and waddled over to him, sniffing at his pants, but not climbing on his lap.

"What are you staring at?" Dominic asked Theo with a scowl on his face. Theo just stood there looking at Dominic, not moving any closer. Theo let out a low growl and his tail puffed up.

"Stop it," Dominic said, as he swatted the kitten away. My eyes widened and my jaw dropped as Theo faltered backwards a step before turning and running back to me.

"Dom!" I was aghast. "He's just a kitten. He doesn't know any better," I said snuggling Theo against my chest until he started purring; then I set him on the floor.

"Sorry," he said, flipping his jet-black hair out of his eyes. "I just really don't like cats."

Finding myself at a loss for words for the second time today, I just stroked Theo's fur for a moment before suggesting we go downstairs for food. I put Theo in his crate before heading down to the kitchen. I went to the fridge, grabbed the pitcher of homemade iced tea, some crackers and some cream cheese and set it on the table. I started spreading the cheese over a cracker and offered it to Dominic. He gladly took it and popped the whole thing in his mouth.

"Pig," I laughed, smiling.

"Mwat?" Dominic said, grinning with his mouth full. "Don't you like see-food?"

Quinn laughed, but Cooper just rolled his eyes. Cooper wished they could go back in time ten minutes to when it was just Quinn and Theo. He much preferred the kitten's antics to Dominic's.

From Cooper's view behind the veil he watched Quinn move to the counter, dampening a cloth to presumably wipe up the crumbs Dominic had spat across the table. Knowing the veil kept him shielded from human eyes, Cooper decided to entertain himself by making faces at Dominic and doing some really stiff dance moves, like a tourist might do at Buckingham Palace when trying to get the royal guards to crack a smile.

Dominic leaned towards Quinn and gave her a long kiss. Quinn's cheeks blushed a deep red.

"What was that for?" She breathed deeply, trying to bring the room back into focus. "Not that I'm complaining," she said with a big grin on her face.

"Just because," Dominic said as he went back to eating his crackers.

Behind the veil, Cooper fumed, wishing that Dominic really *could* see him, so that he could flip him off and have the satisfaction of watching Dominic charge at him and try to tackle him only to be blown to smithereens by the veil. The image of Dominic turning to dust calmed his temper, but only slightly.

*　*　*

CHAPTER
14
★

On Friday night the twins, Dominic and I were all at my place getting ready for the dance. Thomas had finished getting ready first, which made sense since his costume only had two articles of clothing involved. Elsbeth and I were in my room and the boys were waiting in the living room while we changed. She had me close my eyes while she put on her costume. Elsbeth loved fashion and I knew she had made her entire costume by hand, but I had no idea what she was going to the party dressed as.

"Okay, open your eyes!" she said brightly. I obliged and took in her costume in all its glory

"Wow," I breathed. I was awestruck. Her costume was phenomenal. She created a dress based on the style from the 1940s.

It was a white hoop-dress with white lace. The skirt was tiered, and the lacey bodice was short-sleeved. She had even found a cameo, cinched belt, and matching hair bow. It was incredible and I told her as much.

"You really like it?" Elsbeth asked, giving a twirl.

"No, I *love* it! It must have taken you forever to make." I noticed the details and all the hand stitching.

"Yeah, but it was worth it. There's something else though that I haven't told you…" Elsbeth's cheeks flushed with embarrassment.

"I invited ShowMeTheMonet to meet me at the dance. Things have been going really well online and I wanted to meet him in person," Elsbeth confided, her face riddled with worry that I would be upset that she had withheld this information from me.

My first instinct was to tell her how foolish it was to meet a stranger from online, but she was doing it in a public place, and we would all be with her… I did however express my concerns to her anyway and asked her if she was nervous. What if he wasn't what she expected?

"I am really nervous, but he seems great and I may as well meet him before my feelings develop more. I don't want to get attached if the guy is a complete troll," she said scrunching her face.

I burst out laughing, and then quickly tried to calm myself when I saw that she wasn't laughing with me.

"I'm sorry, I'm sorry. I'm sure it'll be great. He's probably a super stud and you two will hit it off and live happily ever after," I said smiling at my friend. Although I was obviously exaggerating, her face lit up at my prediction.

"I really hope so! He just gets me. I mean we talk for hours and he makes me laugh and makes me feel so good."

My stomach clenched at her happiness. Dominic made me laugh, but we never talked for hours—at least not about anything substantial. I found myself feeling slightly envious at her connection with a guy she hadn't even met in person yet. Her giddiness was more than I had felt with Dominic for a while. *Gah, get over it, Quinn. So, what if you don't have long deep talks? You still have a lot of fun anyway.*

"That's awesome. How will you know it's him if you've never met him?" I wondered aloud. "Won't it be impossible with everyone wearing costumes?"

Elsbeth beamed at me. "Well, you see... his costume kind of goes with mine." I thought her lips were going to crack from how wide she was smiling.

"No way! He made a costume too?"

"Well his costume is off of some costume site, but it should go along well with mine, regardless," she said, smoothing out her dress and straightening her hair bow.

Feeling it was safe to steer the conversation away from her mystery man, I asked her to help me with my hair. I had gotten my bangs cut recently, so now they went straight across my forehead like the original Lois Lane. Elsbeth picked up my curling iron and expertly gave my hair the long loose curls I wanted for this costume. I was already in my blouse and pencil skirt; the hair was the final piece of the puzzle. Once my hair was finished Elsbeth looked at me and took in the entire ensemble.

"Holy crap, Quinn, you need to wear your hair down more often. You're a total babe."

"Yeah, I guess I do look pretty good, don't I?" I smiled, appraising myself in the mirror.

When we were satisfied with our appearances, we went downstairs to meet the boys. Dominic had slicked his hair to the side and back like Clark Kent, with the signature "S" strand at the front, curled loosely on his forehead. He didn't want to wear the tights, so I had the idea that he should wear the shirt that had the Superman symbol underneath his Clark Kent outfit, with the buttons undone as if he was halfway into transforming into his true self and not his daily disguise and his alias. All-in-all he looked super-hot.

"You look incredible," Thomas said to us.

"Agreed," Dominic said, looking at me. "We better leave soon though, or we'll be late to the dance," he pointed out as Gran walked in the front door.

"Leaving so soon?" Gran said as she hung up her jacket. I bent down to give her a quick kiss on the forehead as we walked by.

"We're heading to the dance now, but I'll be home later. Theo's in his cat carrier and I'm sure he'd love it if you took him out and played with him, Gran."

Gran looked at my costume, and then the twins' costumes before her gaze fell on Dominic. She regarded him evenly before pursing her lips.

"Have fun and don't be home too late," Gran said through a pinched smile, casting one last curious look at Dominic before walking into the house. I didn't have time to try to figure out what her reaction to Dominic meant because the three of them had already walked outside.

Dominic's car was only a two-seater, so we all piled into the Mantello's minivan. With Thomas driving it took us almost as long to drive to school as it would have if we had just walked, but it would be nice later to be able to drive home after a night of dancing.

By the time we parked and walked to the front doors of the school there was already a line forming to get in. The dance was for all ages, so almost everyone in our school came out for the themed dance.

"When are you meeting Mr. Monet?" I asked Elsbeth as we waited in line to get in. I looked ahead to see if I saw anyone who looked remotely like they were from the 40s.

"He said to meet him on the dance floor, but he didn't say when. Do you see him anywhere?" Scanning the crowd, it was impossible to tell who anyone was in the colorful mass of costumes.

"No, sorry," I replied. Elsbeth's smile faltered. "I'm sure he'll be here," she reassured herself.

Thomas slowly clued into the conversation we were having.

"Wait, who are you looking for?" he asked, shock and confusion registering on his face.

"Well… I didn't want to tell you until we were already here just in case you weren't happy with me."

Elsbeth then filled him in on meeting Mr. Monet.

"You're meeting a random guy? Why would you do that, Elsbeth?" Thomas looked furious.

It was rare to see Elsbeth flustered.

"Well, it's better than if I was to meet him on my own, isn't it?" She put her hands on her hips and glared at him, daring him to deny it.

Thomas just mumbled and glared at the crowd, presumably scanning the pool of people for anyone who looked strange or threatening.

The gymnasium was decked out in every stereotypical Halloween decoration known to mankind as we entered. There was fog on the floor and creepy music in the background of whatever pop song was playing on the speakers. Orange and black streamers covered the ceiling; cobwebs on every wall. It actually looked really awesome—and a tad bit creepy.

"Do you want to dance?" Elsbeth yelled over the pounding music.

"Sure!" I shouted back, taking Dominic's hand as we all made our way to the dance floor.

Everyone was pressed against everyone else; one giant mob jumping in time to the music. It was hard to tell who everyone was with such elaborate costumes. I let my body sway to the music. I was not a good dancer, but I was having such a great time, whipping my hair around and dancing with my friends.

After the song was over, Elsbeth pulled me down to her height so she could talk into my ear. "Do you see any signs of him yet?"

I quickly surveyed the dance floor and looked back at her nervous face. I shook my head. She just pouted and nodded in response. We danced to a few more upbeat songs before taking a break and heading to the refreshments table.

The punch was being served out of a bubbling cauldron, dutifully being monitored by some of the teachers of Rosevale High to ensure no student attempted to make more of a potion out of the punch than originally intended.

I looked down to see there were fake—yet edible—eyeballs in my cup, a little disturbing, but surprisingly delicious. I barely had time to toss back my bubbling potion before Elsbeth was pulling me back towards the dance floor.

"I don't think he's coming, so I need you to dance with me. I need us to dance and dance and dance until I forget all about meeting my mystery man," Elsbeth said, twirling around with her eyes closed, trying to wipe all remaining hope from her system and focus on the now.

And that was when I saw him— whatever his real name was—standing in the middle of the dance floor looking around. I caught his eye, pointed at Elsbeth then waved him over.

"Uh, I think you should open your eyes now," I shouted down to Elsbeth, stopping her mid spin. She opened her eyes to see him standing right before her. She gasped and brought a hand to her mouth.

"Well my, my, my," she said in a fake Southern drawl, just barely audible over the music. He leaned down, taking her hand and bringing it close to his lips as if he was about to graze the back of her hand with a gentle kiss, but then he stopped and lowered her hand slowly.

"May I have this dance?" he asked. Elsbeth looked at me and I nodded telling her it was fine and that I'd be close by. The two of them walked to the center of the dance floor. I turned and walked back to the table where I had left Dominic and Thomas. It was a little quieter over there and my ears were thankful for the break.

The three of us watched Elsbeth interacting with whatshisname. Thomas scowled protectively and Dominic wore an amused expression on his face.

"He's cute," I said to the boys. Dominic shrugged. Thomas said nothing.

"I don't trust the guy," Thomas stated.

I tried to reassure him that we were right here, and that he seemed nice.

"Or, he could be a serial killer," Thomas pointed out, so serious that it made me laugh. He looked over at me incredulously.

"Sorry, that's not funny, but I really think it'll be fine." *Plus, if she was in any danger, I'd know it.* I thought to myself, wishing I could reassure Thomas more.

The music changed from the upbeat pop songs to a slower song. Dominic and I walked back to the dance floor, leaving Thomas glaring at "what's-his-name".

Normally I'd feel super bad about leaving Thomas alone, but his anger seemed to be occupying him enough that he wouldn't be bothered by—or even notice—our absence.

I wrapped my arms around Dominic's neck.

"Il mio," he whispered in my ear as I settled my head against his muscular shoulder. I smiled as we swayed together, shifting our feet slightly so we ended up making small circles in our little section of the dance floor. Elsbeth was glowing as she danced in her guy's arms. That envious pang struck again, but I brushed it off and pressed myself closer to Dominic.

Cooper watched as they danced. Never did he imagine he'd be capable of feeling for someone the way he felt for Quinn and never did he ever consider that his feelings would be unrequited. *Why does she have this hold over me and why can't I make it stop?* He brooded. Anger was easier than acknowledging all the other emotions that threatened to bubble to the surface as he watched the happy couple.

"Ugh," Cooper said out loud, pulling his fingers through his hair in frustration. *I don't know if I can do this…*

Cooper paced behind the veil. If he quit her case, Neil would be in charge of her safety and he really wasn't responsible enough. Cooper would always wonder if she was safe, but here staying was torture. He cared enough about her to put her needs before his own, even if every fiber of his being was begging him to leave.

As we swayed to the music, I couldn't explain this feeling—or lack of intense feeling. In my dreams I always felt such an overpowering love for Dominic, but I didn't feel it in my daily life. I felt strongly for him, but I should have butterflies flying out of my wazoo with the amount of love I felt in my dreams. Or at least I think it was love?

Whatever it was, I didn't feel it when awake. I liked him, I *really* liked him and being in his arms felt nice, but my dreams had me confused. Was that feeling going to develop with Dominic? How long did it take to know if you were in love? Should I have felt it by now, or was it normal to still be in the like-stage? Ugh, all of these thoughts were giving me a headache. Not the psychic kind of headache, thankfully, just a plain old stress headache.

"Are you okay?" Dominic asked me. I hadn't realized we had stopped dancing.

"Sorry, I just got distracted," I said to him.

"By what?" he asked. I looked around the room trying to find a suitable thing to be distracted by and my eyes landed on Elsbeth and the mystery man locking lips.

"By *that*," I said, my eyes bugging out of my head.

"Get off my sister," Thomas growled as he pushed chat-forum-guy away from Elsbeth.

"Uh oh, this can't be good." I rushed after him.

"Thomas, what the hell!" Elsbeth screamed, shoving her brother, not that it seemed to budge Thomas even an inch. When her shove had no effect, she stood in between her brother and her date.

"You don't even know this guy, Elisabetta!" Thomas said angrily, using her full name to bring his point home. Elsbeth's eyes glowered.

"I certainly do know him! His name is Tanner. He's in his first year of university studying art. He has an older brother named Brad. He loves classical music and still watches Disney movies!" Elsbeth said with a huff. "It's my life, *Tomasso*. Just because you don't have one of your own doesn't mean you can butt into mine!"

Thomas's fury was now mixed with hurt at his sister's harsh words. He turned on his heels and pushed his way through the crowd as far away from us as he could get. Elsbeth was too mad to be sorry, but I knew later she would regret her cruel words she said to the brother who was just trying to protect her.

"I better go after him," I called out to Dominic, placing my hand over his. "I'll be right back."

Dominic nodded as I weaved my way through the crowd in the direction Thomas had gone.

I scanned the crowd trying to find Thomas, but I couldn't see him anywhere. Who would have thought when we got his costume that I'd actually be *trying* to find Waldo? Where could he have gone? I checked the hallway and even knocked on the men's room door, but there was no sign of him anywhere. *Maybe he went outside to clear his head.*

I went out the front door of the school and searched the front courtyard as well as the parking lot. Thinking that he may have gone around back, I started walking around the side of the building. I could hear the low bass of the music coming from the gym. I saw a shadow being cast from around the side of the building and rounded the corner to investigate. The back of the school was dark, except for one streetlight glowing in the distance.

The L-Shape of the back of the school was the only thing that made it look different from an office building. I started walking along the back wall of the school, but I didn't see a single soul.

Suddenly I felt all the hairs on the back of my neck stand on end. I turned to look behind me and Mindy was standing there with her hands on her hips glaring at me.

Her shadow stretched outwards smothering me in darkness.

She was dressed in a green tube top and matching skirt. She looked like a belly dancer, except she couldn't be a belly dancer because she had something draped around her neck and the skirt was all wrong. I squinted trying to see what was around her neck and it was a huge snake.

Remembering my dreams, my pulse immediately quickened, even though I knew it was fake.

"All alone, are we?" Mindy asked with a sneer, her lips contorting into a sickening grin. I could smell the booze on her breath, even though she was still about six feet away from me. I honestly didn't want to have to deal with her tonight and I surprised myself by answering back in the same snide tone.

"Alcoholic, are we?" My frustration overruled logic in that moment.

"Watch your mouth," Mindy growled back, taking a step forward.

Well, she may be drunk, but she's not stumbling. I guess she's not as drunk as she smells. Instinctively I took a step back.

"Calm down Mindy. Why don't you just go back to whatever spiked punch bowl you just came from," I said, rolling my eyes, wishing that the hairs on my neck would stop trying to fight their way out of my skin.

"Oh, don't you worry about me. I'm *exactly* where I want to be," she said grinning menacingly.

I didn't know whether it was her costume, the lighting or the fact that it was Halloween, but something in that moment had me stepping backwards again, trying to put distance between us.

I took a peek behind me and realized that I had walked myself into the corner of the L-shaped wall. There was nowhere to go unless I ran past Mindy... *or learned to fly in the next ten seconds,* I thought.

"Seriously, why not just go back inside, Mindy and leave me alone," I said, peeved.

"Leave you alone?" Mindy started to laugh, a dry sarcastic laugh as if what I just suggested was the most ironic thing she had ever heard.

"I'm sure you'd rather..."

"Shut *up!*" Mindy suddenly growled. "Don't tell me what I'd like. You have no idea what I'd like." She lashed out and slapped me hard across the face. I was so shocked I couldn't even move. I brought my hand to my cheek trying to ease the stinging.

"Do you have any idea how long I've been waiting to do that?" Mindy said, her grin becoming more sinister by the second. I started moving my jaw around, surveying the damage. I must have bitten my cheek because there was a slight copper taste in my mouth.

"What the hell, Mindy! If this is because Dominic chose me over you, then you should really take it up with him," I said. The words were barely out of my mouth when she lunged at me pushing me so hard my head cracked against the wall. I slumped to the ground. I reached up and touched the back of my head, my fingers coming back damp with blood.

"You stupid girl. Think you know everything. Thinking that you've *won* him. He'd be stupid to stay with a pathetic girl like you. You're nothing, you hear me? Nothing!" She spat the word at me.

I got up off the ground. I was shaking and really scared now, but I couldn't let her see I was afraid.

"You're insane! Stay the hell away from me."

I pushed past her and started running towards the side of the building. I needed to get around the corner and call for help. I just hoped I was faster than the inebriated Mindy. I could see the corner up ahead. If I could just get there, I'd be fine.

I was about six feet from my intended target when I was pushed forcefully from behind. I threw my arms out to brace my fall and asphalt tore into my palms. Tiny pebbles stuck to the torn flesh on my knee and palms. I stayed on my hands and knees for a moment, trying to catch my breath.

"Looks like Lois Lane is a little out of luck," Mindy sneered. I might have been amused by her alliteration if I wasn't fearing for my own safety.

"Where's your Superman now, huh?" She took another step towards me.

I turned and scooted backwards away from her as she went to kick me again. My pencil skirt was making it difficult to move quickly. My once beautiful hair was now matted against my face with sweat and dirt. She swung her leg forcefully towards me and I threw my hands up in front of my face, bracing for impact.

But instead of the piercing pain I expected to feel from her stiletto heel, I instead saw a bright flash of light. I lowered my hands slightly and saw that Mindy was sprawled on the ground as if someone had pushed her. She was furious now as she jumped up and started running in my direction. I flinched, bracing myself again when I heard a shout.

"NO!" Dominic screamed as he saw what was about to happen. The booming sound of his voice startled both of us, which gave him time to put himself between me and Mindy before she could hit me again.

"Well, well, well…If it isn't Quinn's very own personal Superman," she slurred. Her eyes were pits of fire as she glared at Dominic. Since Dominic was acting as my shield, I took this opportunity to stand up. She saw me moving and took a step towards me. Dominic sidestepped to block her way.

"I said, leave her alone," Dominic growled, his voice sounding darker and more threatening than I had ever heard it. I shuddered involuntarily.

I could say with complete certainty I'd never want to run into an angry Dominic in a dark alley—or anywhere else for that matter.

Even though I knew he was protecting me, I couldn't help but be a little unnerved by the sinister tone of his voice.

Mindy tried to push past him, but all she accomplished was ripping a few buttons off his top so that the Superman 'S' was now fully visible. Then again, maybe getting him out of his clothes was her new goal, since that I was out of reach.

"*Get. Out. Of. My. Way,*" Mindy spat venomously.

"Make me," Dominic spat back.

She went to run around him, but Dominic grabbed her around the waist as she clawed and screamed, trying to get away from him and get to me.

"Get inside!" he yelled at me as he restrained her.

She looked at me over Dominic's shoulder and screamed, "he won't always be around to protect you!"

I turned around and ran back to the entrance of the school. Once inside I ran straight to the washroom. I stared at my reflection in the mirror. I still look frightened, but based on the pain my body was feeling, the damage was not as bad as I had expected. My hands and knees were pretty badly scraped, but once I pulled down and smoothed my skirt, you couldn't tell. I rinsed out my cuts then ran some water over my face, wetting my bangs as well as the small cut on the back of my head before standing under the hand dryer to re-style my hair. Once I felt that the worst was covered up, I took a steadying breath and made my way back to the dance.

When I walked back into the gymnasium, Elsbeth, Thomas and Tanner were sitting at a table. Elsbeth saw me first.

"Where have you *been?*" Elsbeth asked, confused and concerned.

"I went looking for Thomas after your fight and couldn't find him," I answered honestly, leaving out the entire part about psycho-Mindy attacking me.

"Oh, sorry, Quinn," Thomas said a bit bashfully. "I just went to the punch table to calm down then came back. We talked it out. Everything's okay. Tanner's actually alright now that I've talked to him a bit. Everything worked out in the end—no harm done," he said, smiling.

"That's great." I smiled back, hoping that it looked believable. *No harm done,* I thought sarcastically as my body throbbed and stung where I had been cut. *Right.*

"You were gone for a while, so we sent Dominic to go find you," Elsbeth said. "Where is he?"

"Oh…um…he's…" I started, trying to figure out what I'd tell them.

"Here I am. I had to go to the bathroom," he said. I breathed a sigh of relief and was thankful that he didn't tell the whole table what had just happened outside. I'd tell the twins later as to not spoil their evening.

"How long are you guys wanting to stay?" Dominic asked.

"We were just waiting for you actually. The dance will be over soon, and we don't want to get stuck in the parking lot," Thomas said simply.

"Okay, I'm ready too," I told Thomas as Elsbeth gave me the, 'I need to say goodbye without a crowd' look, so I ushered the boys out into the hallway.

Dominic pulled me in for a quick kiss.

Elsbeth joined us shortly after with her cheeks glowing and her lipstick more than a little smeared. Thomas looked away and continued towards the van. He might be less wary of Tanner now, but it didn't mean he wanted to see his sister's post make-out glow.

They dropped me off and Dominic walked me to my door.

"Call me if you need to," he whispered in my ear before letting me go. I gave him a slight nod. He squeezed my hands and then said goodbye to Thomas and Elsbeth before headed to his car.

I bolted into the house, locking the door behind me. I leaned against the inside of the door and slid down to the floor and started to weep. I hadn't realized how much that attack took out of me until I was away from everyone else's stares.

I pinched my eyes shut and let the tears fall. The cheek that she slapped didn't sting anymore, but I felt a brief sensation along my cheek bone, a feather-light tingling. With my eyes still closed and streaming with tears, I placed my hand on my cheek and rested it there. I didn't know how long I sat there, but eventually I pulled myself up the stairs, threw my blouse and skirt right into the trash with a slight sob, threw on my baggiest pajamas and went to sleep, covers curled tightly around me.

Cooper shook with fury after seeing Mindy slap Quinn. He kept his rage under control until he saw Quinn scrape along the pavement. He couldn't restrain himself any longer and *flew* through the veil and sent Mindy flying backwards. Technically her life had not been in peril when he intervened, and he knew his actions had crossed the line. This was the only time Cooper had ever been almost grateful for Dominic's presence. He stayed close to the veil until Quinn was safely in her house. Then she did something he didn't expect her to do—she wept. Cooper couldn't stand to see her cry.

Her eyes were closed, and her body was shaking. Cooper tenderly reached through the veil and ran his thumb along her cheek and wiped a stray tear away, wanting to make it all better for her, knowing he was doing all he could —no, all he was *allowed* to do—to help her.

Only when she was fast asleep did Cooper finally relax a little, knowing that she'd at least be alright… at least until tomorrow.

* * *

CHAPTER
15

★

Ah, the sweet familiarity of my colorful dreams with their swirling shades and hues; a golden light; a peaceful soupy sleep as the colors mixed and blended in my mind. A color would flow to the surface, to the very center before being swooped back under by the current before being replaced with another swirling color. The dream was so peaceful, so calm, so rejuvenating, so sandpapery…*Wait, what?* I groggily swam to consciousness to find Theo licking my face and purring loudly; like someone was shaking a baby's rattle in my ear.

"Ugh, Theo," I mumbled sleepily. "No." I started swatting at him, trying to get him to stop the affectionate attack on my face. He started nipping at me, mistaking my swatting at him for a game of catch-my-fingers.

"Ow!" I said, his little razor-sharp teeth instantly making me more alert. I rolled over and looked at the clock. I had only been asleep for two hours. My senses suddenly snapped awake when I heard the distinct sound of gravel crunching outside. I slowly got out of bed, grabbed my cell phone and moved quietly to the window. I had the blinds angled so that I could look out without having to adjust them, but no one else could see in. I stood by the window and looked down at my front lawn.

☠

Slade came up behind Viper, forcefully turning his partner to face him. "What in Death's name are you doing here? Need I remind you that the Temptress gave us strict orders to lie low? What part of *keep your head down* is unclear to you?" Slade demanded. "Leave now. Orders are orders."

"Staking out the weakling's house is not a big deal, Slade. Calm the hell down, man," Viper countered. Slade dragged Viper by the arm behind the cover of the tree.

"I am not going to fail this seventeen-year mission and risk the lives of our kind because you have decided to become careless," Slade snapped. Viper pushed Slade away forcefully.

"Watch it, Slade," Viper said icily. Slade slammed Viper back into the trunk of the tree, right onto a pointed branch. Viper winced as the branch tore at flesh.

"I made you what you are, and I can unmake you just as easily," Slade said, his voice dripping with contempt as he pressed his forearm against Viper's throat, slowly cutting off the air supply. Viper just stared angrily at Slade, unfazed by the lack of oxygen. "And you best not forget it," he said, adding more pressure to Viper's airway.

★

As I looked out through my slotted blinds, I saw two distinct shadows arguing. I picked up my phone and called Dominic as the two figures disappeared behind the big tree in my front yard.

"Hello?" Dominic answered on the fourth ring.

"Dom, I think there's someone outside my house," I whispered into the phone.

"What!" Dominic sounded startled. "What do you mean? Like a neighbor or something?"

"I don't think so. I think they've been here before. There are two of them." Fear welled up inside me. After what happened with Mindy, I was even more paranoid than normal.

"Where are they now?" he asked with concern.

"They are behind the oak tree in my front yard. They were arguing about something, but I couldn't hear what they were fighting about."

"Go and check the locks and stay back from the windows. I'm going to drive over and check it out. I'll be there in ten. I'm sure it's nothing. Sit tight, I'm on my way," Dominic assured me.

"Okay," I replied before hanging up and slipping my phone into my pocket. I backed away from the window and tiptoed down the hall to check on Gran. She was fast asleep in her room when I peeked around her door, so I headed downstairs to check the locks.

Once I was sure everything was secure, I went back up to my room and picked Theo up before peeking back out the window. I didn't see them anymore, but I knew I wouldn't feel at ease until Dominic verified that no one was lurking outside my house.

A few minutes later I saw his car's headlights round the bend. He turned off his headlights and parked down the street a bit. I saw him step out of his car and walk around the tree, and then walked into the backyard. I felt my cell phone vibrate and I quickly answered it.

"Hello?" I knew it was Dominic because I saw him dialing before I answered his call.

"It's all clear," he assured me.

"Thanks, Dom." I breathed a sigh of relief.

"No problem. Are you alright? I know today must've been tough for you."

I assured him that I was okay, just a little shaky.

"I don't blame you. Mindy shouldn't have done that," Dominic said, with an edge to his voice. I almost smiled at how protective he sounded.

"She was drunk and I'm really okay now. I just want to forget about the whole thing," I confessed.

He looked up at my window and blew me a kiss.

"Thank you," I said with a smile then a yawn. "I think I'm okay to go back to sleep now."

Dominic chuckled lightly. "I'll always be close by, Il mio," he said softly, making me blush as I said goodnight.

"Night," he replied before hanging up. I watched him get in his car and leave before I crawled back into bed.

Theo jumped on the duvet and curled up into the crook of my hip and we both settled in for the rest of the night. I was glad for Theo's presence. It was nice to have a little company making me feel safe—even if it was a cuddly feline whose only power would be licking an intruder to death. I let the sound of Theo's rhythmic purring lull me back to sleep.

★

I looked up at the wide expanse of sky above me. There were millions of stars scattered across the night sky. I was in complete awe. Never in my life had I seen so many stars! The sight took my breath away. I couldn't even find any individual constellations because there were too many stars. Shooting stars cascaded down the dark backdrop adding to the splendor. You'd never see this number of stars in Rosevale—too much smog and pollution. *But this,* I thought to myself, *is the most beautiful thing I have ever seen.*

I sighed in contentment as I leaned back against his chest. He kissed my hair and linked his fingers through mine. I traced his scar on his thumb and smiled to myself, remembering how he got it. *That's what you get for teasing a crab and using your fingers as bait.* I let out a small giggle.

He grumbled playfully knowing that I was mocking him and then he ruffled my hair. I tried to squirm away from him because even though I deserved his retaliation, I hated it when he messed up my hair. He laughed and grabbed me, wrapping his arms around me. I giggled and protested, trying to escape, knowing that if I was not careful, he'd start tickling me, which was basically worse than death itself. I went limp in his arms, hoping that if I stopped fighting, he would too. It worked.

I snuggled back in his arms so I could see the stars. I felt his fingers rest under my chin as he went to lift my face to his. There were so many butterflies in my stomach I was surprised I didn't fly away right then and there. I closed my eyes waiting for the moment his lips would touch mine. My heartbeat quickened in anticipation then finally…

Beep, beep, beep. The sound of my alarm jolted me from my vivid dream. *You've got to be kidding me. Just when the dream was getting to the good part!* It was dreams like that one that made me wish I could sleep through school. I had longed for those butterflies and if the only way to feel them was when I was asleep, heck I'd become a modern-day sleeping beauty—anything to experience that feeling again. I rolled out of bed, knocking Theo to the floor with a soft *thud* followed by a soft mew as he looked up at me with a confused expression in his face.

"Sorry, boy," I said, leaning down to scratch his head. He rubbed against my hand, all memory of him being tossed to the floor completely forgotten and forgiven. I slipped on my slippers and I stumbled downstairs in my pajamas following the smell of pancakes that wafted up the stairs. My body was still stiff from last night's altercation.

"Mmm, it smells delicious, Gran!" My mouth started to water as I watched her load up a plate with fluffy pancakes. I slathered them with heaps of butter before drowning every inch in syrup. Gran put a pot on for tea then joined me at the table, picking up her crossword puzzle. As I ate, I tried to build up the courage to ask Gran something that had been on my mind.

Gran looked up from her crossword puzzle, sensing my shift in energy and took her glasses off and rested them on the table.

"What is it, Quinnie dear?" She narrowed her eyes slightly, trying to get a read on what topic I might be about to broach.

"When did you realize you were in love with Granddad?" I asked tentatively as I absentmindedly stirred my tea. Gran surveyed me momentarily before leaning back in her chair. Her eyes moved towards the ceiling as she traveled back in time in her mind, recalling her life with Grandpa Henry.

"I don't remember the exact moment I realized I loved Henry, but I remember every moment afterwards." She smiled to herself. "He was the love of my life, your Granddad was. I had never been with anyone quite like him. He made me a better person and we brought out the best in each other. He knew my every secret and we accepted each other for what we were—our flaws and all.

His quirks were what I loved most about him; that, and the way he made me feel. I don't know if true love exists, but what I felt with him felt truer than anything in the world. Being with him was as natural as breathing. It wasn't always easy, but it was always worth it." She paused, her face aglow with the memories of my grandfather.

After a moment she continued. "He would've walked through fire for me and me for him. Some days it felt like my heart was going to explode in my chest from how full of him it was. And other days my heart felt like it was going to break when I thought of how one day, I'd have to be without him." Her smile dropped slightly, remembering the pain of losing him.

"How did you know you were in love with Granddad?" I asked her completely enraptured by the love my Grandparents had for each other. The sadness in her eyes was still there, but there was a twinkle in her eye as she started to explain. I could almost see her heart swelling at the thought of her Henry. She twisted the wedding ring she still wore before answering.

"When you're in love the world takes on a whole new light. All the colors seem brighter somehow, birds chirping sound like a beautiful melody and everything in the world is perfect, even if before him it wasn't. I realize how crazy that sounds, but every day with Grandpa Henry was like that for me. I have never felt more beautiful or alive than the time I spent with your Granddad."

By the time she finished she had tears in her eyes and a big smile on her face. I sat there in silence taking in every word she had said to me.

"Oh, sorry dear. Listen to me prattling on," she said, waving her hand and standing up to clear the dishes.

"Don't be sorry, Gran. That was beautiful. It was exactly what I wanted to know." I had a smile on my face and in my heart.

Gran smiled warmly at me. "Why did you want to know?" She regarded me evenly. "Do you think you're in love?"

"No, I don't, especially after hearing about you and Granddad. I've actually been thinking that I *should* feel some of those things with Dominic, but I don't. I like being with him, but I don't have the feelings like you just described," I said, my shoulders slumping.

"I want to love him. I just don't know if I ever will."

"That's okay, Sweetie. You don't have to love him. You will feel that way some day, and if it's not for Dominic, it'll be for someone else," Gran said, patting my shoulder comfortingly.

"But I *want* it to be with Dominic. Maybe it'll happen as we get to know each other better."

"Maybe," Gran said, turning back to the sink and filling it with soapy bubbles. "I still want to meet him properly."

"Could I invite him for dinner tomorrow?"

Gran paused only briefly before agreeing that would be a good idea. As always, she had more than enough.

"I can even make my famous homemade pumpkin pie. I'll have to go buy some whipped cream tomorrow. My pie just isn't the same without it."

"Oh yummy! I'll go ask him now." I grabbed my phone and went upstairs to send him a text. I was suddenly nervous at the idea of them sitting down to talk together. I knew Gran would be able to give me insight into my relationship, I just wasn't sure what she'd say or if she'd like him. This was all so new to me. I had never brought a boy home before…

I texted back saying 6pm before running downstairs to tell Gran the good news before going to visit the twins for the afternoon. Elsbeth had an official date with Tanner tomorrow and wanted my opinion on her clothing options (also known as I nod and say everything looks great and she chooses whatever she wants anyway). I also figured I needed to tell them about what happened with Mindy... although I'd probably just shorten it to one angry push and not the full-on attack. No need to get them all worked up over nothing. She was just drunk and temperamental after all. It was a case of bad timing on my part and good timing on Dominic's.

Elsbeth and Thomas reacted just as I thought they would to the news about Mindy going crazy. Both of them were furious and more than a little concerned.

"Why didn't you tell us right then?" Elsbeth demanded.

"You should've gotten her in trouble! She can't just go around shoving people. Not to mention the fact that she was drunk at a school function!" Thomas added furiously.

"Guys, it's okay. It's just a few scrapes, nothing I can't handle. Plus, getting her in trouble would only make things worse. Then she'd want retaliation for my retaliation and that's an endless cycle I don't want to start," I said, reassuring my two best friends that I had it all under control.

"Next time she even comes too close to your personal space, you tell us," Elsbeth said, her lips set into a firm line as she tried to keep her anger in check.

"I promise, but I really don't think there'll be a next time." I hoped that Mindy's reign of terror had reached a plateau and that there really wouldn't ever be a next time.

* * *

CHAPTER 16

★

Dominic arrived precisely on time as usual. He seemed to be really 'anal retentive' when it came to details and timing, but in the case of meeting my Gran for the first time, I was thankful for this quirk. He rang the doorbell and I ran down the stairs to answer it. Through the semi-frosted glass, I could see Dominic standing there with a smile on his face. I opened the door and his smile widened.

"Hey, Dom, come on in. Gran's just finishing dinner." Even though it was a chilly November evening, Dominic still wasn't wearing a jacket. I swear, for a smart boy he sure was dumb sometimes. "Get in here before you freeze," I chastised.

Gran came to the front hall to greet him. They shook hands and she smiled politely at him. I could tell that Gran was still hesitant when it came to Dominic, but I was glad she was giving him a chance. He was my first boyfriend so this whole process was new to both Gran and me.

"Dinner's served. Come on in and take a seat," Gran said, leading the way.

She had made steak and potatoes with mixed vegetables. It looked and smelled delicious.

"This looks incredible, Mrs. Aurelia," Dominic commented, as he sat down. He leaned over to scoop some potatoes onto his plate when my Gran cleared her throat.

"I'd like to say grace first," she said, looking at Dominic with a slight sternness. I choked back a laugh, never in my entire life had we ever said a formal grace before a meal. I said nothing, wanting to see how it played out.

Oh Gran, what are you up to?

"I'm so sorry," Dominic said smoothly and apologetically. Gran reached out for Dominic's hand as well as my own. It was at that moment that I realized what she was doing. My sneaky grandmother was tapping into our energies! I pinched my lips together and slowly shook my head as Gran bowed her head in prayer for maybe the first time in her life. I followed suit and bowed my head, mostly to hide my smile from Dominic.

"Dearest Lord, we thank Thee kindly for Thy bountiful harvest. The process of growing and harvesting is a sacred thing indeed. Without Thy spiritual water and Thy precious sun, the heavenly spread that is before us would not exist. From the deepest depths, I sincerely thank Thee, Lord. Amen."

"Amen," Dominic and I said in unison, as Gran let go of our hands. I took a deep breath to ward off my laughter before looking up. Dominic was sitting perfectly still, most likely waiting for further instructions so Gran wouldn't scold him again. I leaned forward and dug in first. Dominic quickly followed my lead.

"So, Dominic," Gran asked, once Dominic's plate was full and he had started to eat. "Tell me a little about yourself."

"Well," Dominic said, swallowing the bite he was chewing, "I go to school with Quinn. We have chemistry together." Dominic smiled at me and I blushed under his gaze—the double meaning of his wording apparent in his tone.

"Chemistry class, that is," he said with a grin, then paused and looked at Gran, realizing that she expected him to continue.

"My family owns the vineyard on the outskirts of town. I'm an only child. I like all kinds of music and long walks on the beach," Dominic said with a smirk.

Gran smiled at him and he smiled back, completely oblivious to the fact that she was just being polite, and she was not at all amused. I worked my lower lip in nervousness, trying to figure out how to convince Gran that Dominic was a good guy for me to be with.

"Dominic is incredibly smart," I interjected. "He's at the top of our class." I figured highlighting his academic accomplishments might help her feel more at ease about him being with me.

"Quinn's also is at the top of our class, but I'm sure you already know that. You must be very proud of your granddaughter." He reached across the table to give my hand a quick squeeze.

"I am very proud of Quinn," Gran said, giving me a smile—the first genuine smile I had seen from her all evening.

"She's one of a kind." She reached out and gave my other hand a squeeze.

With one of my hands in each of theirs, I couldn't help but feel like I was being pulled in two different directions. I released my hands and continued eating.

"So, Dominic, what are you planning on doing next year?" Gran asked. *Wow, she's not holding back with the questions, is she?*

"I think I'm going to take a year off and figure out what I want to do with the rest of my life. Maybe go to college the year after, something in the trades perhaps. I like to work with my hands," Dominic replied.

"So, you have no specific life plan?"

"Gran," I said in a warning tone, surprised by her attitude. Being unnecessarily blunt wasn't normally Gran's style. I noticed his eyes darken momentarily, but just as soon as I noticed it, it was gone again.

"No, Quinn, it's alright. I will make my place in the world, even if it isn't in the way that most people see fit. I am determined and goal-oriented," Dominic said matter-of-factly. Gran just nodded in response.

The rest of dinner went like this with Gran firing question after question at Dominic. He answered all my Gran's questions—some which bordered on interrogation—fluidly and fully, artfully dodging any of the questions that he found to be too personal. He couldn't have answered the questions better if he had scripted all his responses. I felt really good about how it was going, but I still was not sure about what Gran would tell me when he left.

Gran started to clear the table and was just placing the leftovers in the fridge when a headache struck me. I groaned slightly and put my hand to my forehead, partly from pain, but mostly from frustration. My psychic flashes had the worst timing ever, always interrupting my life at the most inconvenient of times.

Dominic looked at me and asked if I was alright. I nodded slowly. The sudden headache pounding against my skull made it difficult for me to think clearly.

"You forgot to pick up the whipped cream for the pie, didn't you?" Gran said to me in a scolding tone that to someone who hadn't known her for years, would have sounded like genuine frustration.

"Yeah, I just remembered it now," I said, trying to pass off my sudden psychic headache as an annoyed grumble. "Sorry Gran," I apologized, even though this was the first time she had ever mentioned me getting whipped cream. The world went quiet for a moment as a rush of pictures flooded my mind.

"Well this just won't do," Gran said with her hands on her hips. "Dominic, would you be a dear and run to the store to get some whipped cream? My pumpkin pie isn't the same without it."

Dominic looked from Gran to me as if he was trying to decide if there was more to what was going on than he was aware of. I took my hand away from my head and clasped my fingers together in my lap to keep from instinctively rubbing my head. I plastered a smile on my face and said, "Oh would you Dom? That way Gran and I can have some girl talk before dessert."

"No problem, ladies. I'll be right back," Dominic said, looking suspiciously between the two of us before pushing his seat back and heading to the door.

As soon as he shut the front door, I ran to get my jacket. I knew if I went out the front door I might run into Dominic, so I turned and doubled back through the kitchen to the back door.

I paused in front of Gran to make sure she understood, but the words weren't even out of my mouth when she called out quickly, "Go ahead, dear. Be safe."

I sprinted through the neighbor's backyard towards the river that ran near my house. I needed to get to the elderly gentleman I saw in my vision, preferably *before* he slipped down the bank and into the river. If I got there too late, I didn't know if I could pull him out by myself… and that was if the current didn't get to him first. I dug my feet harder into the ground, thankful that it hadn't snowed yet.

Up ahead I could see the shimmer of the streetlights reflecting on the water and the faint outline of a man with a cane walking along the riverbank. I had almost caught up to him and I breathed a sigh of relief. *He's still on the bank, thank goodness.* My relief was short-lived when I saw him lose his footing and tumble down the steep embankment.

"No!" I screamed aloud as I threw my hands out to try and catch him. I stumbled down the slope after him and cringed when I heard the sound of the man and his cane hitting the water with a splash. I skidded to a halt at the edge of the river. The man was a few feet out and clinging onto a nearby rock for dear life as the frigid current tried to pull him downstream.

The rock was close to the shore and I knew he wouldn't be able to hold on much longer.

"Hold on, I'm going to get you out!"

I dropped to my knees and reached out to him.

"Grab my hand and I'll pull you out!" I shouted. He reached out to me with one hand and I locked my fingers around his wrist and inched him around the rock a bit so I could do the same with his other wrist. I started to pull, but the current was stronger than I was, and he didn't budge. If I let him go, he would surely be swept down the river.

"Please, if anyone or anything out there can hear me, now would be a great time for some divine intervention!" I said aloud. I took a deep breath, leaned back and pulled with all my might.

"Kick if you can!" I called to the man as I pulled and pulled. I had heard stories about how in emergency situations people's adrenaline kicked in and made it so that they could do things that defied the laws of normal human abilities. It wasn't until that moment that I actually understood what that must be like. My adrenaline must have spiked through the roof in that moment because suddenly I had the strength of two people. I imagined two strong hands covering my own and helping me pull him out of the water. I was holding his wrists so tightly and concentrating so hard I could've sworn that I could actually see two hands covering my own. Two strong hands, tanned from being outside, callused, but gentle. Suddenly my heart started to beat faster.

I gave one hard pull and was able to overpower the current long enough to drag the man back to shore. I took out my phone and dialed 911 telling them where I was and that we needed an ambulance. I hung up and put my phone back in my jacket pocket.

"Th-th-thank you, Miss. You're my angel," the man said with gratitude, his teeth chattering from the cold.

"I just did what anyone would have. No need to thank me." I wasn't used to someone actually *appreciating* my sudden appearance and intervention.

"I don't know what I would've done without your help. I'm so lucky you happened to be out for a run when I fell," he said, still shivering uncontrollably.

Yeah, lucky, I thought to myself. If I hadn't wasted time getting a jacket, I could've been here in time to prevent the whole thing. I shook my head. *He's safe and that's all that matters.* I looked up and saw that his shuddering was getting worse and I snapped back into rescue mode.

"We need to get you to a hospital. The ambulance is on its way, but we need to get up the hill. Can you walk?" I asked the man.

He looked from side to side in confusion. "My cane. I need my cane." His teeth were chattering. My stomach dropped at his words, remembering how I saw it fall into the river alongside him.

"I think it got swept down the river. We'll never find it now. You'll have to lean on me to get up the hill."

I helped him to his feet, and we turned to start climbing the steep incline.

"My cane," he said cheerfully pointing to a spot a few feet away from where I had pulled him out.

"What?" I scrunched my eyebrows in confusion, but I couldn't waste time thinking about the accuracy of my memory. I grabbed the cane in my free hand and the two of us slowly made our way up the embankment.

As we reached the top, I could hear sirens in the distance. I looked at the man and handed him back his cane before turning to leave.

"But wait," he said, as the ambulance pulled up. "How can I ever repay you?"

"Next time you're out for a walk, don't walk so close to the edge!" I gave him a quick hug and received a very cold peck on the cheek before I turned and sprinted towards home. Hopefully I could still make it back before Dominic did.

Cooper stood by the line of trees and shook his head, sending water droplets flying everywhere. Hopping on one foot with his head tilted to the side, he tried to get the river water out of his ears. *Damn, that water was cold,* he thought to himself. Helping Quinn pull the man from the river was effortless, but deciding to jump in the freezing water to retrieve a cane that had already started sailing down the river was an entirely different matter. He knew he had to get a change of clothes soon or he'd catch a chill. Even though Coordinators were less susceptible to illness than humans, he still couldn't risk being in less than ideal health while on duty.

The dry Cooper headed to his room and grabbed a change of clothes from his closet and a towel from the back of his door before teleporting to the forest behind his house. He stood facing the drenched version of himself, threw the bag of clothes at sopping wet Cooper, who swiftly caught it. He stood staring at himself for a second. *I'll never get used to this 'one mind, two bodies deal,* both Coopers thought to themselves. And with that, Cooper thought his dry-self back home to his family, before tossing his soaked clothes on the ground and stepping into his dry gear. *There, that's much better.*

★

I was exhausted and my jacket was damp on the side that I used as a human crutch, but I kept jogging, needing to get home. I slowed to a walk as I went through the back door and into the kitchen and flopped myself into my chair just as I heard Dominic's car pulling back into the driveway. I shrugged off my jacket and tossed it to Gran, who was standing in the doorway ready to hang it back up. I smoothed my hair and tried to steady my breath and gulped down the glass of water Gran put out for me, which helped calm me down. Dominic came back into the kitchen carrying two cans of whipped cream.

"Sorry it took so long," he said. "I had to go to two different stores. Apparently, some elderly woman came in and bought the last of their whipped cream earlier today, so I had to go to the convenience store."

"I'm sure she wasn't *that* old," Gran said, as she took the whipped cream from Dominic.

"And thank you so much. You're a lifesaver," Gran said to Dominic before turning to wink at me. I rolled my eyes at Gran before standing up to get the plates for dessert.

"What happened to your pants?" Dominic asked. I looked down and saw that I had mud and grass stains down each leg.

"Oh, uh..." stumbling to try and think through what to say. "Maybe just some old stains that didn't wash out."

Dominic looked at me suspiciously. I could tell he wasn't sure if he believed me.

"Quinn, could you have gotten dirty from the garbage you put in the bins outside just a few minutes ago?" Gran suggested nonchalantly. Boy, she was a smooth liar. I needed to ask her to teach me her mysterious ways.

"Probably. Too bad, I liked these pants," I said, with a shrug. Dominic was still looking at me as if he was trying to piece things together, but I just ignored it and started cutting the homemade pumpkin pie.

"Did you want some?" I asked Dominic as I put a large piece onto a plate.

Even if he didn't believe me about my pants, he seemed content not to push the matter, for which I was thankful. I put a dollop of whipped cream on top before sliding it over to him. I cut Gran and me each a piece and then dug in.

When it came time to leave Gran and Dominic parted with another stiff handshake. Gran went to the living room and settled into her recliner as Dominic and I made our way to the foyer. My wet jacket was hanging in the open closet so I positioned myself so that when Dominic looked at me, he wouldn't be able to see my obviously damp jacket.

"Did that go as well as you hoped?" he asked, with a troubled look on his face.

"We survived it and that's all that matters," I shrugged in response. "She'll warm up to you over time." *I hope,* I silently added to myself. I leaned up and gave him a kiss goodnight before he headed back to in his car.

As I closed the front door, I could see the sun starting to dip behind the horizon; it would be nighttime soon. My gaze fell upon the big oak tree in my front yard as the memory of the strangers outside my house replayed itself in my mind. I could feel my heartbeat accelerate and I walked slowly towards the tree where I thought I had seen the figures the night before, taking in the tree and its surroundings to see if there were any signs that anyone had been there.

I didn't see anything that would indicate suspicious activity and was turning back to the house when something caught my eye. I reached over to a branch and plucked off a shredded piece of fabric. The texture of the material told me it was leather—brown leather to be exact. And it looked like the piece of leather had been torn, almost as if someone's jacket had gotten caught on the branch. I shuddered at the realization that someone had been close enough to my house to have gotten caught on this branch. I slipped the tiny piece of fabric in my pocket before heading back inside.

I couldn't shake the sense of unease I had been feeling lately. I'd definitely be triple checking the doors and windows tonight.

I walked back inside to ask Gran her thoughts, but she was fast asleep in her chair with the television blaring in the background. I could have woken her up to talk about it. Goodness knows my nerves would have liked the assurance that it was all in my mind. However, I found myself not wanting to tell her. I wasn't sure why… maybe she'd think I was being foolish. Or maybe she'd overreact and become a strict parental figure thinking I was unsafe outside on my own. So, instead of asking her what her thoughts were, I just left the piece of leather stashed in my pocked, turned down the TV, and put a blanket over her to make sure she didn't catch a chill.

Even though she was the grandmother and I was the granddaughter, for my whole life we had taken care of each other; after all, we're the only family either of us had left.

Once I was certain Gran was comfortable, I did a slow walk around the house, checking every door and window to make sure they were secure before I went up to bed. Being extra safe tonight couldn't hurt.

Theo was pawing at the door as I approached my room. Poor guy had been cooped up for hours, while Dominic was here. His little *"meow"* broke my heart.

I opened the door and Theo jumped into my arms as I bent down to pick him up. I nuzzled his face and apologized for leaving him trapped in my room before I put him on my bed so I could change.

As I was turning my jeans inside out, the fabric that I had found stuck to the tree flittered out of my pocket and fell to the floor.

I picked it up and rubbed my fingers along it, trying to somehow place who or what it could've come from. I put the piece of leather in a box on my dresser, unsure of what it meant, but knowing I didn't want to see it anymore.

I shuddered as I closed the lid. No point in worrying myself sick over it—at least not until I knew more. All I could do right now was sleep. After such a hectic evening, it was the only thing I wanted to do.

* * *

CHAPTER

17

★

I woke up earlier than normal on Monday morning, eager to talk to Gran about Dom.

"Well, he's very charming," Gran started. I would've smiled at the compliment; except I sensed a *'but'* coming.

"But…" Gran said with a pause, "Charming isn't necessarily a good quality to possess. He seems nice, but when we held hands…" Gran trailed off.

"I *knew* you were up to something!" I exclaimed.

Gran's eyes sparkled as she smiled at me before sobering. "But, when I had both your hands, I tapped into his energy and there was nothing there."

"I don't understand," I said to Gran, my eyebrows pulling together.

"When I tapped in, there was nothing there— literally. As in I couldn't get any read on him whatsoever," she explained.

"What? Nothing? How is that even possible?"

Gran went on to explain that sometimes with people who are very guarded, or with people who are blocking out memories or parts of their past, it can make it almost impossible to get a read on them.

I didn't like that Gran couldn't get a read on him. I was kind of banking on her being able to give me more insight into this relationship.

"It is possible this will change in time," Gran said, "if the reason is because he's guarded, but I can't be certain that is the case here."

I could still feel a tiny spark of hope flickering in my heart. "Other than that, what did you think from what you could tell?"

"As I said, he seems nice enough. I want you to be happy. Just be careful," Gran said with parental concern written all over her face.

★

On the way to school, Elsbeth gushed about her amazing date with Tanner and thanked me for helping her choose the perfect outfit. Thomas asked how dinner went and I told them everything… well, everything minus the psychic flash and Gran reading his energy.

As we approached Rosevale High, I felt that something was off. Thomas and Elsbeth must have sensed it too because we all slowed down our pace. Everyone's attention appeared to be captured by the same thing: they were all crowded in groups reading the Rose Voice.

"What could be so interesting in the paper?" Elsbeth wondered aloud. I heard the wind rustling something at my feet and I looked down and saw a discarded newspaper.

"Well, there's one way to find out." I picked up the paper and flipped to the front page.

Thomas and Elsbeth huddled around me as all the blood drained from my face. There, on the front page, was a picture of the man I pulled out of the river just the night before. He was wrapped in a blanket, sitting on the back bumper of the ambulance, talking to the paramedics. I breathed a sigh of relief when I saw that I was nowhere in the picture.

'Millionaire's Evening Ends in a Splash of Good Luck.'

"Wow, he is lucky to be alive. The river is rough and cold this time of year," Elsbeth said, with a mixture of awe and disbelief.

"It says here someone pulled him out," Thomas read, pointing to the article.

"*What?*" My voice shrilly raised an octave.

"Yeah, apparently a young girl pulled him to safety before calling an ambulance and disappearing into the night," Thomas read out loud.

"Ooooh Rosevale's own superhero!" Elsbeth squealed in delight.

"Except instead of a red cape she wore a red jacket," Thomas said, pointing to the description in the paper. I instinctively pulled my red jacket tighter wishing it would disappear with me along with it. *Thank goodness red is "in" this season.*

"Mr. Rosevale is offering a reward to the girl as a thank you," Elsbeth noted.

"What?" I said for the third time in less than a minute, this time with more curiosity than panic.

"Is that all you know how to say?" Thomas asked with an amused look on his face.

I didn't answer right away because my head was still reeling. *A member of the town's founding family wants to give me a reward? What kind of reward? Should I come forward? What if he wants the press involved? How would I explain being in two places at once to Dominic without telling him my secret?*

Thomas tapped my forehead a few times. I looked up at him confusedly.

"What?" I said and when he started laughing, I continued. "Oh, I mean yes, I know how to say other things." Thomas just chuckled. "The article is just shocking, that's all," I explained.

"Well, he's okay and it looks like if the girl comes forward, she may get some kind of prize for being a good sub-Martian."

"Samaritan," Thomas corrected automatically. Elsbeth looked blankly at her brother. "You said sub-Martian like this girl is some sort of underwater alien. The word is *Samaritan*," Thomas explained, emphasizing the word.

"Whatever, Thomas. You know what I meant," Elsbeth said in a huff. "Then again, maybe she's the one who pushed him in," Elsbeth mused. I could already feel the pending argument subsiding.

"Maybe the cops are going to arrest her when she comes forward to collect her 'reward'?"

"You think so?" Thomas asked skeptically.

"It's possible. Maybe they knew who he was and wanted a cut of his riches," Elsbeth posited, her creative mind already twisting the rescue into a premeditated murder attempt. I couldn't help but laugh at the absurdity.

"He definitely just slipped," I said to my friends.

"There's no way we could know that for sure. It definitely could've been a setup," Elsbeth argued.

Knowing that there was no way for me to prove my point without telling them the whole story, I decided not to push it too much.

"I just don't think anyone would be cruel enough to push an old man into the river, just to run down and hopefully get there in time to pull him out before he got pulled downstream. If she hadn't made it in time, he'd be gone, as would any chance of her seeing reward money."

"Good point. There'd be much easier ways to get money, like becoming his mistress," Thomas wiggled his eyebrows suggestively.

"Ugh, don't be gross! That man is ancient," Elsbeth said, her face distorting in disgust.

"Desperate times call for desperate measures," I said, laughing joining in on Thomas's theory.

"Ew, stop it, stop it!" Elsbeth covered her ears.

Thomas and I definitely would have continued to torture her with unwanted visual images if the bell hadn't had rung at that exact second. I shoved the article hastily into my bag and we followed the stream of students inside.

★

"Gran thought you were charming," I said to Dominic as a way of greeting as I slid next to him.

"I can be quite charming." Dominic beamed. "I'm glad I passed the inspection."

I wouldn't go that far, I thought, but instead I just agreed with him.

I pulled my notebook out of my bag and as I did the newspaper article got caught on my spiral bound notebook and fell to the floor.

"What's that?" Dominic asked, leaning down to pick it up. On the off chance that he hadn't yet read it, I found myself reaching down hastily and grabbing for the paper. I wasn't quick enough. Dominic's lightning-fast reflexes beat me to it. He started to peruse the article and scowled.

"I can't believe it," he said.

My heartbeat quickened. "Can't believe what?" I asked hesitantly.

"That a millionaire would slum it by the river in town when he could be walking on water or limo racing or whatever rich folk do."

"Wouldn't you technically be included in that category Mr. My-Family-Owns-A-Vineyard?" I said, with a half-smile, hoping to distract him long enough so we would stop talking about the article. He shrugged off my comment and kept reading.

"Looks like you and this girl have a similar taste in clothes." he said. "She has a red jacket just like you."

I leaned over and pretended to read the description. "Guess that's what happens in a small town with only one shopping center. I'll have to make sure to go out of town next time I shop."

It looked like Dominic wanted to say more, but Mr. Linton started his lesson.

He stared at us for a moment before slowly and seriously saying, "things in this life are not always as they seem." His words sent chills down my spine.

"In this experiment we will be using water to create fire," Mr. Linton explained. Murmurs of confusion ran through the class wondering how it would be possible for water to start a fire. He raised his hands up to quiet us down.

"If you would all wait a moment, I will explain and dispel your curiosity with my vast wisdom of chemical reactions," he continued. "In this case water is only used as a catalyst to start the chemical reaction. But beware! This experiment can be dangerous if not done correctly. So, if everyone would please take out their notebooks and pens and take notes." He turned and faced the whiteboard and began to write.

I was taking a copious number of notes trying to make sure I didn't miss anything if we were going to be doing an experiment that could cause us harm if done incorrectly. Out of the corner of my eye I saw that Dominic had yet to even crack open his notebook. *I know he's smart, but he could at least write* something *down!* But he was just sitting there, admiring me. I resisted the urge to roll my eyes and went back to focusing on taking notes.

Dominic reached over and twirled my ponytail in his fingers, and I swatted his hand away. There was no way I'd be able to take the necessary notes if my super sexy boyfriend had his hands on me.

"I'm trying to take notes," I said a little exasperatedly, *like you should be doing.*

"I just can't help myself," he said innocently.

I turned back to my notes, scrambling to keep up with Mr. Linton's lengthy instructions. When someone warns you that something could be dangerous, it is best to listen intently.

I wrote down the materials, method, and my hypothesis about what I believed would happen when we did the experiment. Dominic ran his fingers along my forearm, sending a–for once unwanted–shiver up my arm.

"Cut it out!" I said a little too loudly. The whole class turned to look at us, including to my horror–Mr. Linton.

"Trouble in paradise?" Krista smirked.

Apparently, I didn't even need to worry about responding to her because one look at Dom's angry face wiped the smirk off her face pretty quickly. If I hadn't been so frustrated with Dominic, I might have smiled at that fact.

"I didn't realize how passionate you were about proposing changes to the curriculum, Ms. Aurelia," Mr. Linton said with an amused look on his face.

"Unfortunately for you, this lab *is* part of our coursework. However, I'm sure you could write a letter to the Ministry if you are really interested in cutting this out." The class chuckled. "But for now, I'd like to continue if that's alright with you?"

Embarrassment stained my cheeks and I bowed my head, wanting nothing more than to disappear into a puddle on the floor. Mr. Linton took my silence as his cue to continue.

I tolerated my peers making a spectacle of me, but never my teachers. There was something so humiliating about being singled out by a teacher. Now I was mad at myself as well as at Dominic. Normally he was all work and no play and then when I was actually *trying* to do work he wanted to play?

When the bell rang, I stormed out of the room without even waiting for Dominic. When I went to my locker to get my lunch, it took all my willpower not to slam the locker door shut.

"Whoa, what crawled up your butt?" Thomas asked as he approached me. I turned to answer him and saw Dominic walking down the hall towards the lockers. I quickly clamped my mouth shut and scowled over Thomas's shoulder. Thomas gave a quick glance behind him before turning back to me.

"Ahh, I sense that someone is soon to be in the proverbial doghouse," Thomas astutely noticed and gave my shoulder a quick squeeze.

Elsbeth arrived at the same time as Dominic.

"So, I was thinking that we could all go out for lunch. I'd *kill* for a burger and a shake right now."

Dominic and I were staring silently at each other—neither of us looking particularly pleased.

"Wait… I missed something. What's going on?" she asked. Thomas just steered his sister away despite her words of protest and confusion.

"We're getting burgers!" Thomas called back before heading around the corner and out of sight.

Dominic and I stood like that, staring at each other, for what felt like an excruciatingly long time. I didn't want to say anything for fear I'd start a scene right here in the middle of the hallway. Eventually I just turned to walk away. We were obviously getting nowhere, so there was no point in wasting my entire lunch period.

"Quinn, wait a second," Dominic said, with a slight edge to his voice. I turned around feeling nervous about what he'd say and what I'd say back. We had never had anything close to a fight before and I didn't exactly know what to expect.

"What?" I said with some attitude, putting my hands on my hips.

"I was about to ask you the same question. What happened in class?" Dominic asked.

If I was a cartoon character, steam would have been pouring out of my ears.

"Well, let's see… I was writing notes, like you *should've* been doing, and you just wouldn't take no for an answer," I said, my eyebrows almost shooting off the top of my forehead by the time I finished speaking.

"Don't be so melodramatic," Dominic said with a condescending air to his voice. "You were taking notes and I was listening. The lab has like three steps," he said with a dismissive wave of his hand. "Plus, I thought you wanted me to show more affection."

"I do!" I said throwing my hands up in the air. "Just not in the middle of a Chemistry class."

"I think that's the *most* appropriate of all the classes to be affectionate in, don't you think?" He grinned.

"Such a comedian," I glared at him. "For someone who says they don't like public displays of affection, you sure chose a strange place to change your mind."

I thought he was going to explode at me based on the fury on his face, but instead he cast his eyes downwards.

"I was just trying to be better for you," he said quietly. "I want to be closer to you."

He looked up at me through his long eyelashes and I felt the fire running through my veins go from a dangerous molten lava to the lesser degree of a forest fire.

"By not listening to me when I say *stop?*" I said, the fire still blazing. "I want you to too, but it has to be a mutual want," I pointed out. I really wanted him to know that it wasn't the fact that he was being affectionate, it was just the timing and the lack of respect for my wishes.

"Beggars can't be choosers, Quinn," Dominic said, condescension oozing from his voice.

"*Excuse me?*" I said, emphasizing each syllable, my voice rising to a shriek, ringing down the empty hallway.

"You know what I mean," he said, a little annoyed.

"No, I don't think that I do know what you mean. You think I've been *begging?*" I asked incredulously.

"In the past; yeah, you've begged. Not that anyone could blame you. I mean, come on," he grinned, gesturing to his body.

"I cannot believe I'm hearing this," I said, before turning on my heels and storming down the hall. Dominic's sigh was audible followed by an expletive I couldn't quite make out.

"Quinn, wait," I heard Dominic call pleadingly, followed by the sound of his feet against the linoleum as he started down the hallway after me. *Jerk.* I ignored him and continued walking.

"Quinn," he called again, his voice sounding closer and more agitated. "Quinn, I said *wait!*" He grabbed my arm and spun me around to face him. His sudden forcefulness shocked me, and I stumbled to catch my footing.

"Let. Me. Go," I growled at him, trying to pull my arm out of his grasp, but it didn't budge. His face was no longer pleading, but furious. His eyes so dark I could barely make out any flecks of green where his irises should have been. I shuddered inwardly but held my ground.

"Let-me-go, now!" I said with more force. After a beat, his face changed and immediately softened, and he looked pained and maybe even a bit ashamed? He closed his eyes and slowly let go of my arm. He looked at me again with his emerald green eyes much calmer than they had been just moments before.

"I don't want you to be upset with me. I need us to be okay," he said dejectedly.

He doesn't want. *He* needs. All about him—and not even one *sorry* to me. His eyes were searching mine, his deep green eyes, pools of swirling colors. I internally shook my head and stared straight back at him. His good looks won't get him out of this one... not this time.

"Well we're not okay," I said bluntly. He looked as shocked by my words as I felt when I heard them. *Maybe I should just forgive him. I mean, he* looks *sorry. I can't stand seeing him look so sad.*

"What can I do to make this better?" He reached out to me as if to take my hand. I instinctively flinched remembering his harsh grip on my arm and tried not to shrink away from him.

"If we're ever going to be okay again, then right now you need to let me be by myself. Can you do that?" I said, my voice shaking with anger.

"Yes," he said reluctantly. And with that, I turned on my heels and headed right outside for home.

I needed a cup of tea, some peace and quiet. By the time I reached the front door, I was barely keeping the tears at bay.

"Gran?" I called out, as I stepped into the house. I knew already that she wasn't home, but I called anyway.

"Gran?" I called out again, my voice a choked sob as I walked up the stairs towards my room. Part of me was relieved that she wasn't here to see me fall apart; but the other part of me was secretly hoping she'd be standing inside the front door, arms open wide so she could hold me and soothe me the way she had when I was a child.

The tears I'd been holding back start spilling over as I pushed open my bedroom door. Theo jumped into my arms as I sank to the floor, not able to stand any longer. He purred and snuggled into my neck, my tears soaking his fur. He didn't seem to mind though, he just bumped his head gently against my face, like he was trying to absorb every last tear with his tiny fur coat. All the hurt I felt from my altercation with Dominic, on top of all the confusion I was already feeling regarding him bubbled to the surface, threatening to drown me.

The sting of his words still lingered: *"Beggars can't be choosers, Quinn"* His voice echoed repeatedly in my mind. *Is that how he really sees me? As some petty beggar? Does he get an ego boost from being with me, the girl who always pines for him?* "Beggars can't be choosers Quinn…"

I was feeling lower than low as I sat there with Theo. I kept crying until the wellspring ran dry. I heard my phone vibrate so I reached over and unlocked the screen, planning on ignoring whatever feeble apologies Dominic had come up with, so that things were better for *him*. I was not ready to hear his apologies—not yet.

But when I flipped open my phone, I saw that the text wasn't from Dominic at all; it was from Elsbeth, so I clicked open the message.

> Hey Dominic told us
> what happened u ok?
> Hes relly torn up about it
> u shud talk 2 him

Anger flared through me again and not just because she had terrible grammar. *Elsbeth was siding with* him? *She wasn't even there when it happened!*

I resisted the urge to throw my phone. I hastily typed back that I was fine before turning off my phone. I could've freaked out at her, but there was no sense in starting two fights in one day. I couldn't believe he told them about our business before I did and that Elsbeth actually had sympathy for him right now. Dominic better have a good explanation for his behavior today if he wanted me to be his girlfriend for much longer, because right now I really didn't know how much longer I could stick around.

* * *

CHAPTER

18

Viper stood down the road a short distance from Quinn's house contemplating whether to approach her or not. The impeccable vision associated with being a Reaper came in handy in moments like this because it enabled Viper to stay out of sight while still watching Quinn.

Viper shouldn't have been there but couldn't resist instilling a little fear into Quinn. Using the Reaper's ability for stealth and speed, Viper quickly ran to Quinn's door and rang the doorbell before speeding down the street to watch her reaction.

Quinn opened the door and leaned down to pick up the envelope Viper had left on the doorstep. Quinn looked around in confusion for who could have left it before ripping the envelope open. Her face blanched with fear before she quickly retreated inside. Viper let out a maniacal laugh of victory.

The cellphone in Viper's pocket started to vibrate.

"The girl is fighting with her beau," Viper said with a smirk before the Temptress had a chance to speak. "She is presently cooped up all by her lonesome. Permission to take her down?" The twisted excitement was evident in Viper's tone.

"Permission denied," The Temptress said swiftly.

Viper's frustration rose. "I am fully capable of completing this aspect of the mission without Slade," Viper snarled into the phone.

"Dare you question my authority?" the Temptress's voice boomed through the speaker.

"No, Mistress, my apologies, Mistress," Viper's voice dropped dramatically, verbally groveling for forgiveness.

"I thought not," the Temptress replied smugly. "Put Slade on the phone."

Viper cringed. "He is not available, Mistress. Do you not think I am able to handle this weak girl? Is Slade that much better than I am?"

She sighed in irritation. "It has nothing to do with your abilities. The timing is wrong. A new plan has been put in motion; the girl may remain alive for now. But you will get your chance at the girl, as promised. I know you abandoned your post, Viper. Where are you?"

"At the girl's dwelling. In my jacket as to not be noticed," Viper said in an attempt to thwart the Temptress's wrath.

"And who, may I ask, gave you permission to leave your post?" the Temptress inquired with a threatening edge to her voice.

"No one, Mistress. It will not happen again." Viper's voice sounded apologetic, but the tone was a lie. Viper's eyes blazed with fury.

"For your sake, it better not. You are lucky you have found me in a good mood today. Normally I would not be so lenient with your blatant neglect of direct orders. If you were with Slade at your post, you would know that we must not cause her any harm until we know more. Do not lay a finger on her, Viper. Those are your orders. Next time I will *not* be as kind as I have been just now."

Viper's mouth opened to rebut the notion that the Temptress was remotely kind, but instead of saying what would undoubtedly mean severe punishment, Viper just said a curt, "Thank you, Mistress." And with that, the Temptress severed the connection.

"As you wish," Viper added bitterly to the dial tone. A brief moment passed before Viper flipped the phone back open and dialed another number.

"What do you want?" Slade said exasperatedly. "Tired of going rogue already?" The smirk on Slade's face was almost audible through the phone.

"Always the comedian," said Viper, without a shred of humor. "You told the Temptress I left my post?"

"I do not know what you are referring to," Slade chuckled.

"Do not feign ignorance with me. The Temptress already told me that you have spoken with her," Viper retorted bitterly.

"She called shortly after you disappeared. I could not exactly omit that you abandoned your post from the progress report, now could I?" Slade laughed.

"Way to have my back, *partner,*" Viper growled into the phone, spitting out the word as if it had a foul taste to it.

"Now, now, it is not *my* fault that you feel you have something to prove. Are you on your way back to our post or are you going to brood all day?" Slade asked.

"I am heading back. The Temptress said I could torture Dominic until he agreed to mend things with the precious Quinn," Viper smiled menacingly. "And I definitely do not want to miss out on this chance."

"Nice try. If you had been where you were supposed to be, you would have seen Dominic speak to those frizzy-haired friends of Quinn's, saying he plans on groveling until she forgives him. No torturing necessary; the Temptress forbade it. Plus, Dominic is much bigger than you are. If I can take you, I am *certain* that he could too," Slade's amused tone only infuriated Viper more.

"I could take either of you and you know it!" Viper spat into the phone, starting to boil when Slade alluded to Viper's combat skills being subpar to his. Slade just laughed in response.

"Maybe you should come here and prove it?" Slade said, egging his partner on.

"Maybe I will," hissed Viper, muscles twitching in anticipation at the thought of pounding Slade's face in.

"See you soon, *partner,*" Slade drawled before hanging up.

The words were scrawled in messy pencil. But the message was clear. Somebody, somewhere, knew my secret. I felt the blood drain from my face. I quickly scanned the area in a panic. Who could've left this note? Did someone see me down by the river? Or did they somehow know about my gift? And if so, what were they going to do with this information?

I suddenly felt very vulnerable and exposed so I quickly shut the door and locked it. Realizing that I had to leave for work soon, I hastily stuffed the note in my pocket and got ready for work. Even though the sun was shining, I found myself looking over my shoulder as I walked. I couldn't shake the feeling that I was being watched. Or maybe I was just paranoid because of the note. For all I knew it was a prank, and no one actually knew anything.

The November air was bitterly cold as I walked to work. I pulled my hood up and tucked my jacket tighter to my body, helping brace against the wind and helping me feel less nervous. It hadn't snowed yet this season, but by the feel of the weather, it could start any day now.

The overhead bells on the café jingled as I pushed through the door to Cup O' Joe's, bringing a blast of cold air in with me.

"*Burr.* Shut that door, crazy girl! You're letting all the heat out!" Jolene said with an exaggerated shiver.

"Sorry," I mumbled as I made my way behind the counter to the break room to hang up my jacket.

"No need to apologize, Quinn! How else would you have gotten inside?" Jolene laughed as she followed me into the break room.

"Why so glum, chum?" she asked as she took off her apron. There wasn't anyone in the café, so we were both able to be in the staff room without ignoring the customers. The room was strategically located so that you could see the front till from the table. I joined her at the table as she sat down for a bite to eat after being on her feet all day.

"Not a great day overall. Dominic and I got into our first fight ever and I'm not handling it very well," I said, resting my head in my hands.

"Don't worry, Hun. I'm sure it'll all work out," she said reassuringly, as she reached across the table to hand me a piece of the cookie she was eating. I gladly accepted.

"Bryan and I fought over directions to a baseball game during our first argument, and now we're married. What did you two fight about?"

I opened my mouth to explain, but the tingling of the overhead bells signaled the arrival of a customer.

Somehow without even looking, I knew in my gut that Dominic had just walked in.

Jolene must've seen the look on my face because she stood up to retrieve her apron.

"You stay. I'll get this one," she said, offering me a sympathetic smile. I gave a small smile back in appreciation and quickly scooted back a bit so he wouldn't see me.

"Welcome to Cup O' Joe's. What can I get for you today?" I heard Jolene ask the customer. In the silence that followed I started to think that maybe my intuition was off.

I peeked an eye around the corner, and sure enough, I saw his familiar mop of black hair and the lean outline of his shoulders that was apparent even through the sweater he was wearing. *At least he's actually dressed for the weather for once,* I thought, before scooting backwards again.

"Is Quinn here?" Dominic asked. Jolene paused for a moment as if contemplating whether to tell him the truth or not

"No, sorry," Jolene lied, trying to get rid of him.

I could picture Dominic's skeptical look in my mind's eye, as he appraised the truth of Jolene's answer.

"She works at 4 p.m. today," Dominic said in response, no doubt consulting his watch. It wasn't a question, but a statement.

"Oh, yeah, she's running late today," Jolene said quickly. "Can I give her a message?" She asked, obviously trying to dismiss him.

"No, it's okay. I'll just wait for her," he said in a businesslike tone.

"Care for a drink while you wait?" Jolene asked him, "I strongly suggest something warm to stave off the cold weather. A hot chocolate perhaps?"

"Iced coffee. Black," Dominic said as he dropped some change onto the counter. "Please," Dominic added as an afterthought.

Crap, I thought to myself. *How am I going to get out of this now? If he's here and I walk out, he'll know I was here and just didn't go out. I mean, I know we're fighting, but I don't want to make things worse.*

I could see Jolene as she turned to put ice in the glass. She lifted her head slightly and caught my eye. Jolene gestured sideways with her eyes and I saw her reach under the counter and switch off the power to the security system before looking back at me to see if I got her hint. I nodded slightly before grabbing my jacket and heading towards the back door that led to the alley behind the café. I cautiously opened it, not realizing that I was holding my breath until I heard the door gently click shut behind me without the alarm going off.

I sucked in a huge breath of crisp air and quickly left the alleyway making a right at the street heading away from Joe's. I crossed the street a little way down and cut behind the building that was directly across from Joe's instead of taking the main street in case Dominic happened to be looking out the window. I couldn't take any chances of having him see me walking from the wrong direction. It would cause too many questions.

I tried to smooth out the tension in my face before pushing open the front door for the second time that night.

"*Burr.* Hurry up and close the door silly girl! You're letting all the heat out!" Jolene called out, an almost perfect replication of our first encounter of the night.

"Sorry," I said, a little out of breath from my running. "Thanks so much for covering for me," I said looking her straight in the eyes, hoping to convey my double meaning and sincere gratitude. She smiled and nodded slightly.

"Anytime, Quinn. I think I'm going to take off though, if that's okay with you?" She searched my face for any sign that I needed her to stay. I slowly shook my head as I walked by her and into the staff room.

"No. I can take it from here." I looked over her shoulder and saw Dominic and raised my eyebrows in what I *hoped* came off as "genuine" surprise.

Jolene and I didn't say much to each other in the back room as she got ready to leave, both of us acutely aware that Dominic's eyes were on us—well me—ever since I came walking in.

"You going to be okay?" she whispered to me, as she shrugged on her jacket. I gave a slight nod and a feeble smile to my boss and friend.

"If you need anything, call. I'll keep my cell on me," she said before walking out of the room.

"See you later!" Jolene called out as she wrapped her scarf around her neck and headed out into the chilly night.

I didn't really know what to say to Dominic, so I just busied myself cleaning the counter, putting on fresh pot of coffee and restocking the tea. I could feel Dominic's eyes on me as I worked, but neither of us said anything. *Oh my God, this is so awkward.* I must've stacked and restacked the paper cups at least ten times before I finally turned to look at him.

"Can I um, get you something to drink?" I asked him tentatively.

He just gestured to his coffee cup. "I'm good."

I was hoping that by me saying anything he'd at least say *something.* I turned my back on him once again and gave my attention to the creams and sugar. I figured I might as well make myself useful and refill the sugar if he was going to just sit there.

"Quinn," Dominic said, his voice coming from directly behind me. His sudden presence at the counter startled me, making me jump straight up in the air, which sent the jar that I was holding crashing to the ground, shattering the glass. I hadn't even heard him get up or walk over to me… not a chair scraping, not footsteps, not a single sound.

"Holy crap, Dom! Don't you know not to sneak up on a person?" I gasped, trying to steady my heart. "You scared me half to death." I slowly maneuvered around the glass and got the broom and dustpan so I could sweep up the broken pieces.

"Sorry, I didn't mean to startle you," Dominic said apologetically.

"Don't worry about it," I said as I bent down to get some of the pieces I missed. In the awkward silence that followed, I started scrubbing at invisible spills on the counter to give me something to do.

"If you wipe that counter anymore, you'll wear a hole right through to the floor," he pointed out tenderly, as he laid a hand over mine to stop my scrubbing. I pulled away at his touch.

"I take it you're still mad at me," he said. *Always with the statements that should be questions. Sometimes his tone got a bit "all-knowing" and "all-annoying."*

"Can you blame me?" I tossed back, throwing the cloth into the stainless-steel sink. I turned back to Dominic and crossed my arms protectively in front of me.

"No, I guess not," Dominic conceded. "That's actually what I came to talk to you about," Dominic paused. "Could we sit down, since no one is here?"

I nodded and led the way to the table that was furthest from the door, but closest to the counter in case someone came in. We sat across the table from each other and I folded my arms again as I waited for him to speak.

"I'm really sorry about today. It was the wrong time and place for me to show affection. And I should have been more attentive to what you wanted, not just what was convenient for me," he started off. And what a good start it was.

"You're right. It was, and thanks." *I wish I could just say everything on my mind, but when I'm near him, the words refuse to flow.*

"Am I forgiven?" he asked, searching my face.

I looked down at my hands that were now knotted on my lap and contemplated whether his apology was enough for us to move on from this, but I was just not sure.

"Quinn… I can't stand the idea of you being upset with me. You consume my thoughts, and nothing means more to me than being around you, being close to you. Please don't push me away. I know I can be a jerk sometimes, but this is new to me, too."

I could feel my resolve crumbling at the sadness on his face. My breath caught as he walked around the table and pulled me up into a kiss. I whimpered at its intensity; never before had he put this much emotion into a kiss. I lifted myself onto my toes so I could reach him better and lost myself in this kiss, no longer aware of anything except the feeling of his lips pressed against mine. There may not be butterflies, but my body definitely wasn't complaining. Somewhere in the back of my mind I couldn't help but think that anyone who happened to be looking in the window of the café would be getting one heck of a show right now.

I tilted my head and pressed my body into Dominic's, reveling in the moment, not sure when, or if, we'd get another one like it. A sudden crash in the café had us snapping apart. I blinked my eyes, still a little glazed over from the intensity of the kiss. I looked over and saw that a huge gust of wind had blown the door open briefly and had sent a chair skidding across the floor. I shivered and pulled my shirt down and fixed my hair, feeling a little guilty almost as if I had just been caught doing something I shouldn't have been.

"I…uh…probably should be getting back to work," I told Dominic, trying to get my brain to focus. I could still feel the heat radiating off my cheeks. If I was the type to wear lipstick it would be smeared across my face. Dominic was looking at me with a smug look on his face, obviously loving the effect he had on me.

"You're probably right. I think I've distracted you enough for one night," Dominic said turning to leave.

"What's this?" he asked picking up something off the ground. I recognized it immediately.

I contemplated not telling him, but if I was going to brush it off anyway, I guess there was no harm in telling him. "Someone left it on my doorstep. Probably some prank."

Dominic regarded the letter for a moment "Let me guess, they rang the doorbell, but when you opened the door there was no one there?"

"I didn't even see anyone, so I have no idea who left it. They must have run away pretty fast."

He nodded. "I've heard of that happening. Kind of like a modern-day ding-dong-ditch. I wouldn't worry unless it happens again." He went to pass it back to me, but I just shook my head saying he could toss it on the way out. He was probably right and there was nothing to worry about.

Dominic leaned down and kissed me one more time sweetly on the lips before heading towards the door. I blushed again and made a tiny sound of protest when he broke off the kiss. He smiled smugly again. Just as he was reaching for the door, it flew open again.

"Look out!" I called out to him, but my warning wasn't needed because his lightning fast reflexes had kicked in and he had reached out and stopped the door just before it hit him in the face. Dominic's eyes were wide with surprise, then flashed quickly to anger before quickly composing himself and looking back at me.

"I'll have to do something about that door before it takes someone's head off! Are you okay?" I stepped towards Dom.

"Don't worry about me. It'd take more than a door to take me out," he said with a smirk, before ducking out the door with a quick wave of his hand. I went over to the door and opened it and shut it a few times. It seemed to be shutting securely so I poked my head out the door to see if the wind was still crazy, but there was barely even a breeze.

✹

Neil sensed the sudden change in Cooper's mood. They were playing one of their favorite games in Cooper's backfield when it happened. *Absentease* was basically a game created by Guardians, for Guardians, even though some other Coordinators did play occasionally. In this game one Guardian was blindfolded. The other Guardian would then try to get close enough to attack the unsuspecting blindfolded Guardian before they could notice and teleport to evade their attack. This game put their senses to the test. At times, Neil and Cooper would up the ante and would even grapple while both of them were blindfolded.

Neil was a complete clown in school, but when it was just the two of them fighting, he could do some serious damage if he wanted to.

Cooper was blindfolded when the mood shifted. Normally, Neil couldn't get close to Cooper before he disappeared—Cooper's senses had always been more advanced than Neil's. However, this time when Neil took a running start at Cooper, he ran right into him. He had expected Cooper to move, so the impact was much harder than anticipated. Neil bounced off Cooper and fell to the ground as Cooper stumbled.

"You okay?" Neil called up to his friend from his spot on the ground. Neil could see Cooper visibly shaking and could almost feel the anger flowing from him. Cooper swore and ripped off the bandana that covered his eyes.

"Sorry," Cooper said, as he ground his teeth together, a sign that he was way beyond angry.

"No problem. Gotta keep me on my toes!" Cooper extended a hand and helped Neil to his feet.

"What made you lose your focus?" Neil asked. Cooper didn't always divulge his thoughts and feelings to anyone, but on occasion Neil would luck out and Cooper would give an inkling as to the goings-on in his head.

Typically, Cooper only lost his focus when he was bi-locating and it seemed that for the past few months Cooper had been losing his focus more than normal. If he was on a mission, he hadn't told Neil anything about it, but then again that also wasn't unusual.

"I was just thinking about how my mom was planning on cooking something tonight and how I'm not looking forward to forcing it down. The next thing I know you're plowing into me. Pisses me off when my mind does that. If I could turn off my brain, I would," Cooper said with an edge to his voice. Neil knew Cooper wasn't being honest, at least not completely.

"Honestly, bud, I don't buy that this is the only thing going on, but I won't force it. If it's a mission, you can tell me. I'm starting to worry about you a bit man. You're losing your edge," Neil said lightheartedly, but his concern was sincere.

"Losing my edge? As if," Cooper said, as he put the blindfold back on.

"Try again. If you tackle me even once before dinner, I'll eat your portion as well."

Neil shook his head and sighed. He paused a moment to regard his friend before doing the only thing he knew had a chance in hell of helping Cooper's mood—he kicked off the ground and launched himself at his friend.

* * *

CHAPTER

19

★

Gran came to check on me before I went to sleep. In her hands she carried a small, worn, velvet-covered box. I had never seen it before and had no idea what it could be.

"What's that?" I asked her as she sat down.

"You have been asking about your mom, and I know I don't have pictures, but this is something she had made for you. I was going to wait until your eighteenth birthday, but after the tough week you've had, I thought it might be nice to have something to help you feel connected to her as you navigate being a teenager." She gently lifted the lid and pulled out a necklace that had a large ruby in the centre encased with golden angel wings.

I nodded and lifted my hair off my neck. Gran fastened the chain and gently let it fall against my collarbone.

"It's beautiful, thank you." I smiled and felt tears beginning to build at the back of my throat. I settled under the covers and fell asleep with the charm clasped tightly in my hands.

★

Tiny bursts of light flashed behind my eyelids; my own personal fireworks display as I slumbered. Then, without warning they stopped. Suddenly, I was standing in a field. I saw a woman in the distance. Her hair hung loosely around her shoulders. She wore a soft blue nightgown, her back towards me. She turned as if she knew I was there. She saw me and suddenly her face contorted into a look of pure terror.

"Quinn," she breathed, her hands reaching out to me. The terror on her face wasn't *because* of me, but *for* me. There was a protective urgency in her voice.

"You shouldn't be here."

"Who are you?" I asked. I wasn't frightened by her presence… she looked almost familiar. I didn't feel threatened in the least.

"You must leave, please. Go back home, but please be careful. You must be on guard. You're not safe. Tell no one what you can do. Please, Quinn," the woman pleaded, desperation ringing pure in her voice.

"On guard? Why?" Could she be talking about the people outside my house; the ones who wore brown leather? Who was this woman and how could she possibly know that?

The woman looked frantically over her shoulder as if she was expecting someone to emerge at any minute.

"Please Quinn, you must leave. You can't be here. Please, Quinn, just open your eyes. Open your eyes, Quinn. Open your eyes," the woman said over and over again.

"Quinnie dear, wake up."

I blinked awake and saw Gran sitting at the foot of my bed. "Are you alright, dear? I heard you tossing and turning up here." Gran placed a hand on my knee.

"I think I was having a nightmare?" I didn't know how to classify the dream I just had.

"About what, Sweetie?" She didn't need to tap into my energy to know that I was uneasy. I hesitated, not knowing what to say. Should I tell Gran? What if she took it seriously and took me somewhere to get away from *"them"*?

I didn't normally keep things from Gran, but lately it seemed like all I was doing was keeping secrets from her: the strangers outside, the piece of leather, the note, this dream.

"Quinn? What was it? You can tell me," Gran reminded me, sensing my hesitation.

"I was in a field and I saw a woman there. Her face was pale, like a ghost," I told Gran at last.

"What did she look like? What happened next?" Gran encouraged me to continue.

I described to her the woman that I saw, right down to the lace trim along the hemline of her nightgown. I felt Gran's hand tighten briefly on my knee.

"Did she say anything you?"

Once again, I found myself editing the truth to the one person I had never lied to.

"She called out my name and reached out for me. Then I heard your voice calling me, telling me to open my eyes." I paused to see if Gran sensed that I was leaving parts out, but her face didn't look suspicious as it would if she had sensed I was lying. Instead it looked sad and a bit worried.

"What is it Gran?"

"I don't want to upset you by saying this," Gran said tentatively. "But that woman you just described—I think it was your mother. The blue nightgown with the lace trim was what she was wearing the day you were born." Her voice was thick with grief.

I was too shocked to even respond. *That was my mother?* I had never seen my mother before, so seeing her at all was a shock to me. *What does her message mean? Who is after me and what do they want?*

"And you're sure you don't have any pictures of her for me to compare my dream to?" I asked, but I already knew the answer.

Gran shook her head. "Maybe I'm a terrible person for not keeping pictures of my daughter, but it was all so sudden. I was so grief-stricken. I only kept the necklace you're wearing."

"What time is it?" I asked. I needed to distract my mind long enough for the tears to subside.

"Just about time to get up. What would you like for breakfast?" Gran asked, knowing that I was not ready to talk more about my mother.

"Cereal would be great," I responded, toying with the necklace.

"Hot or cold?"

"Hot please."

She patted my knee affectionately before standing to go. She took the box with her when she went.

"And Gran?" I called out as she left. Gran turned back to look at me. "Thanks for the necklace."

She smiled lovingly and headed down the stairs. I ran my finger over the necklace. I closed my eyes and pictured the woman—*I mean my mother*—again. I saw the flowing hair and her face. Now I knew why it was so familiar…she had my eyes. *I mean, I have her eyes,* I corrected myself mentally. I traced my fingers along the bright red ruby one more time before sliding the necklace under my shirt, wanting to keep it close to my heart and away from prying eyes. I also needed it hidden for a while, even from myself. I wasn't quite ready to think about my dead mom or her ominous warnings. I had enough problems with the living—without adding drama from the beyond.

The next day at lunch, I could feel the necklace against my collarbone, its presence making it feel like the pendant was burning through my skin.

"Hey Elsbeth?" I asked. Once the words were out of my mouth, I realized I had cut Thomas off mid-sentence.

"Oh, sorry Thomas. Keep going," I said to him apologetically.

"It's okay. I was just killing time, what's up?" Thomas asked.

"I was going to ask Elsbeth if she could draw a picture for me."

"Of course!" Elsbeth said, "What of?"

"My mother."

Dominic paused mid-bite and Thomas choked on the soda he was drinking.

"But how?" Elsbeth asked gently. Her tone told me she was not sure how to broach this sensitive topic.

I twirled the string of my sweater around my finger, pausing to place my palm against the charm hidden just below the fabric.

"I dreamt about a woman last night and when I described the woman to Gran, she said that it sounded like my mother, but since there are no pictures, I won't know if it's her unless I can show Gran somehow. So, I thought of you."

"What happened in the dream?" Dominic asked before Elsbeth could answer.

"She just said my name, over and over again. Then I woke up." *If I didn't tell Gran the entire truth, I wouldn't tell them either.* Dominic looked relieved at my recounting of the dream.

"Does me dreaming of my dead mom unnerve you?" I asked my boyfriend bluntly.

"Honestly, yeah a little. Death isn't something I like talking about and ghosts, kind of give me the heebie-geebies," he said with a shrug.

Thomas looked unimpressed at Dominic's insensitive response. I wasn't too upset with Dominic's reaction. I knew he was kind of detached from his emotions, so I just brushed off his comment.

"How are you holding up? It couldn't have been easy seeing her for the first time," Thomas said with what sounded like extra compassion—most likely trying to counteract Dominic's words.

"It was really strange. I haven't quite wrapped my head around it yet. I'll let you know as I figure out my thoughts about the whole thing," I said, giving my friend a reassuring smile. It was funny how in situations like this, I ended up being the one to reassure *them* that I was okay so that *they* wouldn't worry. Strange how that worked out.

"So, what do you think, Elsbeth? Will you give it a try?"

"Of course, I will, but I'm not really sure how to start? Unless you somehow videotaped your dream?"

"I was kind of thinking I could just verbally describe her to you?"

"Like I'm a police sketch artist?" She perked up visibly. Elsbeth turned and grabbed a pencil from her bag and a clean napkin. She licked the tip of the pencil before posing to write. "So, Ms. Aurelia, can you describe the woman you saw…"

☙

The phone in Slade's pocket vibrated. He pulled it out, glanced at the caller display. He contemplated answering with a cavalier, "Go for Slade," but quickly thought better of it, knowing that the Temptress would not find it nearly as becoming as he did.

"Mistress," Slade said into the receiver.

"Slade. Is Viper with you?" the Temptress asked in her usual clipped tones.

"Yes, Mistress. We are both at our post as you wished."

"Put me on speaker."

Slade pressed the appropriate button on his phone and held it out so both he and his partner could listen in.

"Go ahead."

"Very good. Now listen carefully. The plan is ready to be put into effect. Chestnut heading southwest towards Violet Lane. Go now. You know what to do. I'll expect you here by morning. Do not fail."

"Yes, Mistress," Slade and Viper said in unison before the Temptress disconnected the call. And with that, the two Reapers silently began their pursuit.

The sun had just dipped below the horizon by the time they had their target in sight. Slade slowed his pace slightly as they approached, with Viper following suit. Slade gestured to his partner indicating that their target was up ahead and that it was time to close in.

After almost two decades of working together, they knew each other well; each movement was now predictable. They seemed to move as one unit as they wordlessly flanked their unsuspecting victim. His muscular shoulders hunched slightly to ward off the wind. A slight dusting of snow covered his mop of dark hair. Although his eyes were cast downwards, Slade knew that behind those lids rested two green eyes and that those normally alert eyes did not see the threat that was approaching.

Slade passed the man in a blur of moment, completely unbeknownst to the younger gentleman. Once Slade was in front of his target, he whipped around abruptly causing the man to collide with him. The man was pushed back half a step from the unanticipated impact.

"Oh sorry, man. Didn't see you there," he apologized to Slade.

"That was the point," Slade sneered menacingly as Viper drove a syringe into his back. His mouth opened as if to cry out, but the words were lost on his lips as he crumpled under the weight of the solution that was now surging through his body. His eyes started to droop, his body becoming a pliant puddle where he stood. Neither Reaper made a move to cushion his fall as his body collapsed with a heavy thud onto the cold ground.

"Man, he falls hard" Viper smiled in satisfaction.

"That is the folly of the human race, always falling hard. All it does is get them into trouble. Useless swine," he said with disgust as they both studied his unconscious form.

"How do you suggest we transport him to the warehouse? My vote, we drag him every inch of the way," Viper said, not holding back a single ruthless impulse.

"The Temptress expects us by morning or that would be my vote as well," Slade smiled sadistically as he crouched down and emptied the man's pockets of his belongings, making sure to turn off his phone before holding up a pair of car keys.

"Care to go for a spin?"

"Fine, but I am driving," Viper said with a child-like grin and grabbed the keys from Slade.

Viper pulled up in Dominic's black sports car and rolled down the window a crack. "We have a small dilemma."

"What is it now?" Slade demanded impatiently.

"It only has a two-person capacity," Viper said, gesturing at the two seats in the interior.

"Well, how about the trunk?" Slade asked. They walked around the back of the car, opened the trunk and surveyed the available space they could potentially utilize.

"It will be impossible to fit him in here… at least not in one piece," Viper smiled dangerously.

"Now, now, Viper, there will be plenty of time for that in the future," Slade said reluctantly, but approvingly.

After a moment of consideration Slade turned to Viper.

"Well... *he* may not fit into the trunk, but *you* would," Slade pointed out.

Viper whipped around to face Slade.

"Not a chance in heaven, bub," Viper said glaringly.

"Well, me and my grandiose physique will not fit in there, nor would our incapacitated captive over there." Slade pointed to the inert heap by the curb.

"Or would you prefer to explain to the Temptress why we are tardy when it could have easily been avoided?" Slade questioned, his tone clearly indicating that he knew he had successfully won this argument.

Viper begrudgingly folded into the trunk, leaving a stream of cusses hanging in the cold night air.

"You could at least pretend that you are not elated at this specific turn of events," Viper hissed.

"You are right," Slade said with a smile as he slammed the trunk. "I could."

He effortlessly tossed their victim into the passenger side seat before speeding off into the night.

* * *

CHAPTER

20

☠

The room was dark and damp, the air cold and dense with moisture. The basement of the Fortress was an unfinished labyrinth of exposed pipes and wires. The overhead lights that had not already burned out cast an eerie fluorescent glow over the concrete floor of the warehouse as they flickered ominously. A slender passageway centered the vast space, but crates upon crates of storage containers towered like metal hedges that created an un-navigable maze for those not familiar with the layout.

Slade and Viper stood beside a towering cage that had been built into the furthest corner of the basement to create a cell. Inside the cell, shackled to the wall, was their prisoner. Slade and Viper leaned casually against the stack of crates that stood in front of the cage in companionable silence. The quiet, yet distinct whooshing of the Temptress's skirts alerted the Reapers to their Mistresses' presence.

"Has he spoken?" the Temptress inquired.

"Not a sound," Slade reported, "but then again, he is still unconscious so we cannot expect much."

"Why has he not awakened yet?" Her eyes squinted in displeasure as she surveyed the Reapers.

"I must have given him a bigger dose of tranquilizer than I intended." Viper shrugged. "My bad," Viper said with a grin.

"You are *proud* of your miscalculation?" The ice in her voice wiped the smile off Viper's face. "You are *contented* that you are wasting my valuable time?" the Temptress seethed. She raised her hand and struck Viper violently across the face.

Viper winced at the impact. "Not at all Mistress. It was my most grievous error. I miscalculated his body's human-like fragility. I will go to the Apothecary now for a stimulant." Viper bowed slightly and began to back away.

"You will do no such thing," the Temptress snipped. "It is not Raul's fault you are incompetent."

Viper's face reddened in embarrassment and fury.

"Notify me the moment he wakes." And with the same whoosh that had signaled her arrival, she departed.

Viper grumbled and kicked some loose rubble through the cell bars. The pings echoed across the basement as the pieces scattered.

"No point in moping over your error. You cannot change it now anyway." Slade picked his fingernails casually as he spoke.

"I think that is the most comforting thing you have ever said to me," Viper said with wary surprise.

"I only said it to make you stop whining. Purely a selfish motive I assure you."

"I am truly relieved. I thought you were getting sentimental on me."

"Do not flatter yourself. If I ever chose to be sentimental—which I will not—I would not waste my breath on you."

A faint groan from within the iron enclosure interrupted their conversation. Both Reapers straightened up expectantly, only to relax again a moment later when the prisoner's head lolled limply against his chest.

"False alarm," Viper stated.

"Redundancy becomes you," Slade drawled with a slight roll of his eyes.

Viper ignored Slade's jab. "We will give him another day to come around before taking more drastic measures."

"Another day? Holy hell, Viper, how much did you give him?"

Viper shrugged. "I wanted to be certain he would not wake."

"*Ever?*" Slade knew Viper enough to know that tempers would shortly rise and a fight with his partner was imminent. Before he could throw the first punch, he suddenly spun around to face a patch of darkness partway down the lengthy aisle.

"What is it, Myles?" Slade spoke to the emptiness.

The newest Reaper flinched at the sound of Slade's voice, even though it held more annoyance than anger.

"What... how...?" The boy stuttered a moment as he stepped out of the darkness. "My feet didn't even make a sound!" His disappointment and confusion were evident in his voice.

"I heard you breathing," Slade said simply.

The boy snapped his mouth shut, immediately trying to quiet his breathing. Slade had a brief urge to ruffle the boy's hair, but it quickly passed. He wasn't known as Slade the Blade because he coddled the new recruits. The ice in his stare returned as he addressed Myles.

"Is there something we can help you with, other than noting the technique you lack?" Hurt was written across the boy's face at Slade's harsh words.

"Well?" Viper chimed in after a moment.

Myles quickly swallowed the lump in his throat.

"You told me to keep you informed and I thought you should know that the girl was seen hanging around the vineyard."

"Hmm, this just will not do. The last thing we need is that brat poking around. We may not know exactly why she is a threat to us, but clever and nosy are definitely traits I have noticed she has acquired."

"So, what do we do?" Viper asked, "Seeing as we are not allowed to just get rid of her... yet."

"Myles, you deal with it."

"Of course, Slade." Myles gave a slight bow of his head, then paused and looked up nervously at the pair.

"Uh... how exactly?"

"Is it my job to hold your hand too? I do not care how, just get it done!"

Myles scurried away silently, holding his breath as he ran.

"Could you have not just used *that* to solve the problem?" Viper said, pointing to Dominic's cell phone that sat on the table just out of reach from the cell.

"Just text her and reassure her that her precious boyfriend is alright," Viper spat.

Slade shrugged in disinterest. "I could, but then what would that teach Myles? I cannot do his job for him. He has to learn."

"Always the compassionate one you are."

"Says the pot to the kettle." The two of them smiled at each other. "What a pair we make."

"Have either of you heard from Dominic? He wasn't at school yesterday and he's not answering his phone," I asked my friends as we walked to school.

"No, I haven't. Sorry," Thomas said.

"Me neither. He's probably sick or something," Elsbeth assured me.

"Too sick to answer his phone?" I had gone over the illness possibility in my head, but had nixed it because surely, he would've answered his phone once in the past 24 hours, right?

"It happened to Tanner once. His phone was across the room and he just didn't have the energy to get up and get it."

I pondered her words for a moment. "Maybe, but he always has his phone on him. I've never seen him without it within arm's reach and when I drove by his house this morning, I didn't see his car in the driveway."

The dread I felt in the pit of my stomach told me that there was something seriously wrong. I couldn't put my finger on it exactly. All I knew was I couldn't just sit here and do nothing.

After school I drove straight to the vineyard. I knocked on the large brass door knocker and waited.

"Can I help you with something?" Mrs. Hunter snapped at me when she threw open the door. I recoiled slightly. I hadn't even considered that she'd be home. I had only met her once when Dominic had to run inside and get something and to say it was awkward was an understatement. Gran may not like Dominic, but Mrs. Hunter loathed the idea of Dominic having a girlfriend. I felt so unwelcomed in that brief interaction I had never been back… until today.

"I'm sorry for bothering you. I'm looking for Dominic. He wasn't at school and he's not answering his phone. I'm a little worried about him. Is, uh, is he home?" I said my whole spiel without taking a breath. I was sure I looked as winded and wild-eyed as I felt.

She looked at me uncomfortably for a moment.

"He didn't tell you?" My stomach dropped and my heart started beating against my ribcage.

"Tell me what?" I managed to say, my throat becoming drier than the desert as dread filled my body.

She paused for a moment, considering her words.

"He is with his dad in Colorado."

"He's what? I thought his dad was deployed somewhere?"

"He was recently granted a short leave, so they are spending some time together."

I was still reeling from this new information. "Why hasn't he answered my texts or calls?"

She shrugged. "It's not unusual for them to go off the radar for a while if they go camping somewhere remote. I'm sure he'll be in touch eventually."

"So that's it? Sorry he left and he may or may not check in *eventually?*"

"I'm sorry if you are unhappy with my parenting, but he is my son and will be long after you're gone."

I stepped back as if I had been slapped. I didn't even have the composure to hide my hurt or toss out a clever retort or a polite goodbye. I just left.

✹

It had now been five days since Quinn had last heard from Dominic and she was going crazy. The dark rings under her eyes paid tribute to her insomnia. She was finally asleep, but it was far from slumber. She tossed and turned the entire time, calling out for Dominic. Frankly, it broke Cooper's heart to see her so lost and confused and all over a guy who wasn't even that great; but then again maybe his opinion was a little biased.

If Quinn was his… *Don't even go there, Cooper,* he stopped himself. *It's not possible.* But what his head knew, and what his heart wanted were two different things.

"Cooper, you're up next," a voice called to him.

"What?" Cooper turned to face Neil and smiled a little internally at how he sounded like Quinn when she got lost in thought. Neil looked at his friend quizzically before pointing to the training hologram. "You're up."

"Oh, right." Cooper tried to clear his head as he approached the glowing simulation arena, which today showed the massive overgrowth of the rainforest. Cooper only hesitated a moment before stepping up to the edge of the simulated veil and nodding up to his coach in the overhead booth to signal that he was ready.

"Your Charge is a member of a tribe that is local to this part of the rainforest. Their family grows and cultivates a very potent healing remedy from a rare plant. Keep him safe. Stay within your oath. Do you understand your assignment?" called Barrett, his trainer, over the loudspeaker. Cooper nodded his head again and rolled his shoulders, his wings stretching and fluttering under his skin.

Training always took him out of his head and allowed him to get lost in technique, enabling his instincts and adrenaline to lead him.

Jungles were difficult to navigate. Not only did you have to keep track of your Charge through the thick foliage, but also keep them safe from humans and animals alike. Cities were easier; machines were predictable, but animals were not.

As his Charge carried a box of medicine to their doctor, he was an open target to thieves and the hungry wildlife. The bell sounded, signaling the start of his session.

His Charge had only walked a few steps when Cooper spotted a snake coiling to strike. He flipped across the veil and swung from one branch to another and quickly tossed the poisonous snake out of striking distance, his Charge oblivious to the entire encounter.

The jungle cat was a little harder to dissuade but grappling with Neil had prepared Cooper to swiftly lock his arms around the large feline and wrangle it away without hurting the animal. Coordinators in all their different jobs were taught to *help a lot and harm little*. Every creature had a purpose.

The foliage unfolded like a jungle gym in front of Cooper as he effortlessly maneuvered his way through the rainforest. He swung from vine to vine occasionally flipping behind the veil to reorient himself before jumping back into the fray. By the time the end location was in sight, he had already tackled a vast array of wildlife. He had intercepted two large felines, tossed five venomous snakes and tripped a thief attempting to shoot an arrow at his Charge. Losing his balance, the thief sent the arrow whizzing past its intended target.

When his Charge arrived safely, Cooper's eyes immediately went to the scoreboard. Another perfect score!

Cooper threw his arms up in victory, the adrenaline still coursing through his veins. Catcalls and whistles greeted his ears as he stood catching his breath. He looked around in confusion. The adrenaline was starting to wear off slightly as he looked down at his body. It was only then that he realized that the outfit his wings had given him so that he could blend in with his environment was just a scantily clad fur loincloth.

He immediately dropped his hands to his sides and resisted the urge to cover himself. He shrugged slightly to his appreciative audience as he backed away through the simulated veil allowing his normal clothes to rematerialize.

When he walked back to Neil there was a group of girls hovering around him. Neil was thickly laying on his comedic charm to the female Guardians within earshot. When the girls caught sight of Cooper, they all smiled. Lillian—a blond goddess by anyone's standards—spoke first.

"Shame you had to put a shirt on. The Tarzan look suited you." Her eyes twinkled coyly at him. Cooper and Lillian had a long-time flirtation running—well, until last September that was. Ever since being assigned to Quinn, he hadn't really been able to wholeheartedly flirt with Lillian or any other girl for that matter. He had actually done a good job of avoiding any non-blood related female Coordinators up until now.

"Had to be done," Cooper shrugged. "Wouldn't want anyone catching jungle fever," he winked.

Even though his response earned a soft chuckle and a hair flip from Lillian, the interaction didn't thrill him the way it used to. In fact, it left him feeling kind of hollow.

Neil's eyebrows raised in surprised at Cooper's words. He hadn't seen Cooper in his element in months. The moment gave him a great idea.

"Hey, Lil. What are girls up to Friday night?"

Lillian glanced at her friend Amy, who shrugged slightly before turning back to Neil. "Not sure yet, why?"

"Cooper and I were thinking of getting a few Guardians together and having a bonfire by Coop's back pond. You two should come."

"Sure, sounds great," Lillian said smiling at Cooper.

"Spread the word, Lily-bird!"

Lillian chuckled and grabbed Amy's arm as they walked away, heads bent close together as they talked.

"Since when did I agree to have a party at my house?" Cooper asked.

"Since when have you ever *not* agreed to a party at your house?" Neil threw back.

"True enough," Cooper conceded. It had been a while since he'd hosted anything and maybe it was about time he reintroduced himself to society.

Neil was called up for his turn in the simulator. Knowing the outfit he was about to be subjected to didn't affect Neil. He purposefully stepped through the veil and strutted his stuff while flexing his muscles, docking himself points, but earning many laughs and whoops from his peers.

Although all Guardians were incredibly fit, Neil was a bit scrawnier than most. He made up for it with his seemingly complete lack of caring about what people thought of him. Cooper just laughed and shook his head at his best friend. Maybe a party would be fun. Now he just had to ask his mom. Hopefully she was in a good mood.

✦✦

"Hey mom?" Cooper asked as he walked inside.

"In here, Sweetie," Candice called from the kitchen. He followed the sound of her voice.

"Neil and I were hoping to have some Guardians over for a party out back this Friday…with your permission, of course." Cooper waited for his mother to turn to him and give a brisk, no. After their last disastrous party, she had said there would be no more parties "under her roof". Even Cooper's logical argument stating that they technically weren't under her roof and that they were in the backyard hadn't been enough to calm her anger. His mom turned to face him. *Here it comes…*

"That sounds like it'd be so much fun." She smiled.

"I can't tell whether you're being sarcastic or whether you actually are okay with it."

"I think it's a great idea!"

"But last time I had a party you said—"

"Oh hush," she interrupted. "That was so long ago. It's all forgotten. Go ahead, have a good time." She turned back to her saucepan and began to quietly hum to herself.

"Okay then… I will." Cooper looked at his mother, trying to gauge her mood.

Cooper went to the living room where Cali was reading.

"Is Mom okay?" he asked his sister. Cali looked up from her book and gave her brother a questioning look.

"Yeah, why?"

"She just told me it'd be okay if I had a party on Friday and she sounded like she meant it."

"She's probably just happy you're not being a hermit anymore."

"I'm not a hermit," Cooper said defensively.

"Well, you haven't really seen anyone other than Neil in months. Mom and Nettie were worried about you."

"Well, hell. Why didn't anyone talk to me about it? I could've told them I was fine." Cooper raked a hand through his hair in frustration. He didn't like thinking that he had worried his mom and Nettie.

"Of course, you would have, which is probably why they didn't say anything. You would've been lying, and they would've been making you feel bad about worrying them."

He couldn't argue with their logic, but he still didn't like it.

"I didn't realize anyone had noticed," he said honestly, as he came to sit beside his sister.

Cali put her book down and looked tenderly at her brother. "Of course, we noticed, Coop. But we also know that asking you is pointless."

"I'm sorry for worrying all of you."

"It's okay we just want you to work through whatever it is, so we can have our Cooper back."

He ran a hand through his hair again and thought it was about time to give his sister some honesty.

"I like a girl, but we're not right for each other, so I guess I've just been walking around being bitter. I'm okay now. It's just taken me a bit to accept it that's all. But it's about time I moved on," he said, the truth of his words sinking in.

He hoped that sharing a bit of the truth would help put his sister's mind at ease. "But don't tell Mom," he added as an afterthought.

"My lips are sealed." She smiled as she squeezed his hands. "And Coop? For what it's worth, I'm sorry things didn't work out with your mystery girl."

Cooper's mouth quirked up in a sad grin. "Me too, Cali—me too."

* * *

CHAPTER

21

Slade and Viper had stood watch all night, but there had been no movement from the cell. Finally, just before the sun was due to rise, the prisoner started stirring. Viper was getting impatient and turned to fill a bucket with water from the leaky tap on the wall.

"Wakey, wakey," Viper yelled and sent the water splashing through the bars. The ice water caused the prisoner to sputter and gasp to alertness. He slowly blinked his eyes trying to figure out where he was. He moved to wipe the water from his eyes, only to find his wrists cuffed and shackled to the wall. Panic seized him in that moment, and he started screaming and pulling his arms as hard as he could, trying to break free.

"You are only going to cut your wrists if you keep struggling, but by all means continue." Slade smiled at his captive.

"Where am I? What do you want?" He spoke at last, his voice raspy and dry.

"Shut up. We will be asking the questions, do you understand?" Viper snapped through the bars.

The man's shoulders flinched slightly, but he did not recoil.

"That is better," Viper said with a satisfied grin.

"Now we can do this the hard way… or the really hard way." Viper laughed.

"Tell us what we need to know," Slade joined in.

"And then you'll let me go?"

"I said *shut up!*" Viper screamed, opening the cell door wide and kicking him hard in the knees.

"Enough," Slade said firmly, putting his hand out to stop his partner. Viper's breath came out in puffs, nostrils flaring in agitation.

"What do you want from me?" The voice whispered in a plea.

"Quinn. And you are going to help us."

His eyes widened in horror. "Stay away from Quinn!" His voice came out in a snarl as he tried to lunge himself forward to no avail.

"Aw, how precious. He loves her," Viper said with mock appreciation before glaring back at him. "You make me sick." Viper spat on the floor in front of him in disgust.

"Tell us everything you know about Quinn. Or suffer the consequences," Slade warned.

"Do what you want to me. I won't tell you anything." With that said, he sat back against the wall and became quiet.

Slade turned to Viper and said curtly, "Go inform the Temptress that the prisoner is uncooperative."

Viper nodded and whisked out of the basement.

☠

The shackles on his wrists pulled his arms up at an inhuman angle as his body lay limp and motionless in the cell. For days now they had been restricting his food and water intake, keeping him weak and miserable, yet still he refused to cave.

"If you tell us what you know—and we know that you know something—this could all stop. No more hunger pains, no more time in a cold dank cell, no more darkness. All you have to do is tell us," the Temptress said sweetly through the iron bars.

He looked up through his shaggy black hair and with all the strength he could muster said, "Go to hell."

The Temptress's eyes glowed red in the darkness. She leaned forward and in a voice colder than liquid nitrogen said, "We are already here."

The Temptress turned to address Slade and Viper. "If starving him will not work, try a little tough love."

The Reapers grinned menacingly as they approached the cell. "As you wish Mistress," they both said in unison.

They paced in front of the cell, deliberating what type of torture would best motivation him to talk.

"We could cut him inch by inch until he screams for mercy," Viper suggested.

"We could take a baseball bat to his head to see if that knocks some sense into him," Slade offered in response.

Slade unlocked the cell door and stepped inside. He stood looming over the captive, like a lion and its prey. Slade pushed the man's hair back so he could look at his face.

"Such an interesting eye color. Too bad Quinn will never see them again."

The prisoner tilted his head up and bit Slade hard in between his thumb and pointer finger. Slade inhaled sharply and said a few choice words before slapping him on the side of the head.

"You should not have done that," Slade seethed as he turned to grab an old wooden board that sat by the wall of the cell. The prisoner kicked his foot out and tripped Slade as he walked by, sending Slade's forehead on a crash course to the cell bars. His forehead hit the metal ledge with a sickening thud—a thick stream of blood dripped from his eyebrow down the side of his face.

Viper hissed and quickly struck the prisoner in the head with the wooden plank, slicing open the part just above his eye.

"Or instead of waiting to learn about the girl, we could just kill her now?" Slade spat as he relocked the cell door. The captive just laughed.

"Go ahead and try. She'd see you coming from a mile away," he said, as he spat out the blood that had pooled in his mouth.

"What do you mean she will see us coming?" Viper asked. Slade watched as his face contorted, knowing that he said too much.

"He means exactly that: she will see us coming. She can foresee events. *That* is what makes her a threat."

Slade suddenly realized that every strange situation they had encountered Quinn in now made complete sense.

"Well there is one way to test this theory," Viper pointed out.

"Myles!" Slade's voice bellowed down the hallway to where the boy was standing watch. Within seconds he was standing in front of Slade.

"Yes, Sir?"

"Stand guard here. Make sure the prisoner does not move from that spot. We have somewhere we need to be."

With a low bow, Myles accepted his new post.

Slade and Viper ran out of the basement of the Fortress leaving nothing except for the sound of the prisoner's screaming cries of protest echoing in the darkness.

☠

"Let us get started," Slade said, after making sure Quinn's house was empty. Snow covered the ground and the temperature was well below freezing. Viper started pouring water over the front steps and Slade joined shortly after. Since Quinn's grandmother had salted it before she left, she'd have no reason to check for ice on her way inside. Once the water had been poured, the two of them rounded the corner of the house to watch their experiment unfold.

★

My head was throbbing, not a psychic headache, but a pounding migraine from lack of sleep ever since Dominic went to Colorado. Jolene kept sending me to the back to hydrate, but other than having to pee like a pregnant woman, there wasn't any change. The sun had dipped below the horizon by the time the steady stream of customers came to a standstill. I let my mind wander, wondering what everyone was doing. Elsbeth was probably at Tanner's; Thomas was probably sitting at his desk; and Gran… my head gave a painful throb. *Ow. When will this stop?* I took a big swig of water trying to kick my migraine to the curb. Gran was probably on her way back from the grocery store.

My head throbbed again… the image skipped in and out of focus—like my brain was short circuiting. I rubbed my forehead trying to sooth my brain. The picture in my mind crackled again and flipped back to Gran walking up the front steps with bags loaded full of groceries as if she was moving in slow motion. No matter what I did, I couldn't make my brain speed up. I was certain insomnia had broken my brain. Why was my imagination running so slowly? Then it hit me… I just didn't realize before because I already had a headache: I was having a psychic flash! The picture of Gran moved faster and faster as I watched her slip on some ice and crack her head against the concrete.

I flew out of the break room and out the door, barely remembering to grab my jacket on my way. I heard Jolene's questioning voice, but I didn't stop to explain.

Tears sprang to my eyes, whether from fear for my Gran or the bitter sting of the cold, I didn't know. I swiped furiously at my tears as I ran blindly towards home. It had taken me so long to realize I was having a psychic flash that I was worried I wouldn't make it home in time to stop Gran's accident. The migraine had muffled my usual symptoms that signalled a premonition. What if I was too late?

By the time I rounded the corner of my street I saw that the car was already parked in the driveway. The tears fell harder as I pushed my body to its breaking point.

"Gran!" I screamed as I ran up the driveway. I saw her sprawled on the walkway—deathly still. I slid to a stop and dropped to my knees beside her. I saw a stream of blood coming from her head and staining the snow.

"Gran, please, look at me!" I cried as I laid my hands on her cheeks.

I was sobbing and frantic because she wasn't responding. I started gently shaking her shoulders.

"Gran, please, don't leave me!"

I kept shaking her, until I heard a voice say: *"Stop, she's alive."*

A slight calmness came over me.

"Call for help," the voice said. It was a man's voice I heard, calming, soothing. *Was it an angel?* I didn't have time to question it. I ripped my phone from my pocket and made the call.

★
★

Guardians were attuned to lifelines, so he could tell that Gran was still on the Earthly plan. However, Quinn wouldn't stop shaking her, so he did something Guardians were taught never to do—he spoke to his Charge.

"Stop! She's alive," he said, as he stepped through the veil. He stood directly behind Quinn, his body almost brushing hers.

"Call for help."

He didn't know what to do. Not wanting to leave her alone, he stayed behind her, just out of her sightline while she made the call and waited for the ambulance.

★

"9-1-1, what's your emergency?"

"My grandmother hit her head and is bleeding pretty badly. Please help!"

"Where are you?" the operator asked. I choked out my address to the woman who assured me help was on the way and told me to stay on the line.

Gran groaned and opened her eyes slightly.

"Gran! An ambulance is coming. You're going to be okay," I said to her, just as much as to myself.

"I salted," Gran choked out.

"What?"

"I salted," she said again, pointing a finger, the strain evident in her voice. I looked over to what she was pointing at.

"The salt bag? You salted?" I said again, trying to understand. She mustered a weak nod.

"Okay, you salted." She seemed content that she had gotten her point across and closed her eyes again.

"Stay with me Gran. Gran, look at me!"

She wouldn't open her eyes. The paramedics pulled up and loaded her into the ambulance. I went to go hop in the back with her, but one of them raised a hand.

"I'm sorry miss, you two will have to drive yourselves in. This ambulance isn't big enough for all four of us." And with that, they shut the ambulance doors and drove off, sirens wailing in the night.

All four of us? I looked around in confusion. It was just me, standing, shivering in the cold. My eyes landed on the bag of salt. *"I salted,"* Gran had said. I looked up and realized the entire walkway was coated in a thick layer of ice. *That makes no sense, not if she salted. It didn't even snow today.*

Looking down the street, we were the only walkway with any ice. Maybe Gran thought she salted, but didn't? She did hit her head after all. Maybe she was trying to tell me she *hadn't* salted.

The breeze picked up, lifting up the top layer of snow, sending it spinning in wisps around me.

I quickly went into the house to get the spare set of keys. When I stepped back out onto the porch, I saw movement by the side of the house. The hairs on my neck were standing up. Maybe I should have taken the time to investigate with all the strange that had been happening lately, but Gran was my priority so it would have to wait. There were no footprints, so I told myself not to worry. But as I unlocked the car, I could've sworn I smelled the faint hint of leather on the breeze.

"Did you see that?" Slade breathed after the ambulance pulled away.

"She came out of nowhere. It must be true; she is a Seer! We discovered her secret. The Temptress will be so pleased." Viper grinned.

"This is nothing to be pleased about," Slade said with a frown. Viper looked at Slade, obviously not following his train of thought.

"I do not understand."

"It means any time a human's life is threatened, she will know and have time to intervene, which would make humans safe as long as she is around."

The consequences of her "gift" fully sank in, causing Viper's eyes to widen in horror.

"We must stop her now! We cannot have her around saving the exact race we are aiming to control and destroy."

"That will not be possible. Did you not see who else was with her?" Slade pointed out.

"He just appeared out of thin air. Who was he?" Viper asked.

"I do not know his name, but I know his kind," Slade said with disdain. "He is a Guardian," Slade spat.

"*A Guardian?* She has been assigned a *Guardian*? That means the Coordinators have her on their radar. This is not good, not good at all."

A frown pulled at the corners of Viper's lips.

"We need to inform the Temptress immediately." Slade whipped out his phone and dialed the Fortress.

"What news, Slade?" the Temptress's cool breath asked through the phone.

Slade blew out his breath in frustration.

"We have a problem."

* * *

CHAPTER

22

★

Waiting was always the hardest part—sitting there in the hospital waiting room surrounded by the smell of sterile decay. I had called the Mantello's house, but both twins were out. My headache still pounded away, and I felt horrible. Lower than low. It was my fault she was hurt. Some psychic I was; I didn't even see what was about to happen until it was too late. I buried my face in my hands.

"Ms. Aurelia?"

My head snapped up at the sound of the doctor's voice.

"How is she?" I started to stand up, but she put a hand to stop me.

"She is stable. She needed quite a few stitches and had some superficial scrapes and bruises. Thankfully you found her when you did. Any longer and she would have most likely succumbed to hypothermia."

My eyes welled up with tears. "Can I see her? Please?"

She nodded at me. "Visiting hours end in fifteen minutes and we want to keep her overnight for observation to make sure she doesn't have a concussion."

I swallowed before speaking. "Okay, thank you." I quickly walked to her room, hovering in her doorway a moment before going in. Gran's eyes were closed so I tiptoed to the chair beside her bed. Her eyelids fluttered open at the sound of my footsteps. As soon as our eyes locked, I broke down into tears.

"I'm so sorry Gran! I didn't see it in time and now you're in the hospital and it's my fault!"

She placed a hand over mine to still me and cleared her throat.

"Quinnie, look at me. You have a gift, one that we have yet to fully understand. It is not a sure-fire thing… we've always known that. But you found me this time and that's all that matters. I am alright. Now come here," she said as she opened her arms wide.

I scooted onto the bed and cuddled up beside Gran and tried not to feel guilty that after all she went through today, she was the one comforting me.

★

The hospital finally kicked me out half an hour after visiting hours had ended. I drove home and pulled up to the dark house. I went to grab the bag of salt and saw that it was empty. Gran had salted *a lot* and yet there were still a few inches of ice on the ground for no good reason that I could see. I carefully made my way inside and straight up to my room.

As I lay in my bed I tried not to think about the day, but I couldn't help but replay the day in its entirety. If it hadn't been for my lack of sleep, I might have been able to keep Gran safe. I played with my necklace as I stewed in my guilt, running my fingers along the textured gold wings.

I had been losing sleep over someone who didn't seem to take my wants or needs into consideration, when I should have been focusing on the people that did care about me. It took over 100 sheep and some relaxation music, but I finally drifted off to sleep…

I was in a clearing at the edge of a grand forest. Ahead of me sat a boy… well, if you could even call him a boy; he was closer to a man. At first, I thought it was Dominic, with their similar physiques, but this 'boy' had hair that was a soft warm caramel, but that was the only thing soft about him. He had well-defined muscles and had a quiet rigidity about him, like a cat poised to pounce. He sat cross-legged on the ground, tossing blades of grass into the air, but… it couldn't be grass, could it? He flicked what looked like blades of grass into the open air in front of him and it would then sparkle and fizzle before disappearing—like tiny fireworks.

There was something so familiar about him, but I didn't recognize him from my waking life. I felt drawn to him; his presence a magnet pulling me towards him. I took a step closer, snapping a twig sharply under my foot. He whipped around to face me, without making a sound. I gasped and fell backwards…

I snapped awake to find Theo nudging my face. I pushed him away to no avail, before finally giving up and dragging myself into a seated position, pulling him onto my lap as I moved. Looking at the clock it was way too early to be awake. The sun wasn't even up yet. I tried petting him, attempting to placate him so I could go back to sleep, but he just kept nudging me.

"What'cha doing?" I asked him drowsily. I looked over at his food and water dishes, both were full. He started nudging more insistently, then jumped off my bed and up onto the windowsill. I picked him up and pulled him tight to my chest. Peeking out the window, I suddenly got a flash of an image in my mind. A scythe. I blinked and the image was gone. *What was that?* I shook myself internally. It was a little creepy being home alone.

I grabbed my phone and called Dominic. It rang twice before going to voice-mail. I hung up, knowing there was no point in leaving a message because I had already filled up his voice mailbox.

No Gran, no Dominic… I was completely alone. I curled up on my bed, phone in hand, Theo on my chest. I just wish I knew why Dominic wasn't answering me… I closed my eyes and took deep breaths, willing myself to fall back asleep.

The room was dark and thick with moisture. I could hear water dripping somewhere in the distance. I walked cautiously, watching for puddles and debris to avoid making any noise. I didn't know where I was, but my instincts told me I wasn't welcome here.

In front of me stood a tall iron cell and inside the prison-like cell was a person chained to the wall. At first, I thought it was the golden-haired boy from my dream because of the fit, muscular build, but then I saw that he had dark shaggy hair that looked more like—

"Dominic," I gasped. His head was drooped against his chest and I couldn't quite see his eyes, but I knew that if I tipped his chin up, I'd see two emerald eyes looking back at me. I rushed over to the bars and called out to him, but he didn't stir. I turned to look for a key and I saw his phone resting on the table just outside the cell.

"Don't worry, Dom. I'm going to get you out of here." I scrambled to find the keys or something that would allow me to pry open the bars. I stopped suddenly when I saw a figure approaching in the distance. I scurried behind the crate, hoping that I hadn't been spotted. A boy, no older than 15, walked by me wearing the same color of brown leather jacket as the piece I had found stuck to the tree outside my house. On the back there was a black embroidered scythe like I had seen in my mind earlier.

He opened the door of the cell with a key from inside his jacket and placed an opened water bottle beside Dominic before slowly closing the cell and locking the door behind him.

Once he walked by me and out of the basement or wherever we were, I knew what I had to do: call for help then try to break him out of this inhumane prison. I grabbed at his cell phone, but my hand went right through it. I gasped and tried again, but no matter how many times I tried, I still kept floating through it as if I were a ghost.

I walked up to the doors and attempted to open them, but the same thing happened. So instead, I walked straight through the bars and put two fingers under Dominic's chin, with the futile hope that maybe my presence would become known to him and put him at ease.

Even though I knew I wouldn't be able to raise his eyes to mine so I could reassure him that I'd get him out, I still felt disappointed when my finger flitted through him. There was a patch of dried blood and hair matted to his forehead.

"I'm going to get you out of here, I promise."

Just as I said the last word, I had the most unnerving feeling, like I was falling. The scene blurred out of focus and the next thing I knew I was gasping for air in my bedroom with Theo looking at me worriedly. The clock's glow told me it was seven in the morning.

"Oh my gosh, Theo… I think Dominic's in trouble." I didn't have a headache like I normally did with a premonition, but I had this overwhelming feeling of dread when it came to Dominic and that warehouse. I had to find him somehow. I rolled out of bed and tossed a sweater over my head, then jumped into my pants, tripping as I went. I threw open the door and barrelled right into something hard: a human something.

I looked up and straight into the eyes I had been missing so badly. His hand was still poised to knock.

"Dominic!" I shrieked and buried my head into his chest as I wrapped my arms around his neck tightly. Never had I been so relieved to see him and to know that he was safe.

"Oh, hey there," he said in surprise as he patted my back.

I stepped back and reached up to brush the hair from his forehead. There along his forehead was a cut, just like I had seen in my dream. He flinched.

"Oh, my God, they really did keep you locked in that cold cell."

Dominic flinched from my touch. "I'm sorry. What did you say?" he asked with a baffled look on his face.

"I had a dream you were locked up in a cell in a warehouse somewhere. You had a cut just like that on your forehead. I couldn't see your face, but I could see that gash." I said pointing to his face. "Are you okay? Should we call the cops?"

"Whoa. Slow down. You thought I was *kidnapped*?" He burst out laughing.

Now it was my turn to look confused. He was laughing so hard it took him a minute to compose himself.

"I got this working on my dad's car. I was in Colorado, not holed up in some warehouse-dungeon."

"But… the cut… the dream…" I stammered. My dream had been so vivid and real that I was certain he was in that warehouse.

"Dreams are flights of fancy. Don't waste your time giving meaning to something that is meaningless."

Reality slowly crept up my spine and spread throughout my body. I could feel my mood shifting as his words sank in. If he really was in Colorado and not being held captive, then he had voluntarily left without any word of where he was going or when he'd be back.

"Apparently I've been doing that a lot lately," I mumbled bitterly to myself.

He asked me to repeat myself, but I ignored him. It was my turn to ask the questions. My resolve crumbled as I snapped at him.

"Why didn't you tell me you were leaving before you just disappeared?"

He looked taken aback at my sudden change of tone and said nothing. I just stood there waiting for his response, anger building with every second he didn't speak.

"Well?" I snapped again.

"Well… It was last minute." He had the audacity to shrug at me as he spoke.

"It was so last minute that you couldn't take thirty seconds to send a text? *Enh*, try again." I made the sound of a game show buzzer when a contestant gave an incorrect answer.

"I was out of cell range."

"In your driveway? *Enh*," I buzzed again.

"Well, I was running late."

I squinted at him in disbelief that he was still throwing out excuses.

"Your excuses are feeble at best, Dominic. You're going to have to do better than that." My eyes had narrowed into slits and I was seething.

"I would have called you on my way back once I was in range again, but I dropped my phone and it broke and I haven't gotten it fixed yet because I came straight over to see you."

I didn't have to think of a response because right then his "broken" phone started to ring. We stood staring at each other. My glare was clearly daring him to answer the phone that kept ringing in his pocket. He reluctantly reached into his pocket and swiped to answer the call.

"Oh, so *now* you can answer your phone? And look it's magically fixed! It's a *miracle*," I shouted sarcastically.

My hand flew towards him and I snatched his phone out of his grasp, putting it to my ear.

"You were supposed to be here half an hour ago. What is keeping you?" the voice on the other line drawled.

"*Mindy?*" I screamed into the phone, not believing my ears.

"Oh, it's you," she sighed in annoyance. "Can I please speak to Dominic," she said sweetly, making his name sounding like a caress through the phone. I lost it.

"No, you most certainly may not!" I shouted.

"Fine. Have it your way," she said calmly. "I will not have to worry about you much longer anyhow."

Before I could respond, she hung up. My eyes flew to Dominic's, shooting sharpened daggers at him.

"What are you doing talking to Mindy? I thought you hated her! She *attacked* me, or don't you care?" I demanded. I was so furious; I could've punched him. He had been in contact with Mindy and hadn't even sent me so much as a text to tell me he was alive. Maybe they had been talking this whole time. The anger inside me bubbled over.

"Of course, I care—"

"You know what?" I interrupted him, "save your breath. I'm not putting up with this bull crap anymore. Any guy who doesn't tell his *girlfriend* before he takes off and who is in contact with the person who has made her a living hell, doesn't deserve to have that girlfriend anymore. I don't want to see your lying face ever again. Go see your precious Mindy. While you're at it you can both *go to hell!*"

I chucked his phone at his chest as I pivoted and slammed the door in his face. I stormed up to my room, slammed that door shut too behind me and screamed.

I couldn't *believe* him. How could I have been so blind? I could never love him… I was just dazzled by his stupid charm. "Ugh. I hate him!"

Theo gave a low snarl.

"Exactly Theo!" I screamed again and grabbed my phone and conference called the twins.

"Hello?" I heard two voices answer.

"I just broke up with Dominic," I said concisely, struggling to control my rage.

"You *what?*" I heard them both exclaim in unison. I was pretty sure Elsbeth dropped the phone. Then they both were tripping over each other as they bombarded me with questions. I let them calm down before I launched into my detailed account of the last fifteen minutes.

"I can't *believe* him," Elsbeth growled.

I smiled quickly despite the rage I was feeling.

"Good riddance." Thomas chimed in, his anger about Dominic clearly evident in his voice. Thomas didn't often get mad, but when someone hurt either of his "sisters" he got very protective.

"Our parents aren't home, and the fridge is fully stocked. Get your butt over here so we can do this break-up right."

"Thanks, guys, but I need to go get Gran from the hospital first. Can I come over later?"

"Of course! We will have food, movies, and tissues ready for you once you arrive."

Thomas was always so pragmatic. I laughed despite the rage and hurt I was feeling.

"Thomas, I'm fuming mad. I don't need tissues… I need a punching bag."

Gran was already in the lobby when I got there.

"Hi Sweetie." She gave me a big bear hug before pulling back to look at me.

"Your energy is off, what's wrong, Quinnie?"

I just shrugged, not wanting to stress her out before she even got home. Gran paused a minute, regarding me evenly.

"Break-ups are hard. I'm sorry you had to find that out." She gave me a comforting pat on the back.

"But… how did you know?"

Gran just chuckled. "Intense anger overlaying a world of sadness, regret and confusion? Honey, your energy has heartache written all over it." She laid a hand on my face before kissing me on the forehead.

"What would you say to a cup of hot cocoa?"

"With mini marshmallows?"

"Is there any other way?"

"I'd say that's exactly what I need." I put my arm around her shoulder as we walked to the car.

Later that night I went to the twins' house where a buffet of candy, junk food, and a new box of tissues awaited me. They had rented two movies. We watched the first one, shouting any male or couple that walked on screen. Well, it was mostly them slamming the characters and me seething and attempting to remember to force a smile every once and awhile.

And wouldn't you know it, but Thomas was right—as usual. Halfway through the second movie the anger I felt earlier was replaced by uncontrollable tears.

"Here's your punching bag," Thomas said as he passed me the tissues. I laughed through my tears. Neither twin said anything else. They just let me cry as they continued watching the movie. I fell asleep on the couch long before the end credits played, completely drained.

★
★

Even in her sleep she looked overwhelmed with sadness. She rolled over fitfully, knocking her blanket onto the floor. Within a few minutes she was shivering. Cooper broke his oath for the umpteenth time that week and stepped through the veil, silently picking up the blanket and gently tucking it around Quinn. She sighed in her sleep and rolled over again, turning to face where Cooper was standing.

He knew he should've gone straight back through the veil. Well, he actually shouldn't have crossed the veil at all—but he couldn't help it. He wanted her to be warm… to feel better… to hurt less. He didn't want to stand by any longer when he could be helping her. And as he stood there holding his breath, he realized that he wanted one thing more than anything. He wanted Quinn to see him, to really *see* him. For months he had been falling for this girl, who didn't even know he existed. Maybe if she saw him…

He brushed a stray strand of hair from her face.

"Quinn?" he whispered.

She sighed again and stirred slightly, her eyelids fluttering as if they were about to open.

★

In my dream he was standing there… not Dominic. No, definitely not Dominic. Dominic might be good-looking, but he was nothing compared to this beautiful specimen. His sandy hair looked almost golden, his eyes like pools of caramel. His full lips—oh those lips! My stomach did flip-flops. If only I could paint or sculpt; I would recreate him and keep him with me always. He smiled at me. Butterflies. He always gave me butterflies. This guy. My guy. My heart swelled as he reached towards me, brushing the hair from my face; his touch like a whisper against my skin. I sighed.

"Quinn?" he said, his voice so close, so real.

220

I felt myself being pulled out of my dream. *No, not yet… I want to stay here!* I struggled against my consciousness, not wanting to leave him.

✦

Her eyelids were pinched shut as if she were purposefully keeping them closed.

"Quinn?" he whispered again, trying to rouse her from her slumber. *It's now or never… if you don't do it now, you'll never find the nerve and you'll never know.* Her eyes were almost open now. *This is it!*

Her eyes opened just as Cooper felt two hands yank him backwards through the veil.

No! he thought to himself. He landed on the cool earth with a grunt.

"Just what do you think you're doing?" A chiding voice pierced his eardrums.

"You couldn't have waited another five seconds, Nettie? Jeez." He ran his hand through his hair in frustration. Adrenaline was still surging through him.

"Five more seconds and she would have *seen* you, Cooper!" Nettie stood with her hands on her hips, staring at Cooper with immense disapproval. He just looked at his feet and kicked some dirt around, still brooding that Nettie had interrupted him.

"What were you thinking, deliberately breaking your oath and crossing into the human realm when there was no danger? Were you *trying* to be seen? What is going on with you Cooper?"

"Are you here as the Magistrate or as my aunt?" Cooper asked, with a frown on his face.

"I could have your wings for this Cooper," she said seriously, still angry.

"I guess that answers that question. You say she was not in peril, *Magistrate,* but I disagree."

"I came here to check in with you because you haven't been yourself lately. And now I see why… What

221

threat was so imminent that you had to cross through the veil?" Nettie demanded.

"Well there were no *visible* threats," Cooper countered.

Nettie tilted her head, some of her anger turning into confusion. "No *visible* threats?"

Cooper took a deep breath. "You didn't see her after they broke up. It was like I could actually see the moment her heart broke. She had been crying and she was shivering badly so I thought I'd give her a blanket so she wouldn't freeze to death. Threats aren't always an external force. Sometimes the biggest threat someone faces is themselves."

Nettie's brows were furrowed in concern. She said nothing… which filled Cooper with dread. *She wouldn't really take my wings, would she?* There was nothing more painful physically and emotionally for a Guardian than getting stripped of their wings. Getting any tattoo removed was painful, but Coordinator tattoos were excruciatingly painful to remove. After being administered, the inked wings became a part of the new Guardian. Taking away a Guardian's wings was like having major surgery without anesthesia, which was why most Guardians made sure to remain within the confines of their oath. Cooper's throat was dry. He swallowed nervously.

"Magistrate?"

"Wait…" she said, putting a finger up to tell him to give her a second. Each passing moment felt like an eternity as he awaited his fate. After an agonizingly long time she finally raised her eyes to his.

"Did you say boyfriend?"

"Yes…" Now it was Cooper's turn to be confused.

"You said Quinn and her *boyfriend* broke up," Nettie repeated with some urgency.

"Yeah, what's the big deal? They have been dating since September and broke up today. So what?"

"Cooper… We have no record of any boyfriend."

"Well, then, your Virtualizing Animatron monitor is broken because he's been around, daily for the most part."

"Perhaps… But if he's around again, inform me immediately. I have to go talk to the technicians."

"Sure."

The Magistrate put her hands on his shoulders and stared directly at him. "I'm serious, Cooper."

"Okay," he said, feeling slightly unnerved by his aunt's intensity. "I promise I will tell you if that bastard Dominic is around again."

"And no more breaking your oath, no matter how chivalrous. Your mother may be my best friend and you may be like family to me, but I am the Magistrate, so do not think that I will always exonerate you. Please do not put me in this position again."

"Yes, Magistrate," Cooper said with sincerity. "I'm sorry, Nettie," he added on a personal note.

"I'm glad to hear it. Oh, and Cooper?"

He looked up expectantly.

"I'm sorry, too."

"For what?" Cooper asked, not understanding what she could possibly be sorry for. She vanished without answering, leaving Cooper standing alone, crushed under the weight of his actions and what punishments might be waiting for him in the future.

* * *

CHAPTER

23

★

I can't believe I risked my wings. That thought repeated through Cooper's head over and over for the next two days. It was still on his mind as he set up for his party.

After training he came home and started organizing and planning. He cut the grass, chopped wood for the fire and even created wooden benches for his friends to sit on. The physical labour helped distract him for a little while and continued distracting him while he put up a few tents for people who might want to stay over.

His mom had insisted on cooking for the party, so Cooper steered her towards the few dishes he knew even she couldn't mess up. He assured her that this party would be tame to make up for this last party, which had been a far cry from mellow. Last time, his house was trashed thanks to his fellow Guardians, who left in the same state as his house. They may not be human, but alcohol still affected them. In fact, since they normally didn't eat, alcohol affected Coordinators ten times faster than humans.

Cooper had told his friends that this was a low-key event, just friends hanging out and 'no funny business' as his mother would say. This would be good for Cooper. Maybe he needed time with people—his own kind of people—the ones who could see him and wouldn't cost him his wings by interacting with them. Gran told Quinn she didn't have to go to school if she didn't want to this week with all that had happened, which had made it easier for her to steer clear of Dominic, which incidentally also made Cooper's job easier.

☻

"How can we get rid of her if she will see us coming?" Viper asked Slade as they sat across from the Temptress. She sat silently poised behind her desk, listening as her two strongest Reapers debated their present dilemma.

"If she is unable to see her own fate, we may be able to sneak up on her, but with that Guardian around, defeating her will be much more difficult. One of them will always ruin our element of surprise." Slade's face was hard and defeated.

"Well, we are stronger than her. We will just overpower her in a fight," Viper pointed out, "two on one."

"With a Guardian watching her? That would be more like two on one hundred."

"We will bring more Reapers to even the score."

"We are trying to build up our numbers, not deplete them. We cannot afford to lose anyone right now. A war when we are outnumbered is foolish and counterproductive when we are trying to stay under the radar. The girl is not touchable. Not when she is a Seer."

"Maybe her Guardian will not call for help quickly enough?"

"But we cannot risk our existence being discovered."

"There *has* to be a way," Viper said, pounding a fist on the Temptress's wooden desk.

"Mistress, is there a way?" Slade asked the Temptress, who had remained silent until now.

"There may yet be a way, my children. You are getting caught up in the fact that she will see you coming. What if the impact of the event itself superseded the importance of who it was that caused it?"

The two Reapers considered her words as she continued to speak.

"You witnessed how she reacted when her grandmother's life was at stake. What if multiple lives were at stake? The event will be her weakness, since she has the failing that so many humans suffer from; the overwhelming regard for the lives of others."

"What do you suggest the event should be?" Slade asked, determination returning to his features.

"Well, this is where it gets entertaining."

Slade and Viper's grins grew wider and more sinister as the Temptress divulged her newest plan to them.

"Do you think this will work?" Viper asked Slade afterwards. Slade grinned over at his partner.

"With the delay between putting the plan in motion and the time when the plan reaches completion… it just might. Plus, worst case scenario, many people die."

"So, it is a win-win situation?" Viper smiled slyly.

"Exactly."

Slade and Viper reached their destination with plenty of time to spare. The snow on the ground did not faze the Reapers at all. They stood a few miles outside Rosevale at the crossroads where two rail lines met. The North/South and the East/West lines were the main means of transportation in and out of the town. People used the trains to commute to nearby places for work, to shop, or just for a night on the town—a bigger town that is. Needless to say, the trains were always crammed to near capacity with Rosevale residents.

The two of them stood by the pole that housed the signalling lights that conductors relied on to avoid any collisions.

"How do we disable the light so the trains will collide?" Viper asked Slade.

Slade walked around the device, examining it from all sides before pulling back his arm and punching straight through the red light, sending sparks and glass showering into all directions as the live wires hissed in the crisp air like angry snakes.

"The humans surely have a system in place to warn them of generator malfunctions, Slade." Viper was clearly unimpressed.

Slade sneered and dialed his phone. "Myles, you have hacked the railroad system, correct?"

"Yes boss, I have the security feeds on a loop, and have deleted any warnings from the system before anyone could see them. I also tweaked the schedule so neither train will know to slow down." Myles was typing furiously in the background.

"You may be a loud, mouth-breather, Myles, but you are not as dumb as you look," Slade said before hanging up. This was as close to a compliment as Myles was bound to get from Slade.

"Fine, but just in case your way fails…" Viper trailed off before running to the forest and effortlessly pushing over a nearby tree, causing it to tumble to the ground.

"Show off," Slade laughed, as he helped Viper pull the tree across the tracks to ensure neither train would take the path that would foil their plans.

"Just think, after tonight we will have disproved and dispelled the prophecy and nothing will stand in our way of taking control of the human race."

"We will be unstoppable, but first we need to get through tonight successfully before we are in the clear." Slade warned. "It will not be long now."

It appeared as if most of his graduating class and then some turned out for Cooper's party. He scanned the crowd enjoying the hum of conversation and music, letting it drown out his thoughts for a while. His eyes rested on Lillian as she approached him. She was wearing a tight curve-hugging dress that stopped well above the knee. It was a red number paired with dark blue heels. Why she couldn't just wear a black, flat, comfortable shoe he'd never understand.

"Hey, handsome. You clean up nice. I like the clean-shaven look." She leaned forward and gave Cooper a kiss on the cheek.

"Uh, thanks. You too," he said, a bit flustered. She cocked her head, raised an eyebrow and smiled playfully at him.

"But with *pretty* instead of *handsome*, or whatever," he clarified. She nodded slightly to herself, still smiling.

"Well, thank you. It's nice to know I can still make a guy trip over his words." She breezed past him to go meet Amy, who had just arrived. Cooper turned and walked around the back of his house.

Once in the backyard, he saw that his mother had set up tables with food and drinks on them. He scanned the crowd of people milling about his back field. There had been a better turnout than he had expected with such short notice.

As if reading his mind, Lillian walked up behind him and said, "A lot of people have rearranged plans or are bi-locating so that they wouldn't miss Cooper's Come Back Party."

His lips twitched into a half grin. "Cooper's Come Back Party? Is that what they're calling it?"

"Well, you *have* been out of the social scene for almost three months now."

Cooper's eyes widened in surprise. "Has it really been that long?"

Lillian nodded. "But you're back now." She smiled coyly at him.

Seeing her smile at him like that used to boost his ego and his libido, but it was hard to focus on Lillian when he was simultaneously a Guardian to the girl he was trying to forget.

While standing in front of Lillian his bi-locating self was also watching Quinn—a picture within a picture of the two girls who had captured his affection in one way or another in the last year.

Quinn was presently trying to teach Theo tricks, which was hilarious to watch. Surprisingly, she was making progress with him. He already could shake a paw on command, but he refused to sit when she asked. He actually looked like he was smirking as she demonstrated for him how to sit.

"Smart cat," Cooper grinned to himself as he sat on the grass near the veil. Theo's ears twitched and turned towards Cooper.

"Theo, can you hear me?" Cooper asked aloud, feeling a little foolish. Theo's ears twitched again.

With Quinn momentarily distracted trying to find something to entice him to sit, Cooper decided to test the insane theory that Theo could somehow hear him from behind the veil.

"Theo, sit." To his astonishment, Theo sat.

"Theo, shake a paw," he said.

Theo's ears twitched again as he raised a paw. Cooper couldn't believe his eyes. Theo could hear him! Quinn turned around just in time to see Theo sitting with a paw in the air.

"Good boy, Theo," she squealed in surprise and bent to give him a treat and a pat. "I knew you could do it."

★★

Cooper laughed out loud.

"Should I not be glad you're back?" Lillian asked, looking at Cooper a little hurt. She didn't know that he was laughing at Quinn and not her. Being in two places at once was not always all it was cracked up to be.

"I wasn't laughing at you. I'm just glad to be back in the social scene." He said quickly to pacify her. She smiled, contentedly placated.

"Well, then. Let's celebrate," she said as she held out a glass to Cooper.

"Can't. I'm on duty." He held up a hand to refuse.

Lillian sent him a smoldering and flirtatious look and said, "Are you telling me our top Coordinator can't even handle one measly drink? Wow, you really have gone soft." She smiled at him challengingly. He really should have let that comment slide, but his ego was on full alert.

"Fine," Cooper said, as he took the glass from her and downed it in one swig. He swallowed twice to get rid of the burning sensation in his throat.

"Happy now?"

She smiled at him with a twinkle in her eye.

"Almost…" she reached up and wrapped her arms around his neck and pulled him down into a kiss. His body went tense, his mind screaming that he was kissing the wrong girl, and he drew away from Lillian.

"Is something wrong?" she asked him, cheeks flushed, eyes glossy.

He looked at this girl, this beautiful, tangible girl.

"No, nothing is wrong."

And with that, he pulled her in close as their lips locked once more.

★

I knew I didn't want to see Dominic again, but I also knew it was inevitable. Especially seeing as I still had some of his belongings at my house: a sweater and a few books. I didn't want any reminder of him anywhere. Not wanting to think about it any longer, I tossed his stuff haphazardly into a box and headed over to Dominic's house.

The vineyard was eerily quiet as I pulled up. The lane hadn't been plowed in days by the looks of it, which was odd now that Dominic was back from his trip. I parked on the street and trudged up his driveway, not wanting to get my car stuck in his laneway. The snow came up well past my ankles, so I took my time with each step to assure I didn't lose my footing. The sun was starting to dip below the horizon, making it more difficult to see. My breath came out in visible puffs, like a dragon's might. And with the amount of anger I was still feeling towards him, I wouldn't be surprised if I could breathe fire.

There was no sign of Dominic's car, which was a relief. I dropped the box noisily outside the front door. As I looked at his box of stuff, I realized that I should've seen this break-up coming from a mile away. Just from the sheer volume of his stuff that had migrated to my house versus the amount of my stuff at his house, which by my count was…

hmm… *nothing!* I had never even been inside his house. I should've seen we weren't balanced and that we were fundamentally too different. Did I have feelings for him? Yes, he was hot. Any girl with eyes would be attracted to him, but I know now that I was trying so hard to make something work that just wasn't meant to be. I *wanted* to love him, and I *wanted* him to love me back, but after Colorado I saw a side of him that I had neglected to see before. I saw him for who he was, not the jaded version of who I wanted him to be.

I took a deep breath, squared my shoulders and knocked on his front door, bracing myself. The door must have not been shut properly because as my fist made contact with the door, it slowly opened with the kind of creaking you'd hear in a horror movie. The house was dark when I peered in.

"Hello?" I called out. The only sound that greeted me was my own voice echoing back to me.

"Mrs. Hunter?" I called again. Still no response. I picked up the box and went inside. I placed the box on the ground and looked around the front entranceway. Even though we had broken up—my stomach dropped at the thought—I had always wondered what the inside of his house looked like. No one seemed to be home, so I let curiosity win and decided to take a peek around.

I felt along the wall for a light switch. I flipped it on, but nothing happened. I stood there a few more minutes letting my eyes adjust before I slipped off my wet boots, turned on my cellphone light and walked out around the corner into what I thought might be the living room.

My heart stopped as I looked around the massive room. Something was very wrong here. Every single piece of furniture was covered by big clear plastic tarps and my feet were leaving footprints in the thick layers of dust on the floor. I looked through the living room into the kitchen and saw that there was the same amount of dust in there too. The appliances in the kitchen had been pulled from the walls, unplugged and draped like everything else in the house. The place looked like no one had lived in it in years.

"What the heck is going on?"

⁎

Cooper pulled away from Lillian, knowing he had to tell the Magistrate immediately about Quinn's unsettling discovery at Dominic's house. He took a step back and the world spun around him.

"How much alcohol was in that drink?"

"There was only a little bit of alcohol," Lillian said with a giggle. "But that wasn't all…"

Cooper laughed at her adorable guilty face. *Wait, why am I laughing?*

"Blame poppy," she said mysteriously. Her words barely registering.

"Lil, I have to go," he said reluctantly.

"Why?" She pouted as she wrapped his arms around her waist and pressed up against him.

"I, uh, I don't remember." His head felt sloshy as he leaned in and kissed Lillian again. Something pricked at the back of his mind, something important that he was supposed to do, but in that moment, he didn't care about anything except for the blissful numbness in his mind, and the feeling of a pretty girl pressed against him.

Every Reaper stood in the vast meeting room of the warehouse, waiting for the Temptress to address them. The room was bare except for the platform where the Temptress stood looking out into the sea of Reapers who were gathered before her. All Reapers wore their brown leather jackets, making it impossible to tell one from the other. But even from a distance she could still make out the few features that all Reapers had in common: a muscular build, eyes as black as night, and somewhere on their body the matching tattoo of a scythe, some visible on the wrists, others hidden underneath clothing.

The Temptress addressed her hundreds of followers. "This, my children, is a night to be remembered. The night we assure the success of the mission that has been mandated to every Reaper."

A cheer erupted from the crowd.

"Slade and Viper have tirelessly searched the globe to find the one human that threatens our existence. And they have found her! Tonight, we make sure she will never threaten us again," her voice boomed across the room. Another uproarious cheer rippled through the crowd, as Reapers hollered and punched their fists into the air with excitement. Everyone in the Fortress started cheering and chanting in perfect unison: "Kill the girl. Kill the girl."

With a sickeningly evil grin the Temptress raised her hands for them to quiet down.

"But first, there is one last thing that needs to be done and I am going to need every single Reaper's assistance. Everyone must grab one of the jackets and a pair of colored contact lenses from the stage and make your way to your designated posts."

All the Reapers shrugged the matching jackets over their existing ones, placed the contact lenses in their eyes— and disappeared out the door and into the night.

Although this version of him had not had a drink, the effects leaked over into both of his selves while bi-locating. Suddenly, Lillian's words flooded back to him…

Blame poppy.

Did Lillian put something in his drink? That would explain the giggles and the intense affects he was feeling. He should be mad, but the good feelings of the poppy were blocking all negative emotions.

The Cooper guarding Quinn wasn't feeling the effects nearly as much as he was at his house party, but any splash-over effect was too much when on duty. He should call to have someone replace him, but he was already feeling better. He manifested multiple glasses of water and chugged them trying to clear out his system. He'd let the other Cooper enjoy himself for a few more minutes before sending him to inform the Magistrate about Dominic's empty house.

⁑

Cooper reluctantly peeled himself out of Lillian's arms and apologetically excused himself momentarily.

"I'll be right back."

Lillian pouted in displeasure. "Don't be too long."

Cooper nodded and teleported himself to HQ. Even though it was the weekend he knew Nettie, *er, the Magistrate*—he corrected himself mentally—would be there late tonight. Knowing the secretary had gone home, he just stepped into the pod and sent the thought command to see the Magistrate.

After a moment the writing scrawled across the pod indicating his request was being processed. The orange rings painlessly encircled him, verifying his presence before turning green and sending the pod shooting upwards towards the Magistrate's office. Nettie was waiting in the hallway when the pod arrived.

"What's wrong? Is Quinn alright?" she asked, sounding mildly panicked.

"Yes, she's fine," Cooper reassured her, carefully focusing on his words and footing, not wanting to get in trouble with Nettie again. He was already walking a thin line with her.

Nettie relaxed visibly. "Then what is it?"

"There's been a development with Dominic." At Nettie's blank stare Cooper rephrased his comment.

"Ah, I mean her ex-boyfriend." *Dang talking is hard right now. Focus, Cooper.*

"And?" Her voice was clipped with concern. Cooper recounted how Quinn went to Dominic's house to return some of his stuff and the front door was open and when she went inside the house was completely uninhabited.

Nettie pursed her lips. "Uninhabited?"

Cooper nodded. "Dust everywhere, furniture that hadn't been used in ages, all covered in plastic."

"I was afraid of that," Nettie frowned. "Any sign of him since?"

"No sign of him."

Nettie looked visibly relieved. "Good. Do not let her out of your sight for even a second, do you understand me?" she ordered, with a fierce urgency.

He was slightly taken aback, puzzled at the forcefulness in her voice. Cooper assured her he would.

"Good." Her gaze slid past Cooper and rested on a spot along the wall just beside him. Cooper could almost see the cogs of thought spinning in her mind.

"Is there something you're not telling me, Magistrate?" he asked, sensing that something was amiss.

Nettie remained lost in thought, seemingly oblivious to the fact that Cooper was talking to her. His worry increased slightly at her continued silence.

"Nettie?" he asked again. Using his aunt's name seemed to derail her train of thought and she focused back on her nephew.

"All you need to know is that she isn't safe right now and you need to assure her safety until I know more. I have some work to do, so if that's all…"

"But you'd tell me if something was seriously wrong?"

Nettie hesitated before nodding briefly and retreating back to her office. He followed her down the hallway and paused in her office doorway. He heard her speaking quickly to someone and moved closer to try to hear who she had contacted. She looked up and saw that Cooper was there and quietly moved to the door and closed it, blocking off all noise. Cooper put his hands in his pockets and with a furrowed brow returned to the pods.

Once outside he teleported himself back to his party, where Lillian was waiting.

★

I suddenly felt uneasy as I stood in the deserted living room. I turned to leave wanting to be out of that house as soon as possible. Just as I reached for the door handle my head exploded with pain. The pain was so intense it brought me to my knees as tears sprang to my eyes. The pictures revealed themselves excruciatingly slowly. Snowy, it was snowy. That was all I saw at first, an endless expanse of snow.

Dimly in the distance to my right was the faint glow of some sort of headlight—a train perhaps? Then the same dim light appeared on the horizon to my left. The two images of the trains chugged into fast forward, heading straight towards me on both sides. I was frozen in place as the two trains collided with me and into each other, leaving the air thick with screams and smoke.

Then to my horror the trains that had just crashed into each other exploded leaving nothing but two giant heaps of charred metal. The eerie silence afterward scared me more than anything. At least when people were screaming, it meant they were alive. The image slammed into me over and over again. Two trains on a crash course that was sure to mean the death of many.

"Oh, my God," I breathed. I tried to stand, but the force of the headache prevented me from being able to move right away. The world spun around me as I tried to breathe and collect myself. How the hell was I supposed to stop two trains? And why was Dominic's house covered in plastic and dust? Oh, right… *and how the hell was I supposed to stop moving trains?*

I sat on the floor on the verge of hyperventilating. *I think I'm going to puke.* Thankfully I was used to having panic attacks due to the vividness of my premonitions, so I knew I had to calm my breathing. *Don't panic, everything is fine. Don't panic, everything is fine. Don't panic, everything is fine. Aw, screw it! Who am I kidding? Everything is not fine, now get up and go* do *something!*

I pulled myself into a standing position and hastily put on my boots and stumbled my way back to my car. I pulled my keys out of my red winter jacket, jumped into the car and took a U-turn worthy of an action film before speeding towards the train station.

⋆⋆

"Quinn!" Cooper gasped, breaking away from Lillian's embrace.

"My name's Lillian, but for tonight, I'll be whoever you want me to be." She seductively leaned back in, but she was met only by a brief gust of wind as Cooper teleported away, leaving her standing alone and confused.

Cooper teleported right to the front entrance of HQ, promptly knocking a man over when he appeared directly in front of him.

"Hey, watch it," the man called out as Cooper pushed by him and into the building. "And next time use the field."

Cooper ignored the man's angry shouts as he sprinted towards the pod, throwing himself into the first one that opened. The pod's orange rings fell around him as his brain was screaming to get to the Magistrate's office.

Nettie was on the phone when the alert scrolled across her desk: *Guardian Cooper arriving RE: URGENT.*

"I must go," she said to the person on the other end of the line. "Some new information has arrived. Yes, I'm aware of the severity of this. No, we're not sure if it's them yet, but my hunch is that it is as we feared. I will keep you informed." Nettie ran her pointer finger along her desk to sever the call and rose to meet Cooper as he flew into her office.

"What's wrong?" the Magistrate asked.

"That's just it, Magistrate. I don't know. But something is most definitely very, very wrong."

The Magistrate sat down behind her desk as Cooper spoke. "Speak quickly and don't leave nothing out."

"As Quinn was about to leave his empty house, she fell to her knees screaming in pain as she held her head."

"A psychic flash?"

Cooper nodded. "I think so, but if it was, it was worse than anything we've seen yet."

The Magistrate dragged her fingers along her transparent desk, rapidly bringing up contacts and files and gave the thought-command to call the control room where every human lifeline was monitored on a vast, complicated network of computers.

"Keeper Ryan here. What can we do for you, Magistrate?"

"Keeper Ryan, has there been any influx in risks in the Rosevale or surrounding area?"

The Magistrate waited as Ryan clicked through monitors briefly before responding.

"The Virtualizing Animatron shows no notable influxes." He paused waiting for further instructions.

"If that changes contact me immediately."

"Of course, Magistrate."

Nettie ended the call and dialed in the Coordinator who coached the Guardians as well as assisted the Magistrate in coordinating and allocating Guardians to specific missions.

"Guardian Barrett, here." His voice emanated from the desk making him sound like he was standing in the room with them.

"Guardian Barrett, contact all available Guardians and have them on standby, including your present trainees."

Without questioning why, he immediately agreed.

Cooper coughed uncomfortably.

"What is it, Cooper?" Nettie asked impatiently.

"Uh, that may be a problem."

"And why is that?" Barrett and the Magistrate said simultaneously.

"Well, most of my class is presently in my backyard and most are probably… most likely… not exactly fit for duty at present…"

Nettie scowled and turned away from Cooper.

"Barrett?"

"I'm on it, Magistrate," he said before disconnecting the call.

"What should I do now?" Cooper asked.

"Well for starters, you should go back to your party and detox along with the rest of your classmates," the Magistrate said, shaking her head disapprovingly.

Cooper hung his head in shame, feeling guilty for going against his instincts earlier that night.

"I'm sorry," Cooper said feebly.

"We'll deal with this later. For now, just get home and wait for further instructions. If anything new comes up, tell Guardian Barrett and he'll relay it to me."

She tossed a small earpiece at him. He sprinted out of HQ and quickly teleported to his other self, who then inserted the earpiece before using another thought command to go back to the party.

Guardian Barrett was already in Cooper's backyard shouting instructions when Cooper arrived.

"Every Guardian line up at one of the stations; five Guardians to a station. Once cleared, change into your mission wear and gather around me."

The Guardians slowly stumbled their way into lines. A Healer was situated at each station, ready to cleanse the Guardians' energy and remove the alcohol (and other toxins) from their systems. Cooper moved to the back of a line when Guardian Barrett called for him to move to the front. Cooper walked up to the Healer.

"Hello, Marnie," he said, recognizing the Healer from his mother's book club.

"Lie down," she instructed curtly. Cooper did as he was told to lay face up on the damp grass at Healer Marnie's feet. Marnie picked up two Healer's Rods and held them a few inches above Cooper's head.

"Now please try to keep still. This may be slightly uncomfortable." She slowly started to wave the rods over his body. He could feel every cell of his body start to vibrate as if they were all of opposite polarity and were all trying to separate. Cooper winced. Marnie smiled slightly.

"You'd think a Healer would have more sympathy for her patients," Cooper said, through gritted teeth.

"You'd think a Guardian would know better than to drink while on duty." She looked at Cooper disapprovingly.

Cooper said nothing else as she slowly—tortuously slowly in Cooper's opinion—moved the rods from his head to his feet. An ominous black smoke-like substance was streaming out of his feet.

"What *is* that?" Neil asked, horrified as he backed away from the cloud his best friend was emitting.

"It's the toxins from your weekend habit," Marnie explained without taking her eyes away from the rods.

"So, are you sucking the booze right out of him?" Neil asked, a look of pure disgust on his face.

"Something like that. You're next. Come lie down."

Once Cooper was restored to his normal state of mental and physical health, he walked over to Barrett.

"How many Guardians on standby?"

"Your entire class, plus at least one hundred of the older Guardians. Whatever is about to happen tonight, we're prepared to help if need be."

Hearing the coach's confidence helped alleviate some of Cooper's anxiety. Quinn was still driving, and he had no idea where she was going or what was going to happen or when.

When all of Cooper's classmates had been seen by a Healer, they congregated around Barrett for further instructions. Guardian Barrett stood standing in front of his pupils, who had all taken a knee while they waited. He looked out into the sea of white cloth and alert eyes and addressed the Guardians.

"The Magistrate believes that a large incident is about to take place on the human plane that could endanger the lives of many innocent humans, stealing them from the Earth before their intended time."

The Guardians started to mumble amongst themselves, all wondering what it could be; some excited for the chance to actually participate in a mission, others grievously worried about what might transpire. Barrett let them chatter for a moment, knowing the young Guardians would just continue to be distracted if not allowed to express their excitement, confusion, and concern. After a moment he raised a hand to silence his class.

"To answer your questions: No, we do not know what the situation will be, nor when it will take place. It is our job to be prepared to cross the veil in a moment's notice. For now, I'll ask that you all remain in the field and await further instructions."

After his address he took a moment to observe his previous and current students, all of them in white for the first time since their Guardianship ceremonies. His heart swelled with pride at how far they had come, but he couldn't shake the nagging worry that lingered. With no children of his own, his students had become like family to him and he found his parental instincts kicking in at the thought of them all potentially being on the human plane at the same time. Cooper broke away from his classmates and stood by Barrett.

"If you don't mind, Sir, I'd rather stay close by. I don't want to waste any time trying to find you should we need to contact the Magistrate."

Barrett smiled with pride and briefly clapped a hand on Cooper's shoulder.

"I think that's a wise decision, son."

* * *

241

CHAPTER
24
★

I threw the car in park and sprinted towards the station's platform. There were dozens of vehicles in the station parking lot. Each car held one person minimum, which meant there could be a hundred or more people on the trains. I had to stop this! There was a small crowd milling on the platform. I rushed past them to the ticket booth.

"Sir! Sir… Two trains are going to collide!" I panted through the thick glass. The ticket vendor looked at me for a moment and said, "Miss, the trains are all moving according to schedule."

"You need to listen to me. Two trains are going to crash, and you need to do something about it." My voice rose, attracting the attention of a few passers-by. Slowly some people seemed to recognize me—seeing as I was the town's bad luck magnet and all—and backed away.

"One moment, Miss." The man got up and went to the booth beside him and spoke in hushed tones to his female co-worker. The woman got up and joined the man in the booth where I was standing. She sat at the computer and turned it towards me so I could see.

"There are no warnings in the system and all trains are on schedule as you can see. So, if you are not going to purchase a ticket," she said condescendingly, "I'm going to have to ask you to step aside. I do not want to call security."

"You *should* call security! People's lives are at risk!"

"I'm going to have to ask you to leave and make room for the next customer if you're not going to be purchasing a ticket today."

"I'm not leaving here until you stop the trains! People are going to *die.*"

The woman behind the glass hastily picked up the phone and dialed security. If they wouldn't stop the trains, I'd have to find another way. I turned to leave before security could drag me away. The platform was suddenly very crowded with people. I started to push my way through the crowd to get to the railroad tracks. *I have to stop those trains.*

★★
★

"Barrett!" Cooper said suddenly, grabbing his instructor's arm. "There's going to be a train accident. You need to tell the Magistrate!"

Barrett turned away and pressed a small device in his ear and commanded it to dial the Magistrate to relay the message. He turned to Cooper and informed him that the Magistrate wished to speak to him directly. Cooper pushed his own ear bud and gave the thought command to be connected directly to the Magistrate.

"How bad is it? What are the monitors showing?" Cooper asked.

"No warnings as of yet, Cooper. Are you sure it's a train collision?"

"Yeah, she—" Cooper paused and took a step away from Barrett. "She said she knows people are going to die if it's not stopped. How can the monitors not be showing the threat if she saw it?"

"The monitors show all threats involving natural disasters and all threats created by humans and machines."

Knowing this already Cooper impatiently repeated his previous statement. "So how come they aren't showing anything?"

"Because this threat wasn't caused by nature, machines," she paused before continuing. "...or humans."

Cooper was rarely often caught off guard.

"How is that possible? It's not Coordinators threatening them is it?"

"No, but I have no time to explain. Just keep me informed and be prepared."

"But I don't under—"

The Magistrate cut him off. "Put Barrett on."

"But—"

"*Now,* Guardian Cooper. That's a direct order."

Cooper begrudgingly turned to Barrett. "It's for you," he said, scowling before his line was disconnected.

"Magistrate, it's Guardian Barrett…"

Since Cooper's earpiece had been disconnected, he was forced watched the one-sided conversation unfolded.

"Dear God, are you sure? But how can that be?"

All of the color drained from Barrett's face as Cooper watched.

"Yes, of course. No, I understand. Yes, Magistrate." Barrett clicked off the earpiece and stared blankly ahead, still white as a ghost.

"What is going on?" Cooper demanded.

"We are preparing to intervene" he said.

"Barrett, what's *really* going on?"

Guardian Barrett turned to face Cooper with a solemn look on his face. "It's not good, Cooper."

"What's not?" Cooper looked at his mentor hoping he would tell him what the Magistrate wouldn't.

"That's all I can say, Cooper. I'm sorry." Cooper could see he genuinely meant it.

He turned away from Barrett and stormed away from the group as Neil came up behind him.

"What the heck is going on?" Neil asked him.

"Hell if I know," Cooper grunted angrily, raking a hand through his hair.

"It must be pretty big if they have our entire class in mission gear. Some of these new Guardians haven't even ever been assigned to an official case yet." Neil said, with an air of nervous excitement. "It really gets the adrenaline pumping."

Cooper did not return his friend's enthusiasm; he was too busy brooding and ruminating on what could've caused this and worrying about Quinn being caught in the mêlée.

"What the hell?" Cooper suddenly said to himself in a startled whisper.

"What is it?" Neil asked. Cooper didn't answer. His eyes were bugging out of his head. Every fiber of his being was telling him to merge back with himself so he could be fully present to help Quinn, but he knew he was the only line of communication between what was going on out there on the human plane and to the people of Crysthala.

"Cooper?" Neil called again.

"Cooper? What's going on?" Barrett echoed. When he didn't get any response, he turned to Neil and asked what happened.

Neil just shrugged. "I have no idea... he just suddenly stopped speaking with that shocked look on his face."

Barrett bent to look Cooper in the eyes. "Cooper? Guardian Cooper!" he said more forcefully, but Cooper didn't respond.

What the hell? Cooper had to blink twice as he looked through the veil out at the crowd on the platform. Suddenly there was a rush of movement and the platform filled with people. Each one was wearing a red jacket just like Quinn's and he quickly lost sight of her in the mass of bodies.

"Crap!" Cooper tried peering over the crowd to try to see where she had gone. Finding a needle in a haystack would be easier at this point. He stepped through the veil, momentarily hoping to reorient himself so he could spot her, but there was no luck. He kept jumping through the veil in case she broke free from the pack and became visible, each second growing more panicked when he couldn't locate her.

★

"Ugh, get out of my *way!*" I screamed as I forced my way through the sea of people.

"Don't you understand I'm trying to *help!*" I had no idea where the sudden mob of people came from. All I knew was that I had to get to the railroad track, follow it until I saw the juncture where the two trains would collide, and then flag one of the trains down—somehow. I'd figure that part out once I got there. *If* I ever got there.

I pushed harder against the mob. I could see a clearing straight ahead and threw my full weight into getting past the last few people crowding the platform. I popped out of the fray, stumbling from my momentum. I had only taken one step when my foot collided with a large black box that was on the ground, causing me to trip over it and fall into the snow.

"What the heck?" I heard a sharp snap and hissing noise from behind me and looked back at the crowd. No one seemed to have noticed. The box had some sort of light on it, but I had no time to consider what it could be. I looked left and right wondering which way to go down the tracks. I looked left again; nothing seemed familiar. I looked right and my head gave a sharp pang. *Right it is.* I sprinted down the tracks, constantly looking around for anything that reminded me of the vision I had seen earlier. My phone vibrated in my pocket. I slowed just enough so I could read the message.

> Hey Q! Next stop Rosevale c u l8r!

With all the craziness returning Dominic's items to his empty house, I had completely forgotten the twins had gone out of town today.

"*No!*" I screamed, tears threatening to fall down my cheeks. First Gran, now the twins... *This cannot be happening.*

Up ahead I saw the faint outline of a fallen tree as the sun started to dip lower in the sky. *This is it! This is the place!* My heart felt slightly lighter, now that I had found the spot. I heard the sound of a train whistle in the distance and just like that, any hope I felt evaporated in an instant.

Something was wrong. He should have been able to see her by now. He went through the veil two more times before he realized what was off. Every time he stepped back through the veil to his side of the plane, it was the exact same image before him, the exact same orientation. He watched as the man closest to him walked halfway across the platform before disappearing and reappearing a few feet away before walking halfway across the platform again.

He stopped and stared at the scene in front of him. It was like it was somehow stuck on a loop. *What is going on?* He jumped into the crowd and started pushing his way through. Cooper looked up across the platform and saw that the air at the end of the platform seemed to be shimmering. He needed to call the Magistrate.

"Uh, Magistrate?" one of the Keeper's called out. "We have a problem."

The alarms in the room started going off as red dot after red dot began appearing on the Virtualizing Animatrons, each spot on the screens indicating a human life that was in peril.

"Oh, my God," the Magistrate breathed, shell-shocked. "It's happening."

"What do we do? There must be over a thousand lives in danger!" The entire room turned towards their Magistrate, silently pleading for guidance.

"Keep monitoring, get an exact count. I need to contact Barrett."

She answered on the second ring. Without waiting for a greeting Cooper started talking rapidly.

"Magistrate, something's wrong. I… I lost track of Quinn and—"

"You *what?*" she screamed in a panic.

"There seems to be something wrong with the veil. It's like everything is stuck on repeat."

"Quickly, look around... Do you see a wall that looks like shimmering glass?" she asked, still panicked.

"Yeah, I do. What is..."

"You need to run through it. *Now,* Cooper!"

The platform was long and with the crowd it made it extra difficult to maneuver, but he pushed himself harder, bumping people out of the way as he ran.

★

It was getting darker by the second, I needed to do something fast! The sound of the whistle wasn't too far away now. How was I going to stop the trains? As I got closer, I saw the outline of two people by the fallen tree. My spirits lifted slightly.

"Help, we need to move the tree!" I called out to them as I approached. Because of my panic it took me longer than normal to realize something about their outlines seemed familiar. Hearing my voice, they turned to face me. One look at their faces and I almost fainted.

"Dominic?" I gasped, not understanding. My blood ran cold and my heart threatened to stop beating. *What was he doing here? Why was he with...*

"Mindy?" I gasped again.

"What's going on? What are you doing here... with her?" I felt my heart breaking all over again.

"We were wondering when you would get here," Mindy said smugly.

"You knew I was coming?" It was then that I noticed their jackets. Brown jackets. Brown *leather* jackets. I gasped as my hand flew to my mouth.

"Oh, I think she is catching on," Mindy said gleefully.

"I think you are correct," Dominic smirked in response.

"You were outside my house," I gasped and took a step backwards.

"I knew she saw you that day. That is what you get for not staying hidden better, Viper."

"You were right, Slade, but it all worked out in the end." They smiled at each other.

Slade and Viper? Dominic and Mindy? The image of a scythe flashed behind my eyelids.

I backed away, not fully understanding what was going on, but one thing I did know for sure was I wasn't safe with them.

"Aw, look, Slade. She is all confused," Mindy said to Dominic, with concern that was clearly artificial.

"Too bad we do not have time to explain," Slade said, with mock disappointment. I heard the train whistle in the distance. Time was running out.

"L'ho trovato finalmente. Lei è il mio… I finally found you. You are *mine*. Il mio."

The words that once brought me shivers of delight now filled me with dread.

"I would say it was nice knowing you, but… well… you know how it is," Mindy or Viper—or whoever she was—commented.

Just as I tried to turn and cry out, I felt the sharp pain of something hard hitting my head. The world swam around me before I was engulfed in darkness.

☠

"Quick, Slade, get the rope. The train will be here any moment." Viper called, as she skipped around Quinn's crumpled form, lying on the ground.

"Can I kick her now?" Viper asked.

Slade nodded. "Why not. It will not be as much fun after she is dead."

Viper kicked her a few times in the ribs.

"That is enough," Slade said, as he handed one end of a rope to his partner. She tied it tightly around Quinn's wrists and feet.

"Should we gag her?" Viper asked.

"No, I want to hear her scream."

They tossed Quinn over the train tracks opposite the tree. The two of them cackled and retreated to the forest to watch their perfectly planned destruction from a safe distance.

* * *

CHAPTER

25

Cooper was pushing his way through the crowd for what seemed like an eternity. For every step forward, it felt like he was pushed two steps backwards. Finally, he broke through the crowd and was standing in front of a vast wall. Nettie described it accurately when she said it looked like a wall of shimmering glass. *Now was she being figurative or literal when she said glass?* He didn't have time to find out.

He took a deep breath and ran towards the wall. He braced himself instinctively for impact, but none came. Cooper was halfway through the wall before the pain hit. It was like a million lightning bolts were striking every inch of his body—tiny shards of electricity slicing at his flesh. He bit back a scream and urged himself forward even though his entire being was yelling at him to turn back, to end the agony.

The pain stopped as soon as he had successfully passed through the translucent threshold. He looked down at his skin, but there were no residual marks indicating what had just transpired. He spotted three pairs of footprints heading to the right and he broke into a run following the tracks. He recognized Quinn's footprints instantly and it appeared that she wasn't alone. His heart thudded faster as he ran after Quinn.

He heard the whistle and saw the light of the train in the distance. Another horn blasted from behind him and he turned around to see another set of headlights hot on his tail.

"Barrett!" Cooper screamed. "We need to go *now!*" The volume and urgency in Cooper's voice drew the attention of his classmates causing everything around him to come to a halt.

"Where?" Barrett demanded.

"A half-mile away from the train station!"

"Lead the way!" Barrett boomed.

Running at full force towards the part of the veil that edged his backyard, he quickly pictured the location of the railroad tracks and the image emerged on the other side of the veil.

The trains were nearing each other at lightning speed now, less than a kilometer apart, as the Guardians streamed through the veil behind Cooper. He saw a dark form on the ground up ahead as a train whizzed by him.

"*Quinn!*" he screamed, seeing her lifeless body sprawled across the tracks.

"Cooper don't!" he heard a Guardian call from behind him. "You'll never make it!"

He could feel the wind from the approaching trains as he raced them. The trains moved closer and closer together, less than a football field apart when Cooper ran across the tracks, scooping Quinn up into his arms before sprinting as far away from the tracks as he could. Quinn's eyes opened at the sound of crunching metal as the two trains barreled into each other.

"Explosion," she muttered, before her head lolled backwards as she went unconscious once more.

"Explosion?" Cooper repeated out loud to himself, the meaning slowly registering.

Cooper turned to Barrett, "The train cars are going to explode. We need to get the people out *now!*"

"*Get the humans to safety. The trains are going to explode!*" Barrett commanded the Guardians.

The Guardians rushed to the cars, breaking windows and prying the metal roofs off to allow people to climb out. Those who had been injured or were unable to move were carried out by the Guardians. They started laying people in the field as far away from the tracks as possible.

Hundreds of Guardians worked quickly getting as many living humans to safety as possible before the impending explosion; a sea of white amongst the dirt, blood, and debris. The sounds of sirens wailed in the distance, signaling that more help was on the way.

Quinn's eyes fluttered open and closed again, fighting to stay conscious. She struggled in Cooper's grasp as she pulled against the rope that bound her hands and feet.

"Twins, twins," she sputtered as blood pooled out of her mouth.

Cooper's other self, froze in front of the train car he was standing by and immediately started searching for Elsbeth and Thomas in a panic, calling out for them as he scoured the field and each train car.

"Don't worry, we'll find them," Cooper reassured Quinn, as he broke the ropes that bound her with one hand. Slowly, as if she hadn't realized his presence until that moment, she turned to look at him. Her eyes met his and her face went pale as her eyes grew wide.

"It's you," she inhaled sharply. Cooper scrunched his eyebrows in confusion.

"It's me?" He repeated dumbfoundedly. His heart started beating painfully against his rib cage.

"It's you," she repeated and with a sigh as she fell into unconsciousness once again. Her body was shaking in his arms.

"Quinn?" he said. "Quinn?" More alarmed this time. *"Quinn, can you hear me?"*

Cooper's hearing alerted him to the ambulances' arrival. He ran back towards the train station with Quinn pinned carefully against his chest.

"My friend is unconscious and bleeding badly from her head. We need to get her to a hospital now!"

The paramedics loaded Quinn into the back of the ambulance.

"Are you coming along?" one of the emergency workers asked, as he went to shut the doors. Cooper hesitated for a moment, knowing he should go help the others.

"Yes," he said finally and hopped into the back of the ambulance.

⁑

The other Cooper still hadn't found the twins when the trains exploded. The fiery light consumed the night sky, sending smoke billowing towards the heavens. People were screaming and frantically holding their loved ones.

"Did we get everyone out of the trains?" Cooper asked Barrett. Barrett looked out at the masses of people huddled together in the cold.

"We got everyone out," Barrett confirmed.

"Alive?" Cooper asked. Barrett hesitated.

"We got everyone out," he repeated solemnly.

Cooper's heart sank. *What if something had happened to the twins?*

"We should be getting back, the paramedics will take it from here," Barrett said, laying a hand on Cooper's shoulder. "We did all we could."

"I'll be right behind you. There's just one thing I need to do first."

Barrett paused as if to instruct Cooper to do as he was told, but after what he had just witnessed, he didn't have the fight left in him to scold Cooper. He just nodded and slipped back through the veil.

Cooper walked through the crowd of people, looking at each person to see if they were the either twin. Every time he came across a lifeless body or a crying group of people, a grapefruit sized lump came to his throat as he peered to see if it was someone he recognized. He was three-quarters of the way through the crowd when finally, he saw them—alive, huddled together, crying on the phone to someone. *Thank God,* he thought to himself, as he quietly slipped back through the veil.

⁑

The ambulance bounced down the main road toward the hospital.

"What's her name?" one of the paramedics asked.

254

"Quinn Aurelia," Cooper answered, never taking his eyes off Quinn, who was still unconscious.

"Is she allergic to any medications?"

Cooper pulled up Quinn's file in his mind.

"No, no allergies, but she is afraid of needles."

The two EMS workers look at each other briefly.

"Will she be okay?" Cooper could feel his emotions heightening and he swiped furiously at his left eye that had started to leak.

"She's lost a lot of blood. We won't know for sure what's going on internally until we can get her to the hospital. How long has she been unconscious?"

"I don't know. She was awake a few minutes ago, but then fell back under."

The machine attached to her started beeping wildly.

"She's coding!" one of them shouted. They cut open her shirt and started sticking the AED pads onto her chest and ribs.

"Keep your hands clear," the EMT instructed everyone. She pressed a button on the AED machine and Quinn's body convulsed as the shock went through her.

"No response. Starting CPR."

Cooper stood and looked out at the Guardians that filled his backyard. His mother and sister were there now too, along with other friends and family of the Guardians in attendance. None of the Guardians had manifested new clothes. Every single one of them were soaked: some with water from melted snow, some with dirt, or the blood of the injured. Soon the adrenaline would wear off and the exhaustion would hit, but for now they all stood discussing what had just transpired.

The Magistrate appeared before Cooper and pulled him aside.

"Come with me please." The two teleported to her office where they would not be overheard. Only the

Magistrate and whomever she was touching could directly teleport to her office through her thought command.

"All the Guardians are back on this side of the veil, except one. Can you guess who that is?" she asked, her eyes haunted and exhausted.

"I just wanted to stay with her until someone came to be with her. I changed into civilian clothing. Please. She's unconscious she'll never see me and by the time someone gets around to telling her someone was there she'll just think it was a kind stranger."

Nettie put a hand to her forehead and made a decision she hoped she wouldn't regret. "Fine, but as soon as her grandmother arrives …"

"… I'll step through the veil. Only a few more minutes."

"I really shouldn't allow this, but after today, after the lives she's saved, I wouldn't want her to be alone either."

"Thank you, Nettie," he said sincerely.

"Don't mention it. Seriously. And Cooper? Do not remain a second longer than necessary, alright?"

"I won't. Promise."

Nettie couldn't help but notice that his statement sounded like "I won't promise" but she was too tired too worried about what to do with bigger matters at hand, so she let it slide…for now.

I fought against the darkness, wanting to see that face, the face from my dreams. I knew I had to get to him. No matter how hard I pushed, I just couldn't break through the surface. The harder I fought, the deeper under I was pulled. *No, please! I need to see him! Please!* There was no other light or sound, just the echo of my own voice inside my head.

Since he was not Quinn's immediate family, he was told to remain in the waiting room while they rushed her away. Instead of waiting, he flipped behind the veil to keep an eye on her. She was stable but needed blood. They hooked up bags and tubes and he cringed as they stuck her with needles and an intravenous drip.

After a while they left her to rest and when the room was clear, Cooper stepped back through the veil and went to sit beside her bed and took her hand in his. Once he made contact with her, an electric current ran through his body. He let go with a gasp. Her fingers twitched reflexively as if searching for his; he laced his fingers through hers again and sat mystified at the charge that surged through him at her touch. Not a painful surge, no. In fact, it made him feel alive. Her heartbeat accelerated and the monitor beeped faster.

He didn't want to draw attention to his presence, but as he tried to release her hand, her fingers tightened around his and her heartbeat slowed again. He smiled to himself—she may not be looking at him, but he was finally holding her hand. Cooper wanted to savour the moment knowing very well he may never have this chance again, especially if Nettie took his wings. He could feel how soft and delicate her hands were, softer than he could've ever imagined. His ears twitched as he heard a familiar voice.

"Where is my granddaughter? Quinn!" Gran called in a panic. Cooper reluctantly let go of Quinn's hand and stepped through the veil as Gran entered the room.

Gran rushed to her bedside and clasped her hand tightly. "My brave, brave Quinn!" She wept beside her granddaughter. "My foolish, stupid, brave, Quinn." Gran buried her head into Quinn's hands, kissing the back of her fingers. Shortly after, the doctor came in to talk to Gran.

"She's stable now. It was touch and go for a while, but she should be fine."

"How long until she wakes up?" Gran asked.

"That depends on her. Head injuries are finicky, and we won't be sure of the damage until she wakes. It could be an hour or a day or more. All we can do now is make sure she's comfortable and stable and let her body heal."

Gran nodded solemnly and turned her attention back to Quinn. The doctor left the two of them alone and after a few minutes Gran turned in Cooper's direction and said, "Thank you for saving her."

Cooper's eyes widened as he took a step backwards.

"You can see me?" he said aloud, but she had already turned back to Quinn. Maybe she was thanking the universe or a higher power, but it felt like she had looked directly at him. He had no time to consider it because the press had caught wind that Rosevale's bad luck magnet was actually the one who warned the train station of the impending collision. They had stationed reporters outside her hospital room, waiting for her to awaken so they could get the first exclusive interview.

"Move out of my way!" an agitated voice called out. Cooper turned to see Elsbeth and Thomas pushing their way through the reporters and into Quinn's room.

"No comment, you filthy vultures!" Elsbeth shrieked as she shut the door behind them. "Sorry," she added, when she saw Gran's raised eyebrows.

"No need to apologize, dear. I couldn't have said it better myself."

"I hope it is okay that we're here," Thomas said sheepishly. "We were getting check out downstairs when we heard that Quinn was the one who warned people about the train crash."

"I'm glad you are here and I'm glad you're okay. She'd want you here. Come. Sit down. You two have gone through a lot tonight. I'm going to go grab a coffee. Do either of you want anything?"

They both shook their heads.

"Mom and dad are in the waiting room. We can't stay long; they want to take us home immediately, even though the doctors said we'd be fine," said Elsbeth.

"I can relate," Gran smiled softly looking over at Quinn before she exited the room.

"Hey, Q…" Elsbeth said, moving to sit beside her best friend. "I brought you something." She placed her sketchpad on the table beside the bed. "I finished your drawing. I hope it's right."

Thomas came and sat beside his sister. "You better wake up soon, you hear? We need to thank you for saving us." He smiled weakly.

There was a knock on the door. They turned to see their parents waiting outside. Thomas waved them in and the four of them all stood looking at Quinn. She had always been an honorary Mantello and all four of them were worried sick.

"We should get going," Mr. Mantello said softly to his children. They both stood up, each giving Quinn a kiss on the cheek as they went. Mrs. Mantello walked over to Quinn and gave her hand a squeeze. "Get better soon, sweetheart."

Gran walked back in with coffee just in time to say goodbye to the Mantellos and to promise them she'd keep them updated if there was any change. Visiting hours would be over soon and Quinn was still not awake. Reluctantly, Gran went home for the night, promising to come back first thing the next morning.

"Watch over her," she said towards Cooper again and shut the door before he could respond.

Now Cooper was convinced Gran knew of his existence. He didn't step back through the veil to verify, knowing he shouldn't push Nettie's leniency for a while. So instead he settled onto the grass behind the veil, watching over Quinn as she slept wishing with all his might to see her open those baby blue eyes again.

* * *

CHAPTER

26

Gran came back first thing the next morning like she promised. There was still no change in Quinn's condition. Gran sighed as she settled in beside Quinn with some knitting. Cooper cleared his throat loudly to see if Gran might hear him the same way Theo had earlier this week. Gran turned her head and faced Cooper.

"You can see me?" he asked tentatively.

Gran nodded, glancing up briefly from her knitting. "Yes, I can see you. What is your name?"

"Cooper, ma'am," he responded, a little baffled. Nowhere in his training manuals did it specify what to do if a human could see through the veil. As far as he knew, it wasn't possible.

Gran smiled. "It's very nice to speak with you, Cooper. Thank you again for keeping her safe."

"But, how can you see me?"

"Well I have two eyes, haven't I?" Her smile grew bigger—almost a mischievous grin. Cooper wasn't sure how to respond.

"But humans can't…" He trailed off as he saw Quinn stir and open her eyes.

Gran dropped her knitting and grabbed Quinn's hand. "Quinnie? Quinnie? Can you hear me?"

"Gran?" Quinn struggled to sit up.

"Lie back. You need to rest." She reached over and paged the nurse to inform the doctor that Quinn was conscious. The doctor came in shortly after.

"You've been in an accident. You're in the hospital. Do you know your name?"

"Quinn Aurelia," she said before looking at her Gran. The doctor then asked if she knew day it was.

"Uh… no, but I normally don't know what day it is. It's November something."

The doctor smiled. "I'll come back to check on you in a while. Is there anything you need?"

Quinn shook her head.

"Okay, well, if your pain increases, press that button over here and if you need a nurse it's that button there."

"Thank you," Gran said to the doctor. Once the doctor was out of the room, Quinn turned to her grandmother in a panic.

"The trains, the people… are they okay?"

"Thanks to you, help was on the scene within seconds of the accident."

Quinn relaxed slightly before sitting straight up again. "The twins? Are the twins okay?" Gran placed a reassuring hand on Quinn's shoulder.

"Both of them are fine. The Mantellos were here yesterday to visit and I'm sure they will be back again today. They'll be glad to know you're awake."

Quinn's hand went instinctively to her necklace. An unconscious nervous gesture she'd picked up ever since Gran gave it to her. She felt along her neck, but it was bare. She gasped.

"Where is my necklace?"

Cooper coughed nervously. "It's in my pocket, Mrs. Aurelia, I'll bring it back when she's sleeping."

"It's alright, sweetie. The paramedics had to take it off before they could use the defibrillator on you in the ambulance. It's in my car." Gran lied smoothly.

Quinn visibly relaxed. Gran smiled and took Quinn's hands in hers. After a moment, Gran started to trace her finger gently along the rope burns on Quinn's wrists.

"What happened?" she asked Quinn.

Quinn swallowed and looked at her Gran with tears in her eyes.

"There's something I should've told you months ago. I'm being watched." Quinn worked her lip nervously waiting for her Gran's reaction.

Gran stiffened. "What do you mean watched?"

"A couple times now I've heard and seen or thought I saw two figures standing outside by our oak tree, but I didn't say anything because I wasn't sure. They were the ones who made the walkway icy when you had your accident, I'm sure of it now. I think… I think they know what I can do. I think they've been testing me. They caused the train accident. They tied me up when I tried to stop—"

"Quinn, why didn't you tell me!" Gran hurriedly interrupted. She had never seen her Gran genuinely startled or scared before. Normally Gran was the picture of calm.

"What did they look like? Tell me everything."

Quinn started to sob at the memory.

"Quinn, what is it? Tell me please. I'm sorry, I'm not mad I promise. Just tell me what happened." Gran cupped Quinn's face and lifted her chin.

"It's Dominic." She started crying uncontrollably and hiccupping. "He's the one…just pretending…Mindy, too…not their names…the scythe…" She forced out the words in between heaving sobs.

Cooper didn't think he could be shocked any more than he had been in the past 24 hours, but that just goes to show that nothing was impossible. *Dominic?* How hadn't his senses picked up on Dominic and Mindy if they had been stalking Quinn?

His mind was reeling trying to piece together a puzzle he didn't know how to solve. None of this made sense. His blood started to boil at the thought of Dominic using her and hurting her in any way.

"Dominic and Mindy? What do you mean about a scythe? Sweetheart, this is important. You need to tell me what you saw."

Quinn took a steadying breath. "Their real names are Slade and Viper. They knocked me out and tied me up and left me on the tracks. They *knew* the trains would crash. They wore jackets with a scythe emblem," she managed between sobs.

"Brown leather jackets?" Gran asked hurriedly.

Quinn wiped her eyes and looked confusedly at her Gran.

"Yeah, how… how did you know?" she asked with a sniffle.

"I sensed something was off and I've seen those jackets before. Oh, sweetie, you should have told me. I'm so sorry. I would have never guessed Dominic. I'm so sorry. I'm so sorry sweetie," she said, as she rocked Quinn in her arms and held Quinn there until she fell asleep, exhausted from crying so hard.

✦

Once she was asleep Cooper quickly slipped through the veil and gave Quinn's necklace to Gran.

Gran grabbed Cooper's wrists in a panic.

"Tell the Magistrate they've found her. He'll know what I mean."

"How do you know about the Magistrate?" Cooper asked, flabbergasted.

"Never mind that! Go tell him now!"

"What do you mean tell *him?* The Magistrate is a woman," Cooper pointed out. He immediately sent his other self to HQ to inform the Magistrate.

"What… what happened to Magistrate Raymond?"

"No one has heard from him since April. His wife is Magistrate now," Cooper explained not sure why he was telling her any of this.

"His wife? Raymond's missing?" Gran's hand flew to her chest, tears in her eyes. Quinn started stirring and Cooper flipped back through the veil to avoid being spotted.

"What's wrong Gran?" Quinn asked as she looked up at her sleepily.

"Oh nothing. It was nothing, sweetie. I just wanted to put your necklace back on. Here you go." Gran leaned over and put the necklace over Quinn's head. "Now go back to sleep." She brushed her hand along Quinn's cheek.

Quinn clasped the ruby red pendant close to her heart and fell back asleep.

★

I was standing in a dark room… or maybe not a room. It was pitch black and I couldn't see anything, not walls, not a floor, not a ceiling… nothing. Up ahead I saw a pinprick of light. I walked towards it. The light got bigger and bigger as I approached. As I got closer, I could see it wasn't a ball of light at all, but a vault. As soon as the realization clicked in my mind, it grew ten times its size.

A figure walked out from behind the vault. It was… me? I stood staring at myself, trying not to panic.

"I've been waiting for you," the other Quinn said.

"Who are you? Where am I?"

"I am you or at least a version of you that your mind created when your memories were blocked." She looked over at the vault.

"You have been avoiding the truth; avoiding the full power of your gifts. Inside this vault contains the information you need to fully step into your gift."

"Why was it locked away in the first place?"

"All the answers lie behind the door."

"Will it hurt?" I asked.

"You won't feel a thing," my other self promised.

"In fact, you won't even remember this interaction. We are just here to open the door. How quickly or slowly your gift unveils itself is up to you. Are you ready to unlock the truth of who you are?"

I looked at the towering, dark vault.

"I'm scared," I admitted. "What if I don't like what I find behind that door…"

"Isn't it better to know the truth? Aren't you curious about what you're truly capable of?"

I swallowed before nodding my head. She gestured for me to approach the vault. I stood staring at the lock, not sure how to proceed.

"But I don't have the key." I said to her.

She pointed to my necklace. I picked it up and held it in my hands, feeling it pulse within my grasp.
Walking up to the keyhole I pressed the wing-crested gem into the opening and the door swung open with a burst of light so intense it sent me flying backwards. Then the scene faded…

★
★

"Magistrate?" Cooper called, as he knocked tentatively on Nettie's office door.

"Door's open. Come in."

Cooper walked into the office and took a seat across from the Magistrate.

"Thought you'd want to know that Quinn's awake."

Her face brightened at his words. "That's good news." She looked at Cooper and saw that he wasn't smiling. "What's wrong?"

"Her Grandmother can see me." He watched her face waiting for shock, but it never came.

"And what makes you think she can see you?" Nettie said calmed.

"She spoke to me."

This got a reaction from the Magistrate.

"She…spoke to you?" Her calm demeanor immediately changed. She shifted uncomfortably in her chair. "What did she say?"

"She told me to tell the Magistrate that they've found her. She seemed really panicked."

Nettie's face blanched, but she remained composed. "Did she say anything else?"

"Yeah, and she was under the impression that Ray was still the Magistrate. So, I set her straight, saying he was missing and that his wife was now Magistrate."

Nettie nodded. "Thank you, Cooper. Do not engage with her again. But please inform me if she says anything else.

After a moment he hadn't moved to leave so she said, "What is it?"

"Well, she said that Dominic was the one that was after her and said something about a scythe on brown leather jackets. It seemed to mean something to her Gran. *Who* is after her, Nettie? Who or *what* is Dominic? And you still haven't explained how she could see me?" Cooper was having difficulty keeping his anger in check. Too many secrets and they could've cost Quinn her life.

"I will be giving an address to all of Crysthala within the hour," Nettie said as a way of response.

This confused Cooper and simultaneously filled him with dread. In his entire memory he couldn't think of one time when the Magistrate addressed everyone at once.

"To *all* of Crysthala? Nettie, *what is going on?*"

She ignored his question and continued. "Go spread the word that everyone is to meet in field outside of HQ in an hour. That will be all, Guardian Cooper."

Cooper stood up and stomped towards the door. Pausing in the doorway, he said, "I have a right to know what's going on. How am I supposed to protect her if you keep me in the dark? You *knew* someone was after her and didn't warn me. I keep finding out you're keeping things from me and frankly it's pissing me off." He shut the door noisily behind him.

Nettie flinched at the sound and buried her head in her hands.

Cooper stood with his fellow Coordinators as they waited to be addressed by the Magistrate. An eerie quiet had settled across the vast plane of Crysthala. Although everyone was proud of the work they had done tonight, not all lives were saved and a few humans were taken before their intended time. All the Guardians, Healers, Keepers, Doyens,

Clerks, Initiates, and all other Coordinators were wondering the same thing—what was going on?

The Magistrate stood on a small podium and addressed all the Coordinators at once. Everyone was in attendance: every man, woman, and child.

"First of all, I would like to tell you all how proud I am of you for the efficiently and fearlessly conducted efforts tonight. You all responded quickly to the call of duty and did your part to help save many human lives… and we *did* save many human lives. Please do not forget that. Every life we save is a victory and tonight, we were victorious."

Some people smiled, but most were still waiting expectantly to find out why she had called the entire plane together. People were fidgeting nervously. Even the youngest of Coordinators could sense that something was amiss.

"Secondly, I know most of you have questions and I'm here to answer them. I wish I had better news, but there is something you all need to know." She paused and took a steadying breath.

"Sixty-three years ago, there were a few attacks on humans caused by a woman who refers to herself as the Temptress. She and her small band of followers went looking for humans to build her army. Most refused and when they did, it meant certain death. After a while she stopped trying to tempt them into joining her and started to dispose of them one by one, hoping to cleanse the human race, thus giving her subjugates run of the land and giving herself sole power over humans. Her band of followers became known as the Reapers."

Now the crowd was mumbling and exclaiming in shocked tones to one another. Cooper felt a chill go through him. He—like many others—had heard of the Reapers, but assumed it was all an urban legend.

"The Magistrate at that time did not inform Crysthala of the Temptress and her horrendous acts because it was a small group that we quickly contained. Although we were never able to find the Temptress, we assumed she had either died or gone into hiding. We have been looking for her for sixty-three years—but there has been no sign of her. It seems that in these past decades she has been rebuilding her army. We do not know how many of them there are, or where they are located."

"Can't we just track them on the monitors?" someone shouted, which was greeted by many cheers of agreement.

"The monitors at present are only capable of tracking human lives. The Reapers are no longer human."

The crowd gasped in unison, but the Magistrate pressed forward. "They contain dark qualities which allow them to stay under our radar, which is how our monitors did not pick up the threat until it was almost too late."

"So, what are we going to do?" someone shouted from the middle of the crowd.

"We will broaden our search and heighten the number of Guardians on active duty until we locate her. We will need everyone's help so we can swiftly bring an end to this and ensure the safety of humans once more. Now go home, spend some time with your families and I will be informing you shortly of how each of you can help the cause." And with that she exited the stage and teleported away.

★

"Quinn, you have a visitor," the nurse said, poking her head into the room. Gran had gone to finish my discharge paperwork.

"Who is it?" I asked, since there was no way the twins would be here this early.

"A Mr. Rosevale. Should I let him in?"

I started to panic, but there wasn't exactly anywhere I could hide. I nodded feebly to the nurse.

A few moments later, Mr. Rosevale walked into the room, sinking into the chair where Gran had been sitting moments before and leaned his cane against my bed.

"I'm glad you agreed to see me."

I nodded again, not knowing what to say.

"Do you know why I'm here?" he asked me, a smile playing on his lips. I said nothing. "Let me refresh your memory." He reached into his pocket and pulled out the newspaper article about the night he fell into the river.

"Have you read this article?"

"Yes, I have," I admitted.

"But you never came forward? Why not?"

"I didn't know what you wanted from me and I don't like the press. How did you find me?" I asked.

He reached into his pocket and pulled out another piece of paper and placed it on my bed. It was the front page of the newspaper and in the centre were two deformed trains in a heap of metal and beside it a small picture of me. My eyes widened. *Why was I on the front page?*

I started to read the article. The story was about how I harassed the train employees enough that they started to look into the train schedules and realized one of their control boxes was broken. They had tried to contact the trains, but there was interference with the connection. So, they did the next best thing, sent all the police, ambulances and fire trucks that they could to help the victims—all thanks to the persistence of local Rosevalite, Quinn Aurelia.

"Oh, my God," I breathed.

"I saw your picture in the paper this morning and recognized you right away."

"What do you want?" I asked. "Sorry, that was rude. I just…well, if you want an interview with me, or to put me in the papers again, I will have to decline."

He laughed and shook his head. "I just wanted to thank you for saving my life and show my gratitude to you."

I looked at him skeptically.

"I have set up a schooling fund for you to pay off whatever college you choose to go to after high school."

My eyes bugged out of my head. "You really didn't have to do that, Sir. I…I can't accept that." I said. I was not used to kindness from strangers—especially of this magnitude.

He raised a hand and firmly said, "I will hear none of that. You saved my life and apparently the lives of many other people who live in the town my family founded. Doing this for you is the least I can do."

He stood to leave. "And if I hear or see anything that tells me you're trying to pay for school yourself or try to pay me back, I will go to the press about how heroic you were." He winked at me before reaching out to shake my hand. "Thank you, Quinn, for everything. Rosevale is lucky to have you. How did you know about the trains, if I may ask? Off the record, of course."

I blushed and merely shrugged. "Just the right place at the right time, I guess."

Mr. Rosevale threw his head back and laughed, his eyes twinkling. "Well then, if you ever find yourself in the right place at the wrong time, or the wrong place at the right time and need help, here is my number. Call it if you need anything, ever. I mean it Quinn," he said looking at me earnestly.

I took his card and smiled up at him, "I will."

He took off his cap and bowed slightly. "It's the least I can do. Get well soon," he said as he left.

As I put the card on the bedside table, I saw Elsbeth's sketchbook. I reached over to pick it up when the door burst open and Elsbeth, Thomas came bustling in.

"You're awake!" Elsbeth squealed, as she ran in. Thomas was close behind, carrying a bouquet of get-well-soon balloons and a teddy bear. Elsbeth threw herself onto the bed and pulled me into an embrace.

"Ouch," I winced, into her hair.

"Oh sorry," she said apologetically, pulling back so that she wasn't squishing me anymore.

"It's okay. It's not like I need to go to the hospital or anything," I said with a grin.

"Well, I see your sense of humor survived the accident, unfortunately," Thomas said as he leaned down for an awkward hug.

"Did you see the sketch yet?" Elsbeth asked. She leaned over and picked up the sketchbook.

"What sketch?" Gran inquired, as she walked into the room.

I looked at Gran sheepishly. "I asked Elsbeth to sketch the woman from my dream…"

Gran frowned slightly as she reached for the sketchbook. "May I?" she asked Elsbeth.

"Of course," Elsbeth said nervously. "If it's not right, I can tweak it again."

Gran came to sit beside me before she flipped open the book. Gran and I both inhaled quickly when we saw the picture.

"It's her, it's the woman I saw!" I cried out, my hand flying to the necklace that was now securely back around my neck. It pulsed in my hand and suddenly I felt like there was something I was supposed to remember… was I supposed to unlock a door for someone? I shook my head and refocused on the topic at hand.

"It's my mom, right Gran?"

Gran had tears in her eyes as she closed the sketchbook and put it back on the side table.

"Yes, honey. That's your mother." She looked across the room as if lost in thought.

★

Cooper tried to peer over the bed to see the picture on the sketchpad. Gran looked at him and gently closed the book before he saw the picture.

"I'm sorry, Gran. I know you didn't want any pictures of her."

Gran then turned to Quinn and smiled. "I know, sweetie, but you deserve to have a picture of her…it's just hard for me to look at."

"Thank you, Elsbeth, it's perfect." Quinn turned and gave her the tightest hug she could muster with all the wires and bruises.

★

Once they were gone, Gran picked my backpack off the floor and put it on the bed.

"I thought you might want a change of clothes before we go home." Gran said with a smile that didn't quite reach her eyes. *She is keeping something from you.* The thought flashed across my mind and I knew with certainty there was something big Gran wasn't telling me.

"Since the article in the paper is out… it won't be long until some people figure out about your gift. You are no longer safe. I know I have told you your whole life to keep it a secret, but I've been the one keeping secrets from you. It's time you knew the truth."

I sat up straighter in bed. "What secrets?" A cold sense of dread started to wash over me and my necklace started to feel hot against my skin.

"Now Quinn, you have to understand. I didn't tell you for your own good. I've wanted to tell you every day, but we decided it was best that you never knew." She started to sob.

"What is going on, Gran?" I asked urgently.

"Please, you have to understand," she begged.

"Just tell me," I demanded. I felt my world come crashing down around me as her words sank in.

"Your mother is alive."

END OF BOOK ONE

* * *

ACKNOLWEDGMENTS

A special thank you to OLIVIAPRODESIGN for the
cover design.
https://www.fiverr.com/oliviaprodesign

If you enjoyed this novel, please take a moment to
write a review on Amazon.

#SupportAuthors
#SelfPublished

Make sure to sign-up to receive notifications about the
release of the second novel in this series to find out what
happens next!

Website: www.JessieCabella.com
Twitter: @CabellaJessie
Instagram: @JessieCabella
Facebook: https://www.facebook.com/cabella.jessie